KILLING ME SOFTLY

KILLING ME SOFTLY

MARJORIE ECCLES

THOMAS DUNNE BOOKS
ST. MARTIN'S MINOTAUR
NEW YORK

THOMAS DUNNE BOOKS.
An imprint of St. Martin's Press.

KILLING ME SOFTLY. Copyright © 1998 by Marjorie Eccles. All
rights reserved. Printed in the United States of America. No part
of this book may be used or reproduced in any manner
whatsoever without written permission except in the case of brief
quotations embodied in critical articles or reviews. For information,
address St. Martin's Press, 175 Fifth Avenue, New York, N.Y. 10010.

ISBN 0-312-20469-8

First published in Great Britain by Constable & Company Ltd

First U.S. Edition: December 1999

10 9 8 7 6 5 4 3 2 1

With special thanks to Inspector Garry Cox of the Hertfordshire Constabulary, as ever, but especially for his generous help and good advice in my researches for this particular book.

1

In the quiet flat, high above the sleeping town, Detective Superintendent Gil Mayo was burning the midnight oil, wading through the pile of official waffle which he'd brought home to work on while he waited for news. He'd been relying on strong coffee and Haydn to help keep him awake, turning the volume down out of consideration for Alex, who was sleeping in the next room, but in the end he switched the music off. At that level, it was sending him to sleep. And better not to listen to old Haydn's glorious sounds at all than at half-cock. He sat back, rubbed his temples and yawned as the hands of the bracket clock on the mantelshelf reached half-past two and the rest of his clocks struck and chimed the half-hour, more or less in unison.

He should have heard something, they should have rung by now. But after the vibrations of the last chime died, nothing broke the silence but the rattle of rain against the window.

Not even the weather was being co-operative. Mid-February, the deadest part of the year, a bloody awful month made worse by the unspeakable weather that had set in since Christmas and showed no signs of disappearing. It had rained all night, and by morning the river would have risen by several inches, and though it hadn't yet reached danger level, it couldn't be far off. Several people were keeping an anxious eye on the situation, none more so than Mayo. He had good reason: a surveillance operation which was going on from one of the few derelict warehouses not yet turned into luxury apartments under the Riverside Redevelopment scheme. There'd been a tip-off, convincing enough for him to have put his DI, Abigail Moon, down there with the support team and half the CID. What the devil was happening?

Nothing, was the short answer.

Abigail's neck ached, she was fighting sleep and boredom, cramped into the cold, stuffy car with Deeley, Farrar and Jenny

Platt. The rain beat endlessly against the windscreen, and they'd long since run out of anything new to say.

She wriggled her shoulders to ease the tension. 'Crack the window a bit more, somebody, will you? Last time I was in a vehicle so steamed up was on my first date.'

Farrar laughed dutifully and Deeley amiably wound down his window another inch, then tipped up his flask for any last dregs of coffee. There weren't any. He shifted restlessly. 'Wish we'd brought some sandwiches.'

'You'll survive.' Jenny Platt aimed a telling glance at his well-packed suit, his thick thighs. The squad heavy, Deeley, looking like somebody's minder, the good-humoured butt of CID jokes. 'Two fish, wasn't it, with chips, before we set out?'

'Have a heart, that was hours ago. I'm not a flippin' camel, for God's sake!'

Deeley hated being on obs, especially in a car. He'd rather get stuck in, any day, action being what he was best at. Or at least, watching from the old warehouse with the rest, keeping in radio contact with the DI and the bods in the support team, also parked nearby.

'Here we go,' said Farrar suddenly. Everyone was instantly on the alert, but it was only a shadow of blown rain, wishful thinking.

The second night of observation, and not a peep out of anybody.

'It would be just too beautiful if we got it right, first time, but why do I feel somebody's having us on?' Abigail had demanded of Mayo before they'd left the office that night.

Mayo, too, had been short on sleep recently. 'We're on a hiding to nothing most of the time, these days,' he said gloomily. 'They're running rings round us, out there. But spoof or not, we ignore this and that's just the time something'll happen. Keep at it. Whatever happens, tonight finishes it.'

Mayo couldn't fairly sanction any more overtime, which was galling, but he had the ACC (Crime) on his back over this. The operation had already cost more than anyone cared to think of in terms of time and resources, and Sheering wasn't renowned for high tolerance where budgets were concerned, this not excluded.

But not even he could shut his eyes to what was happening. The drug scene was here, as everywhere else. Small time, compared with the big cities, but more than enough for Lavenstock. Alerted by a sudden upsurge in drug-related crimes in the area – housebreaking, mugging, you name it – vigilance had been stepped up and the Force Area Drug Squad had been called in.

Tonight's observation was targeted on the unstructured group of old houses further along the river bank, on one of those with their feet almost in the water. The Bagots, the area was called, a kind of no man's land between the posh stretch of the river and the disused warehouses and abandoned factories scheduled for redevelopment. On their last legs, the old houses were soon to be knocked down, despite a fiercely pitched battle, developers v. conservationists, which had ended with victory to the developers. A pity, in a way. The group of workmen's cottages, varying in age from eighty years old to two hundred, were romantic-looking and picturesque, if you didn't get too near, huddled together on the river bend, contributing to current nostalgia. But no, it wasn't economic to put them in order, they were too far gone, come down they must. Meanwhile, despite leaky roofs, cockroaches and rats, they were some sort of home to those too old to have any desire to move, or those who could afford nothing better and had no choice in the matter, and to a group of disaffected, rootless young folk. It was on their shaky old house, the one that stood on its own at the end of a row, that the watch was being concentrated.

The Stockwell was only a small river, a tributary of the Avon, little more than a stream in places but always interesting, and never more varied than when it passed through Mayo's bailiwick of Lavenstock. Rising in the surrounding hills, it was for the most part a bubbling watercourse except at the point where, companion to the canal, it widened out and flowed more gently. The smarter houses at that point had moorings and little boathouses at the end of their gardens, amenities which pushed up the prices of these already much coveted, desirable residences, never mind that you couldn't navigate far in either direction: downstream, beyond where it curved around the park like a protective arm, the Stockwell narrowed again and resumed its shallow, lively course over the stones, while in its upper reaches, in the industrialized areas, it was choked with debris, and sometimes disappeared and flowed, dark and secret and unseen, along underground culverts. Still, a river aspect and a boathouse were status symbols, and remained good selling points.

Tonight, swollen with the recent rains, the river slid past them until, further along, it became turbulent, at the point where the steep, mossy, boulder-strewn banks narrowed at Clacks Mill, sweeping under the bridge and thence into the millrace. The old mill wheel, no longer working but still *in situ*, was two hundred years old but there was no danger that it would fall to pieces. It would see out the much newer, rustic-style bridge that straddled the race.

The trees flailed around in the wind, and the rain rattled against the windows of the mill house. In the main bedroom, Clare Wishart turned over in her sleep and stretched out her arm to the empty space beside her, half woke with a little, shuddering moan, tossed uneasily for a while, but presently turned over and slept again. Her son and daughter, in their respective bedrooms, unaware of either the wind or the rain, or the continuous muffled fall of the water, slept the sound, untroubled sleep of healthy teenagers.

Barbie Nelson, whose nightly dreams were vivid, restless and disturbing, and nobody's business but her own, lived far enough away from the river not to be worried about rising water levels. Tonight, her small flat felt snug and secure, rather than irritatingly poky as it usually did. Tonight, she was tired out. It had been a long and busy day at work and, with so much on her mind, she needed sleep without dreams. Before going to bed she'd taken a pill, and while it took effect she'd allowed herself to indulge in forbidden, deeply satisfying thoughts about the future. At last she slept peacefully, secure in the knowledge that her plans were maturing nicely.

In the afterglow of sex, Ellie Redvers was sometimes able to persuade herself that everything was going to be all right, they would work things out so that she and Tim could be together always, and not just for hidden, secret, shameful meetings.

Everything would be resolved in a way that wouldn't hurt Clare, or the children.

But in the colder light of reason, she knew this wouldn't ever be possible. There was no way out of this, not without tearing everyone concerned apart, herself and Tim – well, perhaps – included.

He lay sprawled out beside her, his tall, loose-limbed frame completely relaxed, his sleep untroubled by what had happened that night. He should have remembered that she was sharp enough to put two and two together. But he'd shrugged his worry off on to her, then forgotten it. Nothing ever really worried Tim, or not deeply. Even now, he looked insouciant, his mouth turned up slightly at one corner, as though being charming had become so much a habit with him that he couldn't give it up, even in sleep. His head was thrown back, disguising the faint slackness of his jaw, the lids closed over the laughing eyes so that their inherent coldness could be forgotten, or ignored. His light brown hair fell over his brow in the boyish flop that women found endearing, herself not excepted.

She resisted the corny impulse to smooth it back and slid out from between the covers. Drawing on her dressing-gown, she pushed her feet into slippers and padded softly to the window. The river was still rising. Slap, slap it went against the pilings of the walkway at the bottom of the lawn. But these houses were secure from a silent invasion by water: brand, spanking new, a fashionable development facing the river and, beyond it, the canal. They'd been built above a short slope to the water's edge, a precaution against the danger of flooding, unlike the old houses huddled along the banks a few hundred yards away at the Bagots. There, it might be a different story, come morning, if the rain continued. But further along still, at the mill, they'd be safe enough: Clare, and Richie, and her god-daughter, Amy.

Ellie shivered and drew her feet up under her fleecy woollen dressing-gown, trying without much success to shut her mind to all thoughts of them by concentrating on her own reflection mirrored in the blackness of the window. A small, pale face, saved from plainness by deep brown, thickly lashed eyes above high cheekbones, and what Tim, in one of his more tender, imaginative moments, had once called a heart-stopping smile. Not the obvious picture of a woman who is systematically betraying her closest, lifelong friend, inseparable since they had met on their first day at playschool.

Clare wasn't a fool. She was well aware of Tim's women, there was no way she couldn't be. There'd been too many to hide, for too long. But she'd never, ever, suspect Ellie – would she? In her way, Ellie hadn't been much better than Tim, as far as numbers went. Fair enough, she wasn't committed to anyone – and she'd always drawn the line at breaking up a relationship. Her own marriage had been wrecked by a red-haired model with pouty lips, no hips and legs that went on for ever. Since then, *she'd* always been the one to back out. Either she'd got fed up herself, or she'd seen the signs in her partner. And yet now, as if under some compulsion, she couldn't do it. She couldn't turn her back this time, not with Tim. All the more incredible, since she'd known him for nearly twenty years, and never understood why women fell down before him like ninepins, until one day, at some baleful conjunction of their stars, he'd chosen to pick up the ball and roll it in her direction.

She was totally unable to understand herself, why she'd so far been powerless to do anything to stop the affair. There'd never been much more to it, on his part at any rate, than sexual gratification, never true love – she knew Tim too well for that – and it shamed her. At the knowledge of what she was doing, she felt as though something in her was slowly dying.

But after tonight, she was dully aware that it had gone beyond Ellie and Tim. Clare and the children could well be drawn in. The time had come when she had to act. Very well then, she would. Somehow she'd find the will to do it. But she swore that never again would she allow anyone to do this to her. Which meant that she could see her life going on, futile, pointless, repetitive, until she became too old to attract anyone and then – she'd be alone.

Except for Clare. One thing she could rely on: Clare would always be there.

Some distance away, another woman lay in the dark. She came back to consciousness, opened her eyes, but could see nothing only blackness. She had a violent headache, and felt slightly sick.

She had a vague remembrance of a previous awakening, of

finding herself struggling to move her limbs, and being unable to move. Her hands and feet had been tied. She'd struggled feebly, and felt the bonds chafing her wrists, but her strength soon gave out and unconsciousness overcame her again.

She was lying now on what seemed to be some sort of narrow truckle bed with a blanket thrown over her. Experimentally, she moved her hands, then her feet. They were no longer tied. She tried to sit up, but dizziness and nausea forced her to lie back again.

She stared into the blackness and tried to remember what had happened. She could dimly recall a fierce struggle with someone who was taller and stronger than she was; but nothing more. Where was she, and why had she been brought here? How long had she lain unconscious? Who was he, her assailant?

More importantly, *who was she*?

The sense of non-identity was terrifying. Almost worse than the thought of being left here alone, in this cold, dank, echoing place, perhaps until she died.

The horror of that made her try and sit up again, but her head swam and she had to abandon the effort, defeated by her own weakness. Yet behind the helplessness she sensed a strength and determination that seemed to be natural to her. She would surely feel better presently, and when she did she would get up and explore, find some way out. She wasn't going to die, not yet.

At some time during the night, the wind died down and the heavy rain turned to a drizzle that would later still turn to fog. The river banks did not overflow. And the long night's surveillance by the police brought forth nothing, other than frustration. No one visited, or left, the ramshackle house on the curve of the river.

'Come to bed, you can't stay up all night.'

Alex, ex-sergeant Alex Jones of the Lavenstock police division, stood in the doorway, her dark hair tousled, her face still blank with sleep. 'They'll ring if there's any news. I'll make us a hot drink.'

So she hadn't been able to sleep, either. Mayo's heart smote him. Alex was the sort of person whose inner state was reflected in her looks, and her dark blue eyes had darker smudges under them, her clear, naturally pale skin was paler than it should have been. She didn't look well. Or was he letting his imagination, his worry, get the better of him? He should have more confidence in her innate steadiness, her ability to see things straight.

She'd lately had things on her mind, sure, a big decision to make, but, being Alex, and having maybe made one mistake already, she was still capable of worrying about it. Another blast of rain hit the window panes and she stretched her hand out and pulled him to his feet.

The parrot, Bert, under his night-time covering, stirred and gave a token squawk on hearing voices, rustled his feathers and sank back into his own mysterious night world as Mayo switched out the light.

2

Breakfast at Clacks Mill was always a self-absorbed affair. None of the family were great communicators at that time in the morning, except for Tim, if he were in a good mood. But he wasn't there today.

Clare drank her coffee while running through her lists, checking things to be done and worrying about the fog which had succeeded the rain. She hated these dark February mornings, driving when you couldn't see a hand in front of you, and today the fog would make it worse. The forecast, so far as it could be believed, didn't hold out for much improvement. There was no help for it. She had to get to Miller's Wife, and drive her children to school.

And that heralded yet another argument with Richie. He was seventeen, at Sixth Form College, had passed his driving test a few weeks ago: *why* couldn't he have his own car, a motorbike, some means of transport? Because who, Clare asked in her turn, is going to afford a car for you, just another expense, plus the exorbitant insurance for someone your age?

And because, my darling boy, she thought, but didn't say, in one of the moods you've been in all too often lately, you could kill yourself, not to mention other people. She was prepared to lend him her car occasionally. Meanwhile, being driven in to school by her in the mornings, being dropped off at the end of the lane in the afternoon by the school bus was good enough for now, she told him firmly. Bad for his ego, though, she could see that, and his standing among his peers. And more often than not, one of the same mates, no more reliable than he was himself at the moment, would drive him recklessly home along the narrow country lanes in some clapped-out old banger. Or worse, he'd ride motorbike pillion without a crash helmet. There was no way of stopping that, but . . . oh God, the joys of parenthood! she thought, churning inside as Richie shoved his chair back and thudded upstairs to plot further ways of undermining her resistance. He'd already got his father's tacit consent – providing Clare could find the money – which was the way things worked in this marriage: Tim the easygoing parent, Clare the one who had to make the rules.

None of the emotional turmoil she felt showed, as she drank the last of her coffee and organized her day. She'd learned that it paid to keep her thoughts and her emotions to herself. She had a neat and disciplined face that gave nothing away, and cool, grey eyes. Finely drawn charcoal brows emphasized a delicate skin, she wore her silver-blonde hair in a smooth, square-cut bob. Snow Princess, Tim had called her once upon a time, then Ice Maiden when he became less pleased with her . . . specifically, when he discovered the vein of inherited self-sufficiency running through her, inherited from her father who'd made what Tim was pleased to call all that disgusting money. Forget that much of that same money had made his own present lifestyle possible, it was obscene, Tim said, to be so rich and then be so grudging with it. Forget that it was only through Sam Nash's generosity, plus Clare's own efforts with Miller's Wife, that they were able to keep Clacks Mill.

His own situation, though he refused to face it, was growing more and more untenable. He called himself a financier, though he'd never been serious about it, playing at it as if it were just another game of squash, or rugger. He was a natural gambler, but his judgement had grown poor, he'd borrowed a lot of money, speculating unwisely in the property boom of the eighties, and lost more when the same property values fell. As a Lloyd's Name, he'd come the final cropper, though he still refused to look the facts in the face, believing Micawberishly that something would turn up to help meet his losses. His 'contacts' were growing fewer, more wary. There were too many others, part of the same Old Boy network, on the same merry-go-round.

It was just as well they had Miller's Wife to fall back on, thought Clare, the business she and Ellie had started here in her own kitchen. It hadn't been much more than a lark at first, a pastime for two women who needed to occupy their time rather than make money. Both were excellent cooks, by way of a Cordon Bleu course after school. At first it had been directors' lunches, or catering for small dinner parties ordered by busy or lazy wives. Their success had amazed them. But heavy lunches for directors were out nowadays, on both health and expense grounds, and less money to go around had forced more women to cook for themselves – just when making money had become necessary to Clare. Then somehow a new notion had developed. They had opened a shop in addition, selling the same sort of meals, fresh-chilled or frozen, and so making them more widely available: beautifully cooked and presented with that touch of flair and discrimination which set them miles apart from the ubiquitous TV dinner, but still less expensive than the service previously offered. Affordable as a treat, or for that special occasion, without ruining the budget, the new venture had widened their clientele, and they now had customers from all walks of life. They were also – though they never let it be known – finding outlets in some of the better hotels and restaurants in the area.

It had meant taking on officially approved premises in the town in line with EC directives, and equipping themselves with new technology, and some staff, though it remained essentially a small enterprise. Neither woman wanted it to grow beyond itself. Taking on Barbie at a small wage in return for the flat over the premises had been a stroke of genius, though, and with David Neale now to look after the finances they were well accommodated.

Sometimes, Clare regretted the move. It had been fun, just she and Ellie working quietly and companionably together, here in her own huge, Aga-warmed kitchen. There was something about its special ambience that induced creative cooking, about the long hours spent slicing and dicing, constructing new recipes while they gossiped and planned and laughed together amidst the delicious aromas of cooking food. Oversized by modern standards, a disaster when she and Tim had first come to the mill, the kitchen now had blue drag-painted units and honey-coloured walls, spiced with sharp white paint. Bright curtains at the windows, and the old uneven flagstones replaced by homely Italian tiles. Tim had rolled his eyes over that, but Clare had gone ahead, anyway, not prepared in this case to sacrifice hygiene and convenience for authenticity. The new tiles made the kitchen warmer, they went with the decor, and you didn't get irremovable gunge in between the cracks. 'Well, anyway,' she defended her choice, 'Ellie likes it.'

'Ellie doesn't have to live in it,' Tim had rejoined, after a pause. Clare had said nothing.

He could have driven them in to Lavenstock this morning – he was a better driver than she was, or at any rate, his recklessness was curbed when he had his family with him – had he not been staying overnight at his mother's flat in Edgbaston, as he often did when he was out late to dinner. But Clare didn't care to put that to the test by telephoning him there, and hearing the lies which were still lies, even when spoken in his mother's aristocratic tones. In Sibyl Wishart's eyes, Tim could do no wrong, she would go to the scaffold for him, and though she'd forgiven Clare for Tim wanting to marry her when the extent of her father's fortune had been revealed, she'd never allowed any real friendship to develop between herself and her daughter-in-law. She had cooled off even more when she discovered Sam Nash had no intention of bailing out his indigent new in-laws in return for the distinguished and respected old name conferred upon Clare, and her introduction to the county set – which Clare disconcertingly didn't care about, anyway.

The big wall clock struck quarter to eight and Clare wrote a note for Jackie, the young woman who came to clean for her on Thursdays, another to the milkman. One to herself to remind her to pick up some dry-cleaning. Amy pushed her chair back and carried her breakfast things to stack in the dishwasher. 'Shouldn't we be off a bit earlier, Mum, with this horrible fog?'

'OK, I'm ready, give Richie a shout.' There was ten minutes

yet before they need set off, but Richie would wait at least that long before making an appearance, in order to register his unwillingness.

Amy went to call her brother, barely raising her precise little voice. Yet Clare knew from experience how surprisingly penetrating and commanding it was. A younger version of her mother, with her smooth blonde hair curving round her face in parentheses, Amy was a composed, collected sixteen-year-old. Unlike Richie, she wasn't given to rebellion. Somewhere around the age of eleven, she'd decided she wanted to be a doctor, and since then nothing had deflected her from her ambition. She worked hard at the necessary subjects and did well at them, without being obsessive about it. She was good at games, too, and popular. She didn't dress outrageously, and kept her room tidy. She was such a *good* girl, without Richie's difficult moods, no trouble at all. But it would be nice, sometimes, to have known what she was thinking.

At that point in her mother's reflections Amy, who had cleared the rest of the table and was shrugging herself into her school blazer, suddenly cried out, 'It's Daddy!' as a four-wheel drive scrunch of gravel announced Tim's arrival at the front of the house. A car door slammed. She flew across the kitchen to take his grip as he came in the door, throwing herself into his arms. The fog was still there, thick as curdled cream outside the door, but indoors the sun shone for Amy.

Tim's first thought was to pick up his morning mail from the old majolica dish on the dresser, where it was always placed. His face darkened as he read a couple of letters – one, as Clare had noted from the envelope, from the bank – then stuffed them into the pocket of his Barbour. She looked at him quickly, trying to assess the mood he was in, as he strode across to the stove, held his hands out to its heat. He looked haggard. Maybe he was more concerned about his money worries than she gave him credit for. Despite his obvious tiredness, he said, 'It's really nasty out there, come on, I'll drive you all into town.'

Where had he been last night, that his conscience was pushing him to make amends? Not at his mother's flat, Clare was certain. Richie appeared in the doorway in time to hear the last words. 'Hi, Dad. Can I drive?'

'Let's leave it till you've had a bit more experience before tackling this sort of stuff, Rich, OK?' Tim said absently.

'OK,' Richie responded equably.

And Clare, noticing her son's easy acceptance of the refusal, despaired. She could view Tim dispassionately and hate what she saw, or what he'd become, even wonder how she could ever have really loved him; yet, seeing him with Richie, and remembering the time when her heart, like her daughter's, had done a dance, too, whenever she saw him, she could somehow find it in her heart to try and forgive him once more.

David Neale swung round from the computer screen, his face lit with pleasure when he saw it was Clare who'd brought his morning pot of coffee. He was especially pleased to see two cups on the tray.

'If you've come about the budget, I'm afraid it's not quite ready yet.' He indicated the spreadsheets on his desk. 'This afternoon, maybe?'

'That's all right, David, we weren't expecting any figures yet. I just wanted a chat.'

'Make yourself at home.' He took the tray from her, drew a chair closer to the desk and poured coffee for both of them, remembering that she took it black, unsweetened, adding both cream and sugar to his own.

'Have a biscuit.' Clare offered the plate of cherry shortbread, a batch she'd just now thrown together, pandering to his sweet tooth. 'Your favourites, straight out of the oven.'

He smiled as he took one, and she reflected how easy it was to like him, how well he'd fitted in here. A tall Scot, a little reserved, but with an expression behind his spectacles that was kind and thoughtful. A nice smile with white, even teeth. Always well-dressed, in a conservative way, today in a grey suit, a finely striped maroon and white shirt, a discreetly patterned tie. Business attire, though he needn't have bothered. They were pretty relaxed about dress, here at Miller's Wife.

'One of the nicest things about working here is the food,' he commented, munching shortbread appreciatively. 'Where else would I get home-made biscuits with my coffee?' Occasionally,

19

too, he was roped in as a taster for new lines. Not to mention being able to pick up something to take home for his evening meals. He lived alone and was glad enough not to have to cook when he arrived home at night.

'I hope it's not the only thing that keeps you here. We'd be lost without you, now. Though if anything else turns up – '

'This suits me very well, Clare,' he said quietly.

She thought this must seem very small beer to him after his previous job, but as the financial director to a big international construction company, the frenetic pace had taken its toll, by way of a slight heart attack at an age much too young for it, though it was hardly possible to believe, now, twelve months later, he looked so fit and energetic. A warning, his doctor had called it, but David admitted it had thoroughly shaken him. He was barely forty-five.

His doctor had insisted, however, on the need for him to slow down, and the work here was undemanding. In fact, any reasonably competent clerk could have coped, and Clare had been afraid he would very soon find it boring. But he seemed content, for the moment, to stay on.

'It suits me fine,' he repeated, his eyes following the graceful movement of her arm as she lifted the cup to her lips. She had slipped on a colourful knitted jacket to come upstairs in place of the overall she wore to work in, and its rich, stained-glass colours warmed her skin, reflected blue into the grey of her eyes.

'I've more free time than I ever had,' he continued, 'besides being near enough to walk to work.' He walked wherever he could, worked out twice a week, even played squash. Doctor's orders, Clare guessed, though she'd soon been made aware that the last thing he wanted was concern about his health. 'For heaven's sake, I'm not in a wheelchair, yet!' he'd protested.

She said neutrally, 'Walking to work must be a plus point. I can't tell you what the journey here this morning was like. Thank the Lord I didn't have to do the driving! Luckily, Tim was able to run us in.'

David was conscious of the slight constraint, the wariness that clouded her eyes when she spoke Tim's name, and he himself stiffened with distaste. Had he been made differently, he might have walked round the desk and put his arm around her and reassured her, promised her that she would always have his protection, that she need fear nothing from Wishart, but she was still another man's wife. Despite everything, she remained loyal, misguided though that might be. Clare was a woman who stayed true to her marriage vows, once made, and his Scottish upbringing had not made him the sort of man to encourage her to break them.

She finished her coffee and put the cup back on the tray. 'One thing I wanted to talk to you about, David, was Barbie. Ellie and I think some sort of pay rise should be on the cards. I imagine we can justify it, can't we? She's worth her weight in gold, really – '

'In which case we couldn't afford her at all!' he said drily.

'Too true!' Barbie took jokes about her size in good part. It wasn't a sensitive issue with her, but it suddenly struck Clare that she'd never before heard David join in the general good-natured ribbing they all indulged in against each other. It was a good sign, she thought, he was learning to take things a bit less seriously. She said, 'Barbie'll turn her hand to anything. She's due for a rise.'

'I'll look into it,' he promised. He had his own reservations about Barbie Nelson. She'd been taken on at his suggestion, so he knew what she was capable of, but it wouldn't do for her to get ideas. She wasn't, in any case, doing too badly, moneywise. The flat above the premises more than made up for any inadequacies in salary, in his opinion, and she'd worked her way into the firm's good books perhaps too easily for his liking. Even so, she wasn't as tiresome as most of the string of women who'd worked here from time to time. 'A moderate rise,' he added temperately, picking his pen up and jotting a note.

'Good.' She was collecting the coffee things when he spoke again.

'Clare, if you're free on Saturday, might I ask you a favour? Maybe it's an imposition, I know weekends are a family time, but . . .'

'You should tell my family that! No, no, just joking, they've got beyond the stage where they want to do anything with Mum and Dad in their free time.'

'And Tim?'

'Oh, I think he's planning on his usual sporting activities,' she said casually. 'How can I help?'

'The fact is,' he answered, having banked on Wishart occupying himself as he almost always did on Saturdays, 'I'm thinking of putting my house on the market, looking for somewhere smaller. Since Jane died, I rattle around like a single pea in a large pod. I want to get rid of it.'

'I can understand that.' Her voice was warm with sympathy. 'A place where you've once been happy . . .'

'Yes,' he agreed quietly.

It seemed to have become darker in the office and he leaned back in his chair, stretching out a well-manicured hand to switch on the floor lamp behind him, glancing out of the window as he did so. The fog was still thick enough to obscure the buildings opposite. He frowned. 'Flood warnings out last night. But at least if the rain keeps off, the river levels should stay down.'

'You're not worried about your garden, surely?'

He owned one of the larger properties with a long garden fronting the river. Like the house, the garden was immaculately kept. Clare had never known his wife, Jane, but she'd evidently been a woman of discrimination. The house was beautifully and expensively furnished with antiques, some marvellous paintings and Chinese porcelain, all in perfect taste – but too perfect for Clare's liking. It had felt chillingly like a museum to her, the one time she'd had occasion to visit.

He smiled. 'No, it's big enough to survive a few feet of flood water. The house, too, come to that, though I believe the basement did flood once, sometime in the past. But the garden's one of the reasons I want to move. I'm not passionate about gardening, and I could do with somewhere less time-consuming. I've seen a small property near Brome, in need of some renovation and with a more reasonably sized garden, that might, or might not, do. Seems ideal, on the surface, but at the same time, I'm not sure I want to live out of the town. I know I'm the one who has to make the ultimate decision, but I'd appreciate another opinion. Clare, would you care to look at it with me?'

'Well, if you think I can be of any help, certainly.' She was surprised and flattered.

'Thank you,' he said gravely. 'Would Saturday morning suit you? I could collect you about eleven, and then, afterwards – perhaps you'd lunch with me? Brome Country Club does very decent food, I hear.'

'Oh, I'm sorry, but I've promised to have lunch with my father. The afternoon would be fine, though.'

'No problem. One time's as good as another,' he said easily. 'Shall I call for you at your father's house?'

'Do. I'll make sure we have an early lunch,' she answered, thinking that he should make use of that attractive smile more often. 'I'll look forward to going with you.'

When Clare told Ellie she was going out with David Neale on Saturday, she was put out by Ellie's downbeat reaction.

'Well, Clare, honestly!'

Was she, just a teeny bit, jealous of a perfectly innocent occasion? Ellie, with all her men friends? Jealous of an outing with *David*? A stuffed shirt, she'd called him when he'd first started with them, laughing at Clare's championship of him, unable to see that beneath the reserved Scottish exterior, David Neale was pure gold.

Or was she having an attack of guilty conscience?

'You can't!' she said, looking utterly disbelieving. Which was unfair, and rich, coming from Ellie. But Ellie's mores were her own.

The ancient house at the end of the area known as the Bagots had, once in its chequered history, been an inn. Every now and then, a little more of it collapsed into ruin, leaving a shrinking but still rambling confusion of small rooms and unexpected staircases. It resembled an illustration out of a Dickensian novel, tumbledown, leaning, with roofs sloping almost to the ground, crooked chimneys and sagging lintels. It had what might be described as a floating population, which, it seemed to Jem, might one day be literally true, if the river rose far enough. It was another contributory factor to all the things which were worrying him just now, though it was nothing new. The water which regularly seeped through into the cellar was an ongoing problem.

Tonight, when he'd taken a flashlight and gone down to make an inspection, it had been awash with several inches of water. It didn't bother anyone else living in the house because none of the other occupants ever ventured down the gruesome, slimy steps, not even Morgan.

The damp had risen throughout the house. Clusters of black mushroom growths fruited in the corners of the kitchen ceiling, skirting boards were rotten, and what paper was left on the walls hung down in great swathes, where it wasn't drawing-pinned up. There was a sweetish odour of mould and rot, mingled with other smells, mainly cannabis.

The house today, as always, reeked of it. Luce drew the line at anything else, she was very strait-laced about some things and it was her house, left to her by her grandfather. She was away for a few days, however, and Jem wouldn't trust the newcomers, Ginge and Sheena, not to take advantage of her absence. The house hadn't been worth much when Luce inherited it, but now that the developers had won their battle to pull it down, Morgan told her she'd be quids in, able to name her price, though Jem had his doubts, and even Col goggled at the thought of anyone giving good money to buy this dump.

Jem, Col, and Luce, a well-established trio. Christened Jeremy, Colin and Lucinda, nice middle-class names given to them by their nice middle-class parents. Some of whom might have smoked more than the odd joint in the sixties, lived in squats and worn flowers in their hair, but had now reformed and didn't take kindly to their children following the same pattern.

The three of them, with Morgan, formed the core of the house, others drifted in, as and when. Jem wished they were still on their own, as they'd once been, but Luce had this thing about sharing her good luck with others.

She had her own standards. Usually, whenever she went home on one of her rare visits, she'd wear her most far-out gear, the clothes calculated to cause maximum annoyance to her mother, which meant they'd quarrel and she'd come back cross and moody, unlike her usual sunny self. But yesterday, when she'd had this letter from home, telling how the house had been burgled, ransacked, and her mum left in a state of collapse, she'd been off like a shot, wearing the sort of straight clothes she wouldn't normally be seen dead in.

Morgan had also taken himself off somewhere, though not with Luce, although she was his woman. He'd gone before she got the letter. Jem wished he knew when they were both likely to be back. His giro cheque had come and he had food to buy, for one thing. They mostly ate vegetarian, since it was cheaper, unless there was free food to be acquired, and not having any fridge to keep things fresh, vegetables had to be bought on a daily basis. He would need to calculate how much to buy. Jem was cursed, he sometimes thought, by this feeling of responsibility for everyone, not only for Col. Col was different, though, he needed Jem to take care of him.

And that was another problem. Jem had the chance of some work, only a few hours a week, but the sort of job they all took when they could get it, casual work without too much effort needed, no responsibility and no questions asked. But if he took it, he was worried what might happen to Col if he wasn't there to look out for him. Although Col was so clever, he was sometimes unpredictable, and you could never be certain what he'd take it into his head to do.

3

Abigail Moon looked up from the pile of reports she'd been working on, hesitated, then determinedly swept them all together into a drawer. Sod the lot! She'd been up half the night on that useless surveillance, which in the end had fizzled out like a damp squib, and she'd sworn she was going to leave the office on time tonight if it killed her. Already she was twenty minutes later than she'd intended, having been overtaken by events, a not unheard-of occurrence. She had colleagues who thought she was in clover, working out in the sticks, here in Lavenstock. Let them just try it.

Tonight, however, she was Abigail Moon, private citizen, with the prospect of a free weekend after tomorrow, a woman who was entertaining at home the man who was coming to feature most largely in her life. Ben had told her there was something important he wanted to say to her and if it was what she thought it was, she'd been thinking a lot about what her answer would be. She had a feeling he wasn't going to like it. But, like women everywhere, she felt the need to pave the way, in the traditional appeasing manner, through his stomach. Truth be known, as far as cooking went, he could beat her into a cocked hat (not single-minded enough about it, her mother said, and Abigail was bound to agree) but under pressure she could come up with the goods, and she'd promised herself that for once she'd present him with a meal which wouldn't suffer by comparison. She put the light out, slammed the office door and dashed for her car.

As she started the engine, the car clock lit up, making it plain that she hadn't really left anything like enough time for preparing an elaborate meal. Nor was there any question of speeding home through the country lanes in this fog, which had hung about all day and thickened with the dusk. That was the downside of living out of town. Damn! She wondered if she ought to ring Ben and tell him not to venture out to her cottage tonight. Stop making excuses, she told herself firmly. Ben was a journalist, editor of the local *Advertiser*, and he'd once been a correspondent in far-flung and dangerous parts of the globe and wouldn't be deterred by a little thing like fog. Besides, he could always be guaranteed to raise her spirits, which was something she could do with tonight.

And also, she'd had to stand him up far too many times lately.

A solution presented itself. She could pick up a ready-prepared meal at Miller's Wife, whose premises she happened to be passing, perhaps not entirely by chance. The shopping precinct was nearby, and kept open late on Thursdays, and Miller's Wife had followed suit, ready for customers with just such an emergency as hers. Miller's Wife. Ouch! said Ben, but Ben was a writer.

She told herself it wasn't necessary to feel guilty for short-cutting, she was a woman with a busy and demanding job. And with food of this sort, she was in no danger of serving up anything tacky. Miller's Wife products were superior indeed – and priced accordingly. But tonight was special, and to salve her conscience, she would have time to cook fresh vegetables from those she'd bought in her lunch hour. Moreover, she owed it to Ellie Redvers, whom she'd met at aerobics classes, and begun to make friends with, to extend her custom now and then . . .

The young woman who looked after the shop, typed the odd invoice and sometimes drove their smart little white and honey-coloured van with the wheatsheaf logo welcomed her cheerfully as she stepped inside. This was Barbie Nelson, a big girl with her hair scraped unceremoniously back into an elastic band, and wearing thick-lensed Bessie Bunter specs. Appallingly dressed, as always. OK, she was frankly overweight, but she could have done better than that, although somehow it didn't seem to matter too much, with Barbie. She had a warm and vibrant personality and a chuckling laugh; under the thick, clumsy clothing, the abundance of creamy flesh hinted at generosity.

'Hi, haven't seen you in here for a while,' she remarked cheerfully.

'I've been learning to cook for myself, lately.'

'You and a few others.'

'Like that, is it?' Abigail asked sympathetically, peering into the shiny cabinets. 'Not doing too well?'

'So-so.' Barbie was careful. 'But is anybody, these days? Depressing, isn't it? For a newish venture, I suppose we can't grumble. It keeps us off the dole.'

'Still just the three of you?' There were staff, Abigail knew, a boy for the heavy work, a woman in the kitchen for clearing up, casual help when they were extra busy. Plus a man who took care of the financial side – but she meant the three who really ran the place.

'Most of the time, yes. But it's how we like it, how it works for us.'

Evidently it did in this case, just the three of them. There'd been other young women somewhere in the background on occasions, Abigail knew, but presumably they hadn't jelled.

With Barbie's help, she began to make a careful selection. A lobster mousse, for starters, then came hesitations over the main course.

'Why don't you try the duck with black cherry sauce? It's a new line, but I can recommend it. One of Clare's inspirations, out of this world.'

Barbie looked like a woman who knew and enjoyed her food. Abigail decided to take her recommendation. 'What about a pudding?'

'You won't want much after all that.'

'Right, we shan't! I've some good cheese, and some fruit. It'll be better appreciated, anyway.'

'I like a man who prefers cheese, any day,' said Barbie. There

27

wouldn't have been all this careful thought if it had been a woman who was being entertained, her smile implied. Abigail hoped this wasn't true, but thought rather guiltily that it might be.

'Give my love to Ellie, tell her I'll ring her, fix something up,' she said as she paid for her packages, aware that she'd neglected to contact Ellie for too long, that a budding friendship needed nurturing if it was to thrive.

'Sure. Don't forget to follow the instructions exactly, that's important, and *bon appétit*. Take care. And don't do anything I wouldn't do, mind.' Barbie's rich laugh followed Abigail as she left.

She was pleased with her purchases, and it was barely six. *What* a good idea it had been to pick the meal up here! There were no prizes for slaving over a hot stove. There'd even be enough time now to wash the fog out of her hair and have a leisurely soak.

The weather seemed to have got worse. The sodium lights glowed eerily through the soupy darkness. Buildings loomed either side. She pulled up her collar and headed for her car. Her keys were in the lock when the figure, tall and sinister, loomed up right in front of her. And instead of dropping everything and going into attack mode, she found herself clutching her chilly packages defensively to her chest with her free hand as if that might still the banging of her heart.

'Hello, Abigail.'

'Nick.' She released her held-in breath. 'God, you scared me!' She'd been expecting to see him for some time, she'd heard he was around, and knew a meeting had to come, sooner or later. But she wished it hadn't been now. His timing had never been good.

'Come and have a drink,' he said. 'For old times' sake.'

'I can't, Nick, I'm in a hurry – '

Then she decided that she could manage a quick one, if she dispensed with the soak she'd promised herself, because she wanted – no, *needed* – to get it over, this moment she had, if the truth were told, been dreading.

It was the same pub they'd often used for anonymity in the old days, a noisy one in a street off the Cornmarket. Nothing had changed, the same smell of chips, the same Space Invaders, the same beery crowd. Only Nick Spalding was different, in some way she couldn't pin down, although he seemed no less enigmatic, or unfathomable. Deep, that was Nick. Too serious and intense, but that was nothing new. It was part of what had helped to break them up.

'What brings you back to Lavenstock, Nick?' she asked when he'd put the glass of tomato juice she'd requested in front of her. 'You couldn't wait to shake the dust off.'

He hadn't lost his old manner of answering obliquely, either. 'I've left the force, you know.'

Impossible to feign a surprise she didn't feel. She'd heard about it, and it had always been on the cards, anyway: he'd always been something of a misfit, a maverick, had never worked well as part of a team, though he was an able policeman for all that. She thought about the rumours she'd heard, wondered if they were true, and didn't welcome the thought. He'd been a disruptive influence in her life, and one of her few mistakes, careerwise. She thought he might be disruptive in anyone's life, but it was something she, at any rate, could do without.

'Roz?' she inquired, carefully, forcing herself to ask. She'd only met his wife once, briefly, when recrimination had cracked across the space between them.

'We've split, in a manner of speaking.' He swirled the melting ice in what was left of his scotch round in the bottom of his glass.

It had never been a seamless marriage, but she'd thought it patched up, the damage she'd helped to cause, the thing she'd found it hard to forgive herself for. And yet . . . She made herself think carefully before asking the next question, but he spoke, abruptly, guessing what it was going to be before she could frame it: 'He died.'

She knew he meant the child, his son, Michael, who was the reason he'd gone back to his wife after their unwise affair. A beautiful child with leukaemia. Cured, there'd been every reason to hope, but only in remission, it now seemed. 'Oh, Nick,' she said softly.

'It's OK, I've got used to it.' He brushed aside the beginnings of her sympathy, but the bunched muscles of his jaw denied what he was saying. 'Look, I need to talk to you, Abigail.' His dark eyes, narrow in a lean face, looked around at the packed tables, the loud crowds around the bar. 'A proper talk, I mean, not here.' His hand stretched out towards hers in a gesture that was all too familiar.

Alarm bells rang as she moved it out of reach. 'It wouldn't be a good idea, Nick.'

'You've got me wrong.' He smiled, slightly cynical. 'It's advice I want, nothing else. There's something worrying me.'

Nick, admitting he was worried, now there was a thing! She was intrigued, but she'd been keeping one eye on the big clock over the bar, and the hands had reached now or never point. She had to leave. 'I'm sorry, I can't, not now. Some other time?' She began to gather up her things, her leather shoulder bag and her gloves.

'Tomorrow then? Or when it suits your convenience.'

He'd never been one to plead. In his face, she read watchfulness, but in his dark eyes ... panic? Surely not! 'All right, but I won't be messed around again, Nick,' she warned.

He smiled, the one that appeared when he'd got his way, and she was immediately sorry she'd let herself be persuaded, but it was too late to back out now. 'For a few minutes, tomorrow then, on my way to work.'

'I'm staying at Prospect Street. Meet me there and I'll give you coffee.'

'Prospect Street?'

'Number four. It's property Roz still owns . . .'

The Amhurst girls, as they'd been, Roz and her sister, had money, and property all over the town, left to them by their parents, who'd been killed in an air crash when the girls were still young. Abigail had to think for a moment where Prospect Street was, then she had it, an insignificant little row of houses where any prospect there had ever been was now obscured by the new Marks and Spencer's. But a street which might not remain insignificant in monetary terms if the demands for more car-parking space near the shopping precinct were ever satisfied, and compulsory purchase orders served. Clever Roz, it had been a good move to hold on to it.

Nick watched her through the haze of smoke as she left, noticed heads turning. She had bronze hair, lovely, that used to fall in a glorious tumble of waves to her shoulders when she let it out of its workaday plait. The plait had gone, now she was an inspector – didn't go with her status, he supposed – as had the short, assertive cut she'd adopted for a while. Now it was styled to fall in rippling curves, *haute couture* hairdressing. It looked right on her, spoke of her confidence with herself. Her clothes were better, too. She was on the way to becoming elegant. He wondered why he'd ever let her go.

Witty in a dry, ironic manner, unfailingly good-humoured, with a fund of amusing stories from his life as a newspaperman, Ben Appleyard had worked on many of the large nationals, and several of his former colleagues looked on his present job, editing a provincial newspaper, as a comedown, not worthy of him. He knew it was generally thought that he hadn't shown judgement in taking the position, that it wasn't a good career move. But Ben had had his own reasons. He was as adept at parrying questions about these reasons as he was at balancing the demands of his own job with Abigail's. He was a journalist first and foremost and she was a dedicated police officer; compromise was not always easy. It made for a delicate relationship. The depth of commitment on both sides would be tested tonight, and he wasn't sure how it would turn out. He wondered if she'd guessed, and how she'd respond. She was astute by nature as well as by training, and it was Ben's experience that when a woman provided this sort of meal and took such trouble with her clothes – calf-length skirt, sweater in soft wool, the colour of bitter chocolate, with a necklace of chunky gold nuggets inside the cowl neckline – she generally knew something was in the wind.

'You look like an advert for Gold Blend, dark, strong and sexy,' he said, nuzzling her neck as they sat on the sofa in front of the fire, her legs across his knees, replete and a little sleepy with good food, finishing off the wine he'd brought. She laughed, content for the moment to talk of this and that, gradually falling into a companionable silence. It felt good to be with him. He was easy, comfortable in his skin, tall, dark and thin as whipcord, her sort of man.

She said suddenly, 'Ben, I saw Nick Spalding today. He's back in Lavenstock.'

It was out before she thought twice about it. Mentioning her former lover might have been tactless, had it ever been any problem between them, but Ben kept his ear to the ground and had known about the relationship before he and Abigail had ever become a couple, anyway. 'Does it bother you?' he asked, after a moment.

'No,' she replied, in a way that made him think she wasn't exactly telling the truth: either that or she was trying to convince herself. His senses were alerted.

'What's he doing here?'

'He didn't say, but I've gathered from other sources that he has some idea of starting up a private inquiry agency. A bit iffy, I'd have thought. Especially if he's relying on police contacts. He doesn't make friends easily. A lot of people were wary of him when he was on the strength, and now . . . Ben, what I don't like is that I've heard he's trying to recruit Alex Jones, and that she isn't averse to the idea.'

He raised an eyebrow.

Alex Jones was high on the list of people Abigail considered her special friends, a former police sergeant who'd left the Service and was presently working with her sister, Lois French, in her interior design business. After a shaky start, the indications were that she was beginning to enjoy it. The two women were pooling their resources and their skills, and not doing too badly, Abigail knew. A bit like Miller's Wife, in a way. When women really got their act together, they could be terrific. Abigail wondered just how serious Alex was about giving up this promising new career for the dubious advantages of joining Nick. They'd been seen together once or twice since September, apparently, but Alex hadn't said anything to Abigail. She was a little cagey about her personal life. Not too many confidences got passed on, and both women knew why: for the one very good and cogent reason that the man Alex lived with happened to be Abigail's senior officer, Superintendent Gil Mayo. Abigail thought wryly that if Alex really intended an association with Nick, she had problems in front of her.

'What did he want?' Ben was asking.

'There's something on his mind . . . he's asked to see me tomorrow.' She broke off. A discussion of Nick's affairs, never mind how uneasy their encounter had made her, was hardly appropriate to the present moment. She was annoyed with herself for bringing the subject up at all. 'Well, anyhow, don't let's spoil the evening.'

'Let's not,' he agreed drily, his arm tightening round her.

He was toying with her hand, twisting the heavy gold gypsy ring, set with garnets, that he'd given her last birthday. The firelight flickered round the room, on the oak table she'd so patiently and lovingly restored, on the candles burning low over the remnants of their meal, on the spines of her books and the few pictures she'd collected, and was kind to the empty corners still to be filled. Buying, furnishing and restoring the once-derelict cottage, making its garden, took all the spare energy and resources she had. She'd made shift and she'd had great plans at first, but somehow there never seemed time enough, not to mention money.

He rearranged her legs more comfortably across his knees as he twisted round to face her. 'Hope I'm not going to ruin the evening with what I've to say, either.'

'That sounds ominous – but go on, don't keep me in suspense.' She stared fixedly into the fire, her heart beginning to beat hard. Don't ask me, she thought in a sudden panic, don't ask me for something I can't give.

'I'm not sure how you'll take this, but – ' He took hold of her chin and gently forced her to look at him. Wait for it, Abigail thought. 'I've decided to chuck in my job.'

For the second time that night, she felt winded. She'd been so sure he was going to bring up the subject of marriage, which, up until now, had never been on the agenda for either of them. Until recently, she'd always imagined their particular situation suited him as well as it did her, but then she'd lately sensed a shifting in the atmosphere and had started to wonder uneasily if he'd begun to have second thoughts. Second thoughts right enough, but not in that way, it seemed. She'd misread the signs entirely. She felt *bouleversée*. 'Your job,' she repeated idiotically. 'You've got another one?'

He didn't answer directly. After a moment, he said, 'The trouble is, my book. It's not working.'

The first time Abigail had visited his flat, his initial attempt at writing a book, a political thriller based on his personal experiences as a correspondent in the Middle East, had been merely a

33

pile of manuscript on his desk. Since then it had been published, and had been well reviewed. At the moment, he was trying to get over the difficult second-book hurdle by following up with one even better. But with a full-time job, there was no way it could be easy.

'You're giving your job up to give yourself more time, is that it? My God, Ben! Tell me I've a bourgeois little soul, but that would frighten the life out of me.'

'It's not time that's the problem. It isn't all that demanding, editing the *Advertiser*, not exactly a leading national, which is why I took it. It leaves me with time and energy enough to write in the evenings, but heck, I can't write about something I haven't been involved in. I need to be there, where it's happening.'

She knew now what he was going to say, and she was shutting it out, not wanting to take on board what it must mean.

'For can't, read don't want, if I'm honest,' he went on, typically open. 'But at the same time, I can't live on air. I need a job to support myself.'

'Are you saying you can just walk straight back into your old one?'

'Of course not. But there are openings – Middle East again, I hope. I'm leaving tomorrow for a few days in London to finalize things.'

It had been bound to happen, sometime. He was used to wider horizons than Lavenstock could offer. And it was the spark of excitement in his eyes at the prospect of being once again in the thick of world affairs, of living on the edge of danger, which made her see how restless he'd become. Something she should have seen, but hadn't, perhaps because she'd been too preoccupied with her own career. But that also had been an unspoken part of the bargain.

Right from the start it had been a no-strings relationship, and there could be no recriminations, no comebacks, no tears. She reminded herself that she *liked* living alone, being independent. He would keep on his flat, he was saying, for whenever he was home. He *would* be home, often, things would hardly be any different. After all, there'd been many times when they hadn't seen each other for a couple of weeks. On the other hand, weeks when they'd seen each other nearly every day . . .

'God dammit, I shall miss you, though.'

'Me, too.' She felt bleak. She smiled.

'Abigail? You do see, don't you?'

'Oh, absolutely.' The last thing she wanted was for him to feel guilty on her account. And a quiet voice told her very clearly – and perhaps this was the hardest part to bear – that if the positions had been reversed, she would have done exactly the same. 'It's a pity we've drunk all the wine, or we could have toasted to your success. Wait a minute, though, I have some brandy.'

They drank to his future, to hers, they talked and talked, and finally, when the logs had fallen into ash, he said, 'Come to bed, flower.'

Barbie Nelson took off her thick spectacles and put them carefully on to her bedside table. Then she began slowly to undress, first her heavy, unbecoming trousers and sweaters, then her sleek silk underwear; she undid her hair and let it fall in thick, dark, luxuriant waves to her shoulders. When she was naked, she stood in front of her long mirror, dispassionately assessing her statuesque curves and the creamy, voluptuous skin, as far as that was possible without the benefit of her spectacles. Her reflection was blurred, so that she wasn't dissatisfied with what she saw. But maybe it wasn't altogether due to the absence of glasses: she'd been taught to accept herself for what she was, generous and beautiful. Smiling, she lifted the designer nightdress from where it lay ready across the bed and slid it over her head, smoothing the frothy lace sensuously over her full breasts, and the heavy pale-raspberry duchesse satin over her swelling hips and buttocks. She thought of Tim Wishart, tall, rangy, heartless. She closed her eyes with a great shudder.

Tim Wishart. Was it possible? For a moment, her certainty wavered, but it was for a moment only. Of course it was. Yes, yes, oh *yes*!

4

The small house in Prospect Street had been rented out as furnished accommodation for several years, although it was far better furnished and more fully equipped than the usual run of such. Comfortable and functional, all that needed to work doing so. That was to be expected, its owner being what she was, Abigail supposed. Roz's reputation for efficiency had always intimidated her. Nor had Roz ever flashed her money about, not like her sister, though they both had plenty of it. 'Nice,' she said.

Nick shrugged. 'It serves its purpose.'

But the house, lying overshadowed by the new shopping precinct, was dark, for all its bright paint. Gloomy, in the tiny north-facing front room, had it not been for a table lamp lit against the dank, dismal morning and the flames of a simulated coal fire making it cosy – and rather too intimate. Abigail sat perched sideways on the edge of the settee. No point in giving out any wrong signals.

'Suits me well enough, on a temporary basis,' Nick continued when he'd made and poured coffee. He was smoking again, good intentions gone with the wind, and not asking her whether she minded.

'Rumour has it that you're thinking of settling back locally.'

'Rumour's more or less right, then. But that's as far as I've got,' he admitted warily, 'though I've been sounding out a few people.' She'd heard that, too. Other people, apart from Alex Jones, that was. The Lavenstock police grapevine was nothing if not efficient, and it paid to keep tuned in. But she hadn't heard that anyone else was interested.

'Is it a good idea?' She wasn't pleased at the prospect of having him back on her patch, as a private investigator, or in any other capacity.

'I have my eye on some premises in Hurstfield.'

The next division, safe enough not to be a nuisance. That was better. 'It's going to cost you.'

He looked evasive. 'Sure, but I have an arrangement.'

Did that mean he'd succumbed? After all he'd said about refusing to touch a penny of his rich wife's money? She couldn't see how else he could have amassed enough capital, in so short a time. He didn't throw his money around, but he didn't count every penny, either. What he said next made her think her guess maybe hadn't been so far out.

'I have to contact Roz.' His face darkened. 'Which at the moment is proving damned difficult.'

'Why's that?'

'She seems to have disappeared – and I haven't a clue as to where.'

She drank some coffee, debating what to say. A woman with marital problems to sort out might well decide to drop out of circulation for a while. It was her privilege, and to a woman with means, like Roz Spalding, that wouldn't present any difficulty. 'We-ell . . .'

'Oh, I know! You're going to say she's every right to go off, if she wants to, but it's not as simple as that.' He sat forward, hands between his knees. 'I suppose I'd better put you in the picture. After you and I – after I got back together with Roz, we managed to rub along well enough. At least, as well as most married people,' he added with a spark of his old cynicism. 'In the latter stages, just before Michael died, it was better. I began to think we might work things out permanently . . . and then, afterwards, when it was all over, she suddenly claimed she needed to be on her own, to think, before we . . . Well, anyway, the last tenants here had just left, so she came over and moved in for a short while. In the event, it was for four months. She messed around generally for a bit, took a temporary job.'

Teaching, that would be. Roz had, by all accounts, been a good teacher, it was what she'd trained for.

'And then she *informed* me – a damned letter, not even a telephone call – that she was going away. She needed a different perspective, was how she put it. She mentioned Tuscany, said she'd be in touch.'

'That's hardly disappearing.'

He ground his cigarette out in the ashtray, then sprang up and walked to the window, where he stood staring out with his hands shoved in his pockets, jangling his change. Always a restless man, Nick. His body blocked what little light there was, this dank morning, but it would be gloomy in this room, even in summer, when the sycamore that grew in the tiny front plot was heavy with leaf. She watched melancholy drops clinging to the lifeless branches until he came back to his seat.

'There was something about that letter, something I couldn't put my finger on. I'd promised I wouldn't follow her here, but in the end I did. And didn't like what I found. She'd left the fridge full of food that was going off, for one thing. Anything more unlike Roz, I can't imagine.'

'A sudden decision – '

'There's something else,' he interrupted. 'I found this by the front door.' From the floor near his chair he produced a black suede shoe, a pretty thing with crossed straps and a tiny buckle fastening. 'Just one. What d'you make of that?'

'Maybe she just dropped it in her rush to get away.'

'No chance! When Roz goes away, she *packs*! Efficiently, no loose bits and pieces to scatter around. And as well as cleaning out the fridge and the garbage, she even turns off the water and the gas. None of which she'd done.'

'Maybe she had a plane to catch.'

'Too much in a rush to pick the phone up and let me know? What the hell could have been so important for her to rush away like that without letting me know? Leaving food to go bad, dropping shoes!'

His anger suddenly gave way to uncertainty as he looked at the shoe, still in his hand. His temper was volatile, but while the whirlwind raged, you were wise to keep your head well below the parapet. Was that what Roz was doing? Letting the dust settle? Abigail had every sympathy with her, whatever her reasons for going away were – and she could think of several, the most likely being another man. Presumably she wasn't immune from falling in love. Was it, then, a spur of the moment decision to go away with her lover – understandably omitting to inform Nick?

'Tuscany, you said? What about her passport?'

'It's not in the house, but neither is her handbag, or her other papers. That proves nothing. I've contacted Sophie, as well, or tried to, but wouldn't you know, she's off on her travels again, has been since last autumn, she and that husband of hers. A card came from her, yesterday, posted in Cairo.'

Sophie, Roz's sister. There was a name from the past! Abigail saw her around sometimes, though not often, had heard she was richer than ever, having inherited the old woman's money. Several times married, this time happily, but not cured of her wanderlust, it seemed.

'Why haven't you reported her missing?'

He took another cigarette from the pack, watching her sardonically over the flame of the lighter. 'Oh, come on! You know as well as I do what the reaction would be. Just the line you're taking now – if a grown woman decides to disappear, she presumably has reasons for not wanting to be found. No grounds for searching for her unless there are suspicious circumstances, and an uncleared fridge wouldn't be regarded as that.'

There was no arguing with that. 'Just what do you want me to do that you can't do yourself? You're an experienced detective.'

'I've every intention of carrying on looking for her myself, I just don't want to make a song and dance about it. I'm only asking you to make a few unofficial enquiries, as well, set something in motion. You've access to more information than I have. You carry more weight.'

They'd come a long way since the days when he could persuade her into almost anything. 'I'm sorry, I'd advise you to wait a bit longer, I'm sure you'll hear from her soon.' Abigail stood up. She had a busy day in front of her, and no more time to waste. Yet she sensed that he was really worried, although so far he hadn't convinced her that there was any cause for undue concern. 'Look, Nick, she could walk in at that door tomorrow, and she wouldn't thank you for having chased her.'

'I know that well enough. But I can't leave it like this, you must see that.'

What Abigail saw was that the success or otherwise of his marriage was balanced on a knife edge, but she knew that Roz was a self-reliant lady, who valued her independence. She guessed also that Nick might be desperately afraid that his wife could renege on her promises to support him in his new venture, and that puzzled her.

'What if she's in trouble,' he said suddenly, 'serious trouble?'

Perhaps she'd been doing him an injustice in believing that he was worried about Roz's so-called disappearance primarily because it affected him financially. And after all, who could know what a mother might do after the death of her child? Roz had had a terrible experience, long and harrowing. Hardly surprising if something had finally snapped. Suicide? Was that what Nick was trying to say? But Roz, from what Abigail knew of her, stood for common sense, robustness. She could handle herself.

All the same . . .

Nick was never loath to use emotional blackmail when the occasion warranted it, as she knew to her cost. He could be ruthless in getting what he wanted. She sighed and stood up. 'All right, I'll keep my eyes open, that's all I can promise.'

'Thank you, I knew you'd help.' She tried to ignore what was undoubtedly satisfaction in his eyes. 'But you will be discreet, won't you?'

She gave her assurances, though she had a strong suspicion he hadn't told her all he knew, which didn't bode well for success. What was at the back of all this? she wondered as she made her way in to work. What game was he playing?

Clare hadn't yet gone to bed when Tim came home that night. Amy and three of her friends had spent a strenuous and rowdy few hours playing table tennis in the games room extension to the accompaniment of loud music, but the friends had long since noisily departed in an old banger belonging to one of the boys and Amy had gone straight up to bed.

Half an hour later, she'd heard a car arrive at speed down the drive, drawing up outside with a punishment of tyres on gravel which meant no one else but Richie. A wash of relief swept over her, as always when he returned after driving. He'd called goodnight from the hall, but she came out of the sitting-room while he was still half-way up the open-tread staircase.

''Night, Richie,' she called, then, 'Are you all right?'

He looked pale, sick. She thought at first he'd dented her car, except that Richie would have come straight out with it; then that he was drunk, but there was no smell of drink on him. Drugs! The dreaded word flashed through her mind, every parent's nightmare. She searched his face for the signs that were supposed to be there, but instinctively she knew it wasn't that.

'What's wrong?' she asked, reaching out over the banister rail to him.

'It's nothing, Mum,' he said, avoiding her hand and then bending to give her a hasty, embarrassed, goodnight kiss. 'Just knackered, that's all.' He'd loped up the rest of the stairs, two at a time, and she heard his bedroom door bang shut.

She made a chicken sandwich and a pot of tea, and sat wrapped in an old velvet kaftan, watching one mindless television programme after another, none of them making any impression whatever. She managed to eat half the sandwich, drank three cups of tea, then switched the set off and listened to the solitude. This was never how she'd expected her life to be, spending her evenings alone, worrying about her children, wondering if Tim was going to turn up or whether she'd be spending yet another solitary night, alone in the king-size bed.

Tonight, the house, silent but for its ever-present rush of water, was getting on her nerves. The mill wheel had been jammed to prevent its turning, but she could hear its creaking ghost. She shivered and concentrated on her outing with David Neale the next day. She was looking forward to it with more pleasure than she would have thought. It was a long time since she'd been escorted anywhere by a personable, attentive man and though it wasn't a social engagement as such, she'd planned what she was going to wear as if she were a young girl going out on her first date.

She heard Tim's car draw up as she was carrying her tray into the kitchen. She was loading crockery into the dishwasher when he came in and she was immediately aware that he'd been drinking, though normally he drank little. It wasn't one of his vices.

'Come into the sitting-room, I want to talk to you, Clare.' He directed his appealing, one-sided smile at her, the one which had once made her knees turn to water, but it was a travesty of what it had once been. He looked dreadful, almost as bad as Richie.

'I was just on my way to bed.'

'Come on, you can spare me a few moments,' he said in a thick, cajoling voice.

She shrugged and followed him reluctantly, and perched on the arm of a chair, with her arms wrapped around herself. Let's get this over with, she thought, and then perhaps she might even get the chance to talk to him about Richie. He was Tim's responsibility as well as hers, and he and Richie had always been able to communicate with each other. 'Tim – ' she began.

'I'm in trouble,' he interrupted abruptly, which didn't come as any surprise. Everything over the last week or two had suggested it, she'd seen the usual restless signs, plus an unfamiliar edge of worry. 'Serious trouble.'

'Money again, I take it.'

'Partly – but don't be like that, Clare. It hasn't all been my fault.'

'Most of it has.' For months now, she'd been keeping the household going, paid all the bills, and some of Tim's, too. 'But you've come to the wrong place this time. Money's as tight with me as with everyone else.'

'I'm only asking for a short-term loan, for God's sake! A few days, that's all.' Even when asking for favours, he couldn't hide his petulance, his assumption that it was his right to expect people to bail him out. His voice was unbearably patronizing in its public school arrogance. She shook her head.

'There's your father.'

'No,' she answered quickly, having anticipated this question, and her answer to it. 'No way will I ask him. Don't even think of it.'

'He's helped us before.'

'That's just why I won't do it again.'

'He wouldn't miss it, he's lousy with it!' His face had begun to look ugly.

'He's worked damned hard for every penny, if that's what you mean, and it isn't right that he should be expected to subsidize you, Tim.'

'God, you're a hard-hearted bitch! You care about nothing but that tinpot cooking outfit, you and that partner of yours!'

Instead of retreating into sulks, as he invariably did after one of their contretemps, he advanced towards her, his face congested with rage, and caught hold of her wrist, dragging her upright so that his face was inches from hers, and she could smell the whisky on his breath. He stood over her, big and overwhelming, glaring at her with his arm half lifted, his fist clenched, and she braced herself for the expected blow. Never

42

before had he threatened her with violence, but she would not cower back. A pulse beat violently in her temple, but she held his gaze, and eventually it was his that fell. His arm dropped to his side, he flung her away from him and she lurched back against the chair.

He turned on her a look of such loathing that she felt scorched by it. Then, without another word, he swung round and stamped off upstairs. She held on to the chair for dear life, feeling waves of nausea envelop her. With her hand to her mouth, she staggered to the downstairs cloakroom and was violently sick.

Afterwards, she leaned her forehead against the cold glass of the mirror, her eyes closed. I've forgiven you a lot, Tim, over the years, but this must be the end, she told herself, the end of our marriage, the absolute end of everything.

On Saturday morning David Neale listened to the radio weather forecast as he showered and shaved. There was apparently to be no hope of a quick ending to the persistent clammy fog that still hung around outside his bathroom window, though the faintly optimistic forecast was that the sun might try to break through in the afternoon. But if not ... He was beginning to be worried. His arrangements with Clare might not work out exactly as he intended. Relax, he told himself, relax ...

Part of the cause of that collapse of his, after a particularly acrimonious board meeting, he'd been told, was due to his inability to unwind. His job was too stressful, he must give it up and learn to take things as they came. He'd been advised to take up yoga, find some new interests, quit smoking, and follow a quiet and well-ordered way of life. He'd thought at first he might as well *be* dead.

His parents had been rigid Presbyterian Scots and, since childhood, he'd been imbued with the strong Calvinistic ethic of hard work and duty. He'd reached his position on the board, not because of his brilliance, but through sheer slog and determination. Shy as a young man, he'd never actually relished the cut and thrust of corporate life; it didn't come naturally to him, but he'd always believed he'd managed to keep his end up, that he worked well under pressure. It had taken him a while to begin to admit to himself that he'd always been on the sidelines of that macho power game, longer to accept it and find there were other ways to keep the adrenalin flowing.

His pulses quickened as he thought of the day ahead, but he controlled his excitement as he went over his plans, making a careful selection from his wardrobe, deciding finally on a fawn cashmere roll-neck sweater and a pair of casual, well-tailored slacks that he put aside to wear later, when he went to meet Clare.

She'd left one of her notes on his desk yesterday when he'd been out at lunch time, suggesting the best time for him to collect her from her father's house. He smiled as he took it from his wallet and smoothed it out, and, before going downstairs, he put it in the drawer of his bedside table, next to the photograph of his mother, and every one of the other notes or memos Clare had ever written to him.

He had a cleaning woman who came in twice a week to do his chores, although one not untidy man living alone barely made a dent in the atmosphere. For the most part, he lived in his comfortably furnished study, next to the dining-room, but he always felt he owed it to Jane to see that the rest of the house was kept as she'd once liked it, with the care and attention that showed off the beautiful furniture, collected by her father, and now his responsibility. He walked from room to room, checking that everything was in order, that Mrs King hadn't knocked any of the pictures out of line when she dusted, rearranging in a more comfortable fashion the cushions which she insisted on leaving quatri-cornered along the sofa.

On an impulse, he went in as he reached the door of what had been Jane's workroom, something he rarely did now. It was very much as she'd left it – her battered old desk and armchair, the big table where she used to do her sewing. She'd been an accomplished needlewoman, and the tapestry cushions all over the house bore witness to this. She'd also taken to making her own clothes. He'd never been able to see why she'd rebelled against the designer models he liked to see her wearing whenever she went out with him. But for all they'd been married thirteen years, Jane had never really understood him. Not many women did.

Which was strange, because he liked women and was attentive

to their welfare. He couldn't bear to see them suffer. He'd done his best for Jane, poor, dear, misguided Jane, in his own way, right to the end. He stared bleakly out of the fog-obscured window. He'd never imagined he would miss her so much, that he'd be so lonely. Her ghost walked with him everywhere.

The trick was to find the way out of the shadows, out of despair, to shut off your mind to things too painful to remember. He blinked and shook his head as if to clear it, and the image of Clare came to take its place. Yes, well. Maybe, soon, things would be different.

From here, one could just about see across the murky river. His eyes were drawn like a magnet to the Bagots, dimly outlined in the fog, eyesores which couldn't come down too soon for him. The sight of the decrepit, tumbledown, uncared-for buildings went against his sense of how people should live. The sooner they were pulled down and their inhabitants rehoused in clean, comfortable accommodation, the better he'd be pleased, for their sakes. He was delighted the developers had won the battle. Not only because he had a strong sense of social justice, but also because he had a substantial tranche of shares in their company. He wasn't Scottish for nothing.

He looked at his watch; there were things he mustn't forget to do before he met Clare, duty before pleasure, drilled into him as a child. He had to follow his routine exercises in the basement, update his computer. He was very particular about keeping up with his skills. Miss a day and you soon got out of the way of it.

Abigail was taking a virtuous walk before breakfast. It provided bodily exercise, but a tramp through the fields, with the dank mist hanging low and limiting the view to dismal acres of brussels sprouts, was hardly spiritually uplifting. The rain was holding off, but the fog was clinging and penetrating, despite her big woolly scarf, a knitted hat and thick gloves, with her coat collar pulled up around her ears. She plodded along the narrow field path, thinking about the Ben situation, fidgeting with it in her mind and trying to see how she could make it work for her. Doubtless she would, in time. See the best in it. But not yet.

Her walk seemed suddenly pointless. She wondered crossly

why she'd come this way. Picking your way along the edge of a field, between mud and puddles, was a form of masochism, and the smell of those sprouts was digusting.

After breakfast she felt slightly better, and zipped through her necessary weekend chores, though without much enthusiasm, skipping the corners if the truth be told, since housework was never likely to be her favourite occupation. That done, she faced the question of what to do with herself, feeling like an engine with a broken fan belt. If anyone had asked her yesterday what she would do with two whole free days, she'd have said without hesitation sleep, sleep, sleep ... but that was yesterday, and today here she was, charged with energy and nothing particular in prospect, except many more of the same sort of weekends. The remembered promise to herself about Ellie Redvers came like a lifeline.

She pulled her diary from her bag and dialled Ellie's number. The welcome in her attractive, husky voice was immediately cheering. 'I've just been speaking to Barbie,' she said. 'Hear you called in at the shop on Thursday night.'

'Only in an emergency, I admit. I left myself too little time to cook. I'd better arrange for that to happen more often, the food was delicious!'

'Come and have lunch with me, Abigail. I've got the blues and I need cheerful company.'

It was consoling to know she wasn't the only one, but Abigail said, 'I've got a better idea. Why don't you come out here and help me to eat what I intended to cook on Thursday? It'll give you a break.' Just in time she stopped herself from apologizing in advance for what was sure to be an inferior meal to any Ellie herself could cook, guessing how sick she and Clare must be of hearing such protestations.

Ellie accepted enthusiastically, saying she was longing to see the cottage, which she'd heard about but never seen.

Abigail suddenly saw her hard-won little retreat as it might appear to other people, an uninteresting, square little house overwhelmed by the hill behind it, with drab fields in front, redeemed only by the small garden she'd made. 'Don't expect too much. I'm afraid you won't see it at its best. I look at it through rose-coloured specs but other people need the sunshine to appreciate it, and the garden's looking like nothing on earth this time of year.'

'But it's lovely, lovely!' Ellie exclaimed, in the rather exaggerated way she had, when she arrived in her smart little dark blue Fiat, speaking warmly, as if she really meant it, as if the brave makeshift was every bit as appealing as the cool elegance of her own modern house.

She was appreciative of the food, too. Well, so she should be. She'd realize, if anybody did, the trouble Abigail had taken. She ate with relish and Abigail wondered enviously how anyone with an appetite like that could stay so slim. Thin, not to mince words, and really, not looking very happy. But if it was unhappiness that had hollowed her cheeks and given her that vulnerable, appealing look, it suited her. She was wearing a jacket in a soft tone of burnt orange, a matching checked skirt and narrow chestnut boots, but whatever she wore, Ellie always made other women look as if they tried too much.

'I hear Miller's Wife's suffering from the recession like the rest,' Abigail said, when they were sitting relaxed after lunch, before the warmth of the piled-up log fire.

'Oh? Who told you that?' Ellie was instantly defensive.

'Barbie, when I was in the shop.'

'Well, she shouldn't have, that's hardly the way to inspire confidence in our customers!'

'I expect it was only because she knew I was a friend.' Abigail tried to be appeasing, surprised at Ellie's sharpness.

'Doesn't make any difference, she was out of order.' She frowned, then fluttered her hands in an extravagant gesture of apology. 'Sorry, sorry, I'm a bit touchy on the subject. Barbie's the proverbial treasure, but she does take a bit on herself, and I suppose that *is* what we want. Someone to show initiative, I mean. Clare thinks she's wonderful.'

Which, by implication, meant that Ellie didn't – or perhaps not quite as much.

Ellie seemed to guess her thoughts and smiled ruefully. 'It's just that I can't understand someone as intelligent as she is being content to be, let's face it, nothing more than a dogsbody.'

'Jobs aren't hanging off trees at the moment.'

'Don't I know it,' said Ellie, who, from what Abigail had

gathered, had never known what it was like to be short of a bob or two. 'I suppose we're lucky, you and I, doing jobs we love.'

'Most of the time I'd agree with you,' Abigail returned drily. 'But I haven't exactly loved what I've been doing this week. Up to here with drugs.'

'Drugs?' Ellie repeated, staring into the fire, holding her hands out as if they needed warming. 'That's the pits. You do see the seamy side of life, don't you? But then, nobody's life is perfect.' She was suddenly all huge, sad eyes. 'May I have some more of this delicious coffee, do you think?'

Supplied with a refill, she held both hands around the steaming cup, and went on as if there'd been no interruption. 'My life isn't, anyway. It's far from perfect, at the moment. To be honest, it's a total mess. But I've really made my mind up to do something about it, finally. Last night, it seemed easy – stop it, just like that, the way you're supposed to give up smoking, but there's nothing easy about ending a relationship, is there?' She stared fixedly into the flames. 'Not even when you despise yourself for it, allowing yourself to – ' She broke off abruptly. 'But you'd never let that happen to you, you're far too sensible.'

More than you think, Ellie. Abigail had been the one who'd sensibly ended the affair with Nick Spalding, and she'd felt for months as though whole areas of skin had been scraped off, leaving her raw. Saying so wasn't going to help Ellie now. Even allowing for a certain tendency to dramatize a situation, it was obvious she was in a state, but she hadn't yet reached the point where she was asking for advice.

'Men are bastards, Abigail. Ask Clare, having to cope with the fall-out of – ' She looked as though she wished she hadn't said that. 'Or ask Barbie.'

'Barbie?'

'Oh yes,' she came back sharply, glad to be on another tack. 'When you think about it, there's only one explanation for Barbie, and the way she looks. She's trying to hide it, of course, but there's a man somewhere, take it from me. Underneath all that don't-give-a-damn-how-I-look exterior, she's quite attractive. Haven't you noticed?'

'I've noticed,' Abigail said, at the same moment as the telephone rang.

When she came back from answering it, a few minutes later,

all thoughts of Barbie Nelson, Clare, Ellie's problems, had receded. 'Sorry to be a wet blanket, but I'm going to have to wind this up. Duty calls, I'm afraid.'

Ellie said immediately, 'That's all right, time I went, anyway. Nothing ghastly, I hope?'

'Pretty ghastly for the young lad concerned, and his mum and dad. He was taken into hospital last night with an overdose,' Abigail replied soberly. 'He died this morning.'

5

When he heard of Clare's arrangement with David Neale, Sam Nash had offered to drive over to Clacks Mill on Saturday morning to fetch his daughter to have lunch with him. 'That way, he can drop you straight back home afterwards,' he'd suggested. Collecting Clare like that, Sam thought, would also give him the opportunity to cast his eye around the mill house.

'Where's everyone?' he asked when he arrived, disappointed not to find Amy at home, and was told that she was out shopping for clothes with one of her friends. 'Quite the young woman,' he remarked with a chuckle. It seemed to him not five minutes since he'd dandled her on his knee, or she'd come running out to welcome him with her hair flying when he came to visit with a pocketful of sweets.

'She sends her love, though,' Clare told him, 'and Richie says he'll be seeing you,' she added, a wryly raised eyebrow showing she was well aware of the hidden agenda behind this seemingly innocuous message.

Sam was an affable man who adored his grandchildren and would do anything for them, and he knew what the message meant, too. Richie had been lobbying him about this blasted car he was after, trying to enlist his aid against his mother, but Sam was too old a hand to get inveigled into that sort of situation. He'd told Richie plainly that he thought Clare was quite right, for the time being. To do him justice, Richie, never a lad to bear a grudge for long, had in the end taken it philosophically enough, no doubt he'd expected nothing more. But Sam knew they hadn't heard the last of it, Richie was well aware there'd come a time when they'd have to give in. Like all teenagers, he knew the value of relentless persecution.

And Tim, Clare added, scrupulously taking Sam at his word when he'd enquired about 'everybody', had taken his gun and gone out shooting with John Fairmile, who lived at the farm at the bottom of the lane.

'Hm!' Sam made no further comment, but stood by the window, drinking coffee while he waited for Clare to finish getting ready.

Apart from her lavish herb-and-vegetable plot at the side, there was no garden as such at Clacks Mill – just a gravelled forecourt with tubs by the front door that were filled with flowers in summer, and a short stretch of lawn at the back for sitting out or sunbathing. The natural landscaping of the mossy, tree-shaded banks, the stream rushing between the red sandstone rocks and past the wheel, was pretty enough to need no added embellishments.

Sam had already had a quick check around to satisfy himself that everything was in order, running his eye over the weather-boarding, gutterings, window frames, things in general. The drive needed resurfacing, he noted, there were puddles in the gravel. And something should be done about clearing and making use of that spare land alongside the lane, between the main road and the mill house. A quaggy four and a half acres, overgrown with sycamore saplings, brambles and holly, it wasn't much use for anything in its present unkempt state.

The millstream was high and running full spate over the rocks, and he'd walked along to the bridge over the race, testing it with his weight, shaking the low handrail to make sure it was safe. He was nothing if not practically minded, and felt it his duty to keep his eye on such things, here at Clacks Mill, since he knew Clare's husband never deigned to lower himself to such mundane tasks.

On the way into town they chatted for a while, then fell into a companionable silence. Sam could only guess what his daughter's thoughts might be; if she was under stress, she was determined not to show it by anything she said, but he'd noticed the dark circles under her eyes, the way her hands were clasped tightly together on her knee. And he was pretty sure, when her sleeve had slipped back, that it wasn't his imagination which had discerned a livid bruise on her forearm. He tried to push this new worry to the back of his mind.

'Remember Mary Bellamy?' he asked her suddenly, with a quick, sideways glance as they drew up to a red light.

'Of course.' Mary was the widow of one of Sam's acquaintances who had died some five or six years previously. She was a young-looking woman of about sixty, a retired nursing sister, childless, comfortably off, a good-humoured and practical person with a cheerful smile, whose name had cropped up more and more in Sam's conversation lately. 'She's a lovely lady.'

'Good to hear you say so, Clare, I want you to like her. I'm – er – taking her out to dinner tonight.'

'Are you saying what I think you're saying, Dad?'

He grinned, looking suddenly boyish. In his late sixties, he was still a handsome man, well-muscled and spry, his fierce dark brows and tanned, craggy face a contrast to the crest of thick white hair and bright, quick brown eyes. 'I somehow thought you'd have guessed. Dammit, this isn't the time to say this, I should've waited, but there's something you should know.'

'You're getting married!' Clare guessed, delighted.

He was evidently a little disconcerted that it had been so obvious, but pleased at her reaction. 'She's a fine woman, Clare.'

'She'll be getting a fine man,' Clare said affectionately, and since she couldn't hug him when he was driving, she squeezed his arm and pressed a fingertip kiss on his cheek.

'You could be prejudiced!' he returned, smiling, keeping his eyes on the road.

'I could. But it's wonderful news, you'll make each other very happy, I know.'

He said seriously, 'I wish I could feel as certain about you, m'duck.'

'Leave it, Dad.'

She'd always known how he felt about Tim. He'd never been happy about their marriage and had done his best to stop her rushing into it. 'Give it a bit more time. You've only known him a few weeks, girl,' he'd begged her. But she'd been twenty years old and fathoms deep in love and wouldn't listen, nor even agree to a long engagement. It had been the nearest they'd ever come

51

to a serious row when he'd told her bluntly, 'You're going to regret this, Clare. A fancy county name doesn't hide the fact that he's a womanizer, and weak-willed.'

'Don't – just don't! I know there've been other women, and why not? He's single, unattached.'

Sam knew his daughter. She'd inherited a surprising stubbornness from her mother, besides much else that made him love her, and nothing was worth losing her, especially a row over Tim Wishart. He'd given in gracefully and helped them financially, though judiciously, knowing instinctively that it would be wrong to trust Wishart too far, to allow him to get his hands on too much of his own hard-earned money. Clacks Mill had been his wedding present to Clare. He had made sure the deeds were in her name.

The rumour had soon reached him that his son-in-law had maybe sailed too close to the wind once or twice. Heck, no, there was no maybe about it, to those in the know! Yet the fact that Sam had been proved right on all counts didn't make him feel any better. Clare wouldn't talk about it – and he hadn't helped by not troubling to hide his opinions over the years about Tim Wishart. But she couldn't hide from him how patently unhappy she now was, whatever face she put on it; when Sam thought about what her life must be like, he felt his blood pressure rise dangerously. His hands itched to get themselves around the bastard's throat and throttle the life out of him.

He changed the subject with a reference to her suggestion that they should start their lunch immediately they arrived at his house and get it out of the way before David Neale, whom Sam hadn't yet met, arrived.

'Suits me. It'll give me plenty time to get to the match.' He never missed when Lavenstock United football team were playing at home. 'Mrs Wilton's left us one of her famous soups, I believe. But we needn't drink it.' An adequate, if unimaginative, cook in other directions, Mrs Wilton produced soups which were famous for their awfulness.

In fact, she must have been having one of her better days. She'd left quite a passable light consommé, much improved after Sam, who enjoyed cooking and made his own meals, except for the days Mrs Wilton came to do for him, had added a dash of sherry. And the chicken casserole which followed was decidedly tasty.

'This Neale chap,' Sam began, as they sat in the small, heated conservatory overlooking what in summer was a very attractive garden, with the coffee and cake with which he invariably liked to finish his meal. 'Shaping up all right, is he?'

'David?' Clare concealed a smile at 'this Neale chap'. She was used to the suspicious treatment meted out to any man who came within a mile of her. 'Lord, yes, I don't know how we managed without him. Keeping the books used to be a major headache for us, but it's child's play to him. He can almost make that wretched computer talk!'

Sam nodded. He knew the value of someone like that. His own business had benefited from having a shrewd financial man about the place who knew the ropes, especially in the beginning, when Sam himself had been no great shakes with the paperwork. He'd started his business with one small car-repair shop, gone on to body-building and then to selling cars. He'd gradually acquired a string of garages and later added a small coach-hire firm. His fleet of distinctive dark red buses with the name 'Sam Nash' in gold across their sides was now a familiar sight on the hilly roads all around the Black Country. Though he was retired, he still retained a controlling interest in the business. Kept him on the ball, that and being on the Borough Council, with a bit of gardening on the side to keep him active. Speaking of which, he'd noticed that morning the plants in his borders were already pushing up through the sodden ground. He kept an eye on them throughout the winter, knowing where every dormant plant in the garden lay. He'd worked it, getting it to his liking, ever since he'd brought Clare's mother to live here as a bride.

Clare was asking about Sam's and Mary's plans for their marriage.

'Oh, we're not about to rush into anything. It's hardly a shotgun wedding, you know.'

'Sam Nash, I should hope not!' Clare laughed. 'But where are you going to live?'

'Why here, of course, where else?'

'Does she know that?'

Her father said of course she did. Clare reflected that Mary

Bellamy must indeed be smitten, to be prepared to leave her modern, well-furnished bungalow on the outskirts of the town. Or astute enough to realize that Sam, amenable in most things, would never be prised out of here. This house was unassuming, a pleasant, double-fronted Edwardian villa, one of a small terrace of four in a quiet road near the park. Her mother had made it pretty and comfortable, and they had stayed put while houses around them changed hands for ten and twenty times what had originally been paid. Despite his increasing wealth, Sam had never seen any reason to move. It suited him, there was room for her mother's piano, which he'd taken to playing most days, never mind that he didn't do it particularly well. It breathed a bit of life into the house, he said, stopped him talking to himself to fill the empty air.

Sam let Clare tease him a bit about Mary Bellamy, glad enough to see her cheerful. They lunched together as often as not on Saturdays, usually with the accompaniment of a bottle of wine, and today he'd managed to persuade her to have a cognac with her coffee as well. For a while, she looked happy and relaxed.

Later, Sam watched her depart with David Neale. The man had seemed a decent, reliable sort of chap, but Sam thought he'd interpreted pretty correctly the look in his eyes when they'd rested on Clare, and he hoped that didn't spell more trouble, Clare's situation being what it was. He knew he really shouldn't be so protective about her – but, that bruise! Though maybe another man in her life was what she needed, he thought, sitting at the piano for a few minutes before getting ready for the match, playing 'Bring On The Clowns', one of his favourite songs that Clare's mother had played so often for him. A good man. Yes, maybe that was the answer.

The clock struck the hour. It was time to get ready.

One thing Grace had begged of him before she died: 'Promise me you'll never interfere, Sam. It never does any good, between husband and wife.' He'd promised. He thought it was a good maxim – within certain limitations – but he suddenly knew now that it was a promise he was prepared to break.

*

The meeting in Mayo's office was well under way when Abigail arrived. Present were DI Skellen and his sergeant, Ray Tillotson, from the Force Area Drugs Squad, plus Roger Steele, a detective from the divisional drugs team; they were actively discussing the abortive surveillance at the Bagots on Wednesday night, and why it had gone wrong.

'Your weekend off, Abigail – sorry to have to bring you in.' Mayo's apologies were a matter of form, saying sorry took second place to the subject in hand. 'But as you were in on this originally – '

Abigail flapped a hand in a don't-mention-it way. She'd long since grown philosophical about interruptions to her private and social life. To the hard work and being chronically short of sleep, as well. That was what it cost for a job you were willing to give your eye-teeth to get, even though you sometimes hated it. But it was ultimately stimulating and fulfilling, which was more than you could say for most jobs. And she'd have come in on her wedding day if it meant catching the scum who were responsible for this lad's death. Drug dealing was despicable, the rock-bottom end of a dirty business; it made the hairs on the back of her neck stand up.

She sensed an atmosphere of tension building up in the room. A suggestion was being put forward by DC Steele that they should lose no time in raiding the Bagots, but this was immediately vetoed by Skellen.

Mayo, arms folded across his chest, was obviously of the same opinion as Steele. 'Time to get the priorities right, Inspector,' he reminded Skellen. 'Before any other youngster cops it. We know who the dealer is – so we pull him in. What's your problem?'

'My problem is we've spent weeks on this. There's a new supplier on your patch, and the jungle drums say the dealing's going on from the Bagots. We can bust them any time, but we can't guarantee they're going to grass on their source, and that's who we want.'

'How much longer do we have to wait?'

'We should've had him last Wednesday, we'd good information he'd be there, but word must have got out. We need more time.'

'I'd be asking your informant for your money back, if I were you,' Mayo remarked caustically.

'He's always been reliable enough in the past.' Skellen shrugged, not liking the implied criticism, and looked to his sergeant for back-up. 'We're building up good intelligence, but sometimes it all comes unhinged, despite best efforts.'

'Somebody got wind,' agreed the laconic Tillotson. 'It happens.'

The two men trod a dangerous line, sometimes working undercover, playing with fire. Mayo thought they overdid the streetwise bit. They were wearing the required gear, jeans and leather and scruffy trainers. Skellen sported a grade three haircut and an ear-ring, wasn't as young as he looked. His eyes were the giveaway. There was something about him Abigail tried to remember, a background of trouble, something menacing. His sergeant, a thin, cadaverous man, looked so like a druggie that certain people had been known to wonder if his double life hadn't skewed him in the wrong direction. But he wouldn't have lasted long with Skellen if he had.

'This guy who's dealing, he's small potatoes,' Skellen said. 'He's not part of any organized drug-trafficking that we know of – but there's more stuff getting through to this neck of the woods than there should be, and we've a chance here to get back to the source if we get it right.'

No one said anything for a moment.

'The ACC's not happy about this. "Crime-related drugs-taking"', Mayo quoted, '"is costing this force alone twenty-three millions a year."'

'Yeah,' Skellen said, 'and *forty*-three millions next time he blinks. Catching a two-bit street dealer isn't going to stop that. There's dozens more ready to crawl out of the woodwork and take his place.'

'I know, I know.' Mayo sighed irritably. Skellen was right, of course. It went against the grain, however, to allow drug-pushing to go on under their noses. But it was good policy to let it continue, for months sometimes, never losing sight of what they were after, in an attempt to get a definite line to the supply chain. 'But don't expect me to like it. A kid out there on my patch died last night.'

'I hadn't forgotten,' Skellen said quietly. 'But we'll get nowhere compromising the operation.'

'OK. You win. But for God's sake, pull your finger out, and get something moving.'

'Who was he? The boy who OD'd?' Abigail asked, thinking Skellen looked as though he hadn't finished arguing the point.

'Damien Rogers. Fifteen. Pupil at Woodmill Comp,' the divisional man, Steele, recited. 'Good school, good home. No reason for it.'

Abigail thought of the grey, faceless tower blocks where drugs were pushed as a matter of course, needles were left around for kids to find, where unemployment was the norm, crime was rampant . . . No reason?

'E, was it? Ecstasy?'

'Smack.'

This raised her eyebrows. Not many of his age had the money to spare for hard drugs like heroin. Solvent abuse, glue-sniffing for the kids, the twelve- and thirteen-year-olds, progressing to marijuana, amphetamines, Ecstasy, LSD. Grass, uppers, downers, acid. Pocket money drugs. Anything else usually indicated too much money to throw around. But Damien's parents were an insurance salesman and a hairdresser, with nothing to spare and too much sense to be over-lavish with pocket money. Damien was a certainty for one of the number who'd turned to crime to pay for his habit. A dead cert, unfortunately.

Clare had no need to get out of the car to see that the house they'd come to view was a non-starter. What amazed her was that David Neale, shrewd, sensible and used to a comfortable, even luxurious mode of living, in one of Lavenstock's most upmarket houses, had ever dreamed it would be. Set in a field, half-way down a muddy lane, miles from anywhere, the house was simply lacking in any sort of charm. It had been erected nearly forty years ago for a farmer, from the profits made by selling off his original Georgian farmhouse to a Birmingham company director who fixed coach lamps outside the front door and made the farmyard into a patio. The farmer had been happy enough to end his days in the New House, a brick-built, flat-faced, utilitarian construction with mean windows and an ungenerous roof overhang, standing in a garden which had been mainly given over to cabbages. But who else would be?

Clare told herself the bad impression may have simply been due to the grey lowering skies and the soaking drizzle, but inside, it was no better. Walking from one square, box-like room to another, taking gloomy note of the out-of-date central heating and bathroom facilities, the cold, bare kitchen, she felt it had a mean soul.

'Well?' David asked, watching carefully for her reactions. 'I dare say it'd look a whole lot different with the garden landscaped, it needs modernizing, and a few gallons of paint . . .'

'Depends on how much money you're prepared to spend, of course,' she began cautiously, not wanting to disappoint him, if he'd set his mind on living here, though privately she considered he must be mad if he thought a bit of tarting up would make much difference.

Suddenly, he laughed outright. 'You don't like it, I can see – and you're right, of course,' he said to her relief and perhaps, she thought, to his own. 'I was taken in by the price, and the possibilities of the garden. I can see it won't do.' He wasted no more time on fruitless speculation, but slammed the front door firmly behind them.

While they'd been inside, the lowering cloud had settled into a persistent, heavy rain. Now the heavens opened. Nothing for it but to make a dash, umbrella-less, down the concrete driveway, before diving into his car, laughing and breathless. He peered doubtfully through the streaming windscreen when they'd finally mopped themselves up. 'I'd thought of a walk, perhaps, if we'd had time, but this has put paid to it . . . Shall we look for a café and a cup of tea?'

'Why don't you drive me back home and we'll have tea by the fire?' she suggested. 'No sense in staying out in this weather.'

He hesitated only fractionally, then answered with a quick smile, 'That sounds like a very good idea.'

The car was roomy and luxurious and smelled of warm leather. 'Mozart, country and western, or what?' he asked. He seemed cheerful and not at all put out or disappointed by the outcome of their visit though, as far as she recollected, he'd seemed quite keen on the house when he'd spoken of it in his office. She was sure he'd told her that he'd seen it several times and thought it might be just the thing.

She looked sideways at him as she settled back into her comfortable seat and mellow music swept softly through the car, aware of a breadth of shoulder next to hers, reminding her how athletic he was, despite his desk job. Had he then used this visit simply as an excuse for her company? The unexpected thought pleased her and brought a warmth to her cheeks, but was at the same time disconcerting. He wasn't the sort, David Neale, to use subterfuge. Or was he? She was suddenly deeply aware that she really knew very little about him, but also that she would indeed like to learn more.

'I know of a property which might possibly be coming on the market quite soon,' she told him rather breathlesssly. They were driving towards Lavenstock, the hills either side disappearing into the lowering clouds. It had come to her that Mary Bellamy's place, not too far out of the town, would suit David admirably. 'I can't say any more than that just yet, but I could let you know, if you're interested. It's a very nice bungalow, going out towards Lattimer.'

'Sounds fine. Not too large, I hope? Good, I was brought up in an Edinburgh semi. I'll need a bit more than that to accommodate my furniture, but anything too big is still inclined to give me a guilt complex.'

She thought of the beautiful house by the river, large by any standards, especially for one man, but failed to imagine him satisfied with anything less. Smaller, yes, but not less. Quick to catch her reaction, he explained, with his slow smile, 'My father was an elder in the Presbyterian Church and I was brought up to believe that material possessions were not things to be enjoyed. That sort of attitude's hard to put behind you.'

She'd wondered once or twice about his background, but he'd never talked about it before.

'Believe it or not, but when the parental home was sold up, there was a needlepoint chair worked by my grandmother, still in mint condition. My mother took great pride in the fact that no one in our house had ever been allowed to sit on it!'

Clare couldn't think of a comment that wouldn't reveal what she thought of that. An immediate picture of a dour, joyless

Scottish household and repressive parents had sprung fully formed into her mind, a chilling impression. She looked at him to find him watching her quizzically.

'You're meant to laugh at that! Though it's not as unusual as you might think, par for the course with the Scots, in fact. We're a canny nation. You must have noticed, the way I look after your money.'

She did laugh then. It was extraordinary, how different he was, away from Miller's Wife, how easy and comfortable she felt with him. Perhaps his upbringing had also taught him business and friendship should be kept separate. 'Were you an only child, like me?'

'Yes. It's not always easy, is it? Too much is expected of you.'

'Not in my case. I always remember my childhood as very happy.' And who wouldn't, surrounded by love and good humour, with a sweet-natured mother and Sam for a father?

'I can imagine. I've heard a lot about Sam Nash, and liked what I saw when I met him just now.'

The wipers flicked and the tyres hissed, and they came over the ridge and down into a Lavenstock grey and murky with drizzle, but with no evidence of the heavy rain they'd left behind. She saw the arc lights were on at the United football ground. The match was still being played, they could hear the roar of the crowd as they passed, and she was glad her father's Saturday afternoon hadn't been spoiled.

'Dad'll be pleased they've been able to carry on playing,' she remarked. 'Are you a football fan, too?'

He shook his head. 'Squash is my game. It's my mission in life to get the lads at the Centre interested, but wouldn't you know? All they want to do is kick a ball around a pitch.'

The youth sports and social club, run by volunteers, was the latest function for the disused Hill Street Methodist Chapel. Its sports facilities were far outclassed by the new Sports and Leisure Centre on the outskirts of the town, but she knew Richie and his friends often patronized it, if only for its coffee bar and loud music. 'You deserve a medal, truly, for putting up with that lot,' she told him, meaning every word.

'Oh, I don't know,' he said with a shrug, making light of the time and energy he put into it, 'they're not bad young folk. Bright. Knowing more than we ever knew about everything.

Knowing nothing, all the same, of what's important, won't be told, either.'

'I'd second that,' she said in heartfelt agreement, thinking of Richie.

'Och, why did I come this way?' he exclaimed suddenly, sounding unusually Scottish in his annoyance. 'I wasn't thinking. We've missed the ring road now.'

It would mean a circuitous detour, even after they got through the town centre, which was crowded with shoppers and the milling Saturday street market, straggling out of the Cornmarket and into every adjoining side street. He could only inch the car past traders and shoppers undeterred by the damp, past bright sweaters hanging like rows of prayer flags, then alongside the queues at the mobile butcher who sold the best and cheapest bacon for miles. His hands grew tense with annoyance on the wheel as they slowly manoeuvred past the half-price leather goods and the jewellery glittering under the stall lights at Alf's, next to the reject shoe stall with its piece of cardboard to stand the new shoe on while you tried it for size.

From then until they reached Clacks Mill, twenty minutes later, he relaxed, but didn't say much. Clare didn't mind, aware of feeling comfortable enough with him to let the silence continue. She glanced from the corner of her eye at his profile, liking his strong features, thinking he should wear different frames to his spectacles, or contact lenses; they made him look older, more severe, and tended to hide the kindness in his eyes.

They drew up in front of the house, behind her car, parked next to Tim's Discovery.

'Come in,' she said, but he was checking his watch.

'Look, this must seem very unmannerly, but do you mind if I pass up on that tea, after all? It's taken longer than I thought to get here, and there's someone I must see at four.'

He was suddenly his reserved, courteous self again, and it wasn't difficult to guess the reason for his change of heart. It could only be that he didn't want to have to exchange platitudes with Tim, which was all they ever seemed to manage when they met. She could hardly say: It's only his car that's there, it's only half-past three, it's unlikely he'll be back yet. She smiled brightly. 'Of course not.'

'Clare, thank you so much for giving me your time. I can't

thank you enough,' he said, stiffly correct, then amazed her by touching her cheek briefly. She had the definite impression he would have liked to have kissed it, in the casual way people did, only she thought it might not have been casual, not with David Neale. She stood watching him drive off, feeling an odd mixture of emotions, the chief of which was a flare of such fury and intensity against Tim that she could scarcely get her key into the lock, the sort of anger she rarely allowed to break through. How did he manage it, even when he wasn't there, ruining even the innocent pleasures of a cup of tea by the fire with a friend? Well, we'll see, she thought, marching indoors, throwing off her coat, decision and determination in every step. She pulled herself up. Could she even contemplate such a thing, could she?

Yes, there was a limit to what anyone could be expected to stand. She'd played the victim for far too long.

Morgan came back to the Bagots late in the afternoon. He didn't say where he'd been but he was distinctly chuffed, looking unusually cheerful. 'Where's Luce?' he demanded immediately.

'Gone away for a bit,' Jem answered. 'She had a letter. Her mum's in a tizzy because somebody broke in and pinched all her belongings. They knocked her down, too, her mum, I mean, so Luce dashed straight down there.'

'She *what*?' Morgan's good humour seemed suddenly to be in danger of departing. 'Since when has she ever found it necessary to play the dutiful daughter?' Then he laughed, looking hopeful. 'No chance of Mummy kicking the bucket is there?'

'Not a lot. She was OK, according to the letter.'

Luce's mother, Mrs Rimington, wasn't wealthy, but she owned a nice little cottage near Guildford, and the same grandfather who'd left the old house to Luce had left his daughter a bit of money, too. There hadn't been a Mr Rimington on the scene since Luce was four years old, so Luce and her sister stood to gain on their mother's death, but that possibility seemed unlikely to be imminent. Not from a bang on the head when she fell, which she seemed to have survived.

'When did Luce say she'd be coming back?'

'She didn't. I suppose she's looking after that kid sister and holding her mum's hand. She could've let us know when,' he added, 'if your mobile had been here.' A permanent telephone wasn't an accessory they aspired to at the Bagots.

'That's what a mobile's *for*, to have with you, you pillock! Pity she didn't let me know, I want to talk to her. *They'll* have to go,' Morgan said, jerking his head towards the ceiling, where footsteps could be heard from the room above. You couldn't escape noise, in this house. Carpetless floors and rotten stairs that creaked, gaps an inch wide in the floorboards. 'I don't trust that Ginge.'

Although the house was technically owned by Luce, and she ostensibly decreed how it was to be run, it was Morgan who really controlled things. He was twenty-seven, older than the rest of them by several years, a big handsome bloke with hair waving to his shoulders, high cheekbones and beautiful teeth, deepset eyes, the young Clint Eastwood look that women seemed to go for. Jem envied him that, being dark as a gypsy himself and somewhat vertically challenged, as Morgan put it. Morgan liked a joke – when it wasn't on him – but it didn't do to let that fool you. He knew what was what, and you'd better not mess around with him, or get the wrong side of him. Even Luce had to be careful.

'What's for dinner?' he demanded. 'I'm hungry.'

Jem had somehow been landed with the job of cook, since he made a better fist at it than any of the others, which wasn't saying much. His menus relied heavily on rice and pasta, and whatever he called the resulting dishes, they mostly ended up tasting the same. But he'd taken that job that had come up, after all, and today they had Black Forest gâteau. Better make the most of it, he didn't know how long he could be bothered with the hassle of the job, it was hardly worth it, only a few hours a week, anyway.

'Col's getting some stuff in,' he told Morgan. Seeing the look on his face, he added, 'Don't worry, he won't do anything stupid, he's keeping up with his medication. He's all right.'

'Oh, sure, otherwise they wouldn't have chucked him out of that loony bin, would they?'

Jem was never quite sure when Morgan was being sarcastic. Col had been in a psychiatric unit for eighteen months, and then when the health service cuts had been announced, he'd suddenly been deemed fit to leave and find his own way in life, with the assistance of anyone prepared to help. Care in the community, the government called it. Pass the buck was more like it, Jem thought, but he was glad to have Col living with them again, even though Morgan did go on about him all the time. To change the subject, he said, 'What did you mean about not trusting Ginge?'

'I've heard things,' Morgan said obscurely. 'If we don't watch it, we'll have the fuzz around. Luce should never have brought that stupid pair of gits here.'

Jem was inclined to agree. They were a menace, Ginge and his girlfriend, Sheena. Luce had taken pity on them when they'd been evicted from the squat where they'd been living, and though they'd sworn they didn't do drugs, it didn't take an Einstein to know that they were on something or other most of the time. Sheena was all right when she wasn't spaced out, little and dark and with a soft Gaelic accent, but Ginge was a pain any way round. He was a ferrety-looking bloke who spoke in impenetrable Glasgow gutturals, and Jem thought Morgan was right not to trust him, or the people he mixed with. He moved in circles where they'd sell their grandmother for gear.

6

The kitchen door was hurled open with the sort of last trump sound that normally heralded Richie's entry. The knob crashed into the side of the freezer with a loud metallic clang, and a shower of dead frond from the out-of-reach, moribund fern on top fell down like rain. Clare automatically turned round with a reprimand on her lips, momentarily forgetting that Richie was already there in the kitchen, foraging in the fridge for something to prevent him starving to death until supper time. Her hand froze on the tap and the water ran over the top of the kettle she was filling as the flung-back door was followed by the eruption into the room of Amy, shaking, her face a queer, greenish-white colour, her eyes enormous. She leaned against the wall, speechless.

Clare found herself by her side without knowing how she'd

got there, but before she could ask her what was wrong, Amy began sobbing helplessly. 'It's Daddy, it's Daddy . . .'

'Amy, whatever's the matter? Quick, catch her, Richie, she's going to fall!'

'The bridge,' Amy managed, and swayed gracefully into her brother's arms.

Abigail Moon rapidly surveyed the scene. In sunshine it would be as pretty as an idealized Victorian picture on a birthday card: the old weatherboarded mill with its hipped roof and huge wheel, the rustic bridge, the river rushing between the red sandstone boulders and thence into the race. Now, at the fag end of the afternoon, with the white-overalled police personnel going matter-of-factly about their allotted tasks, their footsteps muffled, moving like ghosts through the opaque, thickening layers of dusk and fog, under the corpse-light from the emergency lighting, it was creepy and shrouded as a Gothic horror movie.

The man's body, clad in classic country gear of cords, green wellies, wax jacket and tweed cap, was slumped in a half-sitting position against the bridge handrail, one arm dangling. His shotgun was wedged between his knees. His face was not a pretty sight.

Abigail had been caught just as she was leaving the office after the frustrating meeting with the Drugs Squad men had wound to an unsatisfactory conclusion, and had rushed over here. She now knew that the dead man was Timothy Wishart, aged forty-four, who lived at Clacks Mill with his family, and that he'd been found by his daughter Amy, who'd looked out of her bedroom window and, seeing his figure huddled on the bridge, had run down to see what was wrong. That was tough on her, poor kid, something a girl of sixteen wasn't ever going to forget, never mind any amount of counselling or whatever therapy was fashionable at the moment.

'When was he last seen?' she asked Carmody.

'Went out late this morning to do some shooting with the farmer who lives over yonder, name of – ' the big sergeant consulted his notes – 'John Fairmile. Didn't get much, apparently, seems he'd only bagged a few wood pigeons and a couple of rabbits.' Carmody's long, basset-hound face lugubriously contemplated the game bag a few feet away from the dead man. 'Don't care for 'em much myself, wood pigeons or any other sort. Not much more than a mouthful when they're plucked.'

He was a big, gloomy Liverpudlian, and never took an optimistic view of anything, but Abigail didn't care for eating small birds, either, for other reasons. Especially pigeons. They were too much associated in her mind with the scavenging, streetwise creatures that hopped in and out of the traffic and roosted in dismal rows on ledges of the ugly Town Hall which overlooked her office, leaving her with a permanent view of what they left behind.

She could hear wood pigeons now, cooing softly, motionless smudges of grey in the leafless trees above the mangled body on the bridge and the dead animals in the bag. She wished she were somewhere else. There was altogether too much death around here, all too horribly reminiscent of the opening scene from that Renoir film – that shooting party, the scene of bloody carnage when birds fell from the sky like rain. She pulled her coat collar closer round her neck. 'Did he leave a note, Ted?'

'As good as. Some letters, screwed up in his pocket. A dunning one, threatening prosecution, another from the bank. An overdraft like that, you don't need any better reason for ending it all.'

The portly figure of Professor Timpson-Ludgate, the pathologist, was still bent over the body. He drew off his latex gloves as he struggled to his feet and looked around for Abigail. When he saw her he crooked his finger. 'Spare me a minute, m'dear, will you?'

She ground her teeth. Why not Inspector, if he didn't like Abigail? M'dear! The nice little woman, playing at being a nasty policeman. Then she decided to forgive him – it wasn't worth the expense of adrenalin, and he probably didn't know any better, at his age.

The Prof's well-known vintage Rover had scarcely disappeared before Mayo put in his official appearance. When they saw who it was, a ripple ran through the men, a smartening up and focusing of attention, they became more purposeful. It was an effect he had, but not because they were afraid of being caught out – he picked his men carefully, drew them together as a team

66

and there were few who didn't pull their weight, out of a consequent sense of self-respect. But he could put the fear of God up anybody found wanting, and there was no telling when he'd be on the warpath, especially nowadays. He was sharper lately, something was worrying at him, either the responsibilities of his job, or personal worries intruding into the demands of a crowded professional life. Abigail didn't think it was work.

The constable with the clipboard recorded his approach, as he had with everyone else. Mayo ducked under the tape and walked across to where she stood waiting for the SOCO team to give her the nod that it was OK for her to take a closer look at the body on the bridge. She wasn't falling over herself to do so, she could smell blood and maybe cordite, and the vomit of the youngest PC, who could be forgiven for being sick, since it was his first death by shotgun. She searched in her pocket for a Polo mint. It sometimes helped.

'Tim Wishart? Should I know him?' Mayo asked, joining her.

'He married Sam Nash's daughter.'

'*The* Sam Nash?'

'U-huh. He's with her now. Wishart's father was Freddie Wishart. The England cricketer,' she added, before realizing that such an explanation was probably unnecessary to a Yorkshireman.

'Good God.' Mayo searched his memory. 'Didn't he blow his brains out, too?'

'Yes. Only . . .'

'Only what?'

'Only T-L thinks he didn't . . . the son, I mean. He's pretty sure someone else shot him.'

The Super let out his breath between his teeth.

Someone had attempted to make it look like suicide, only not very successfully. Someone knew enough about the manner of suicides to have propped the twelve-bore shotgun between the victim's knees, to have crooked his finger around the trigger, but the pathologist had been of the opinion that it was an amateur attempt. For one thing, the spread of the pellets as they entered the face suggested the gun had been fired from more than arm's length. Would-be suicides made sure by putting the barrel under their chin, or even in their mouth. This was only a preliminary hypothesis, he'd been quick to add, which would need to be confirmed by the autopsy, and backed up by the ballistic report, but T-L wasn't a man to make wild guesses, only educated surmises based on long experience. He was more often right than wrong, but he was human, and therefore fallible. However, he was also an expert and a respected authority, at the top of his profession, and he didn't expect them to doubt him for a minute.

'How long's he been dead?' Mayo asked, looking around. Apart from the chimneys of a farmhouse faintly visible some distance away across the river, presumably the Fairmile dwelling, there was no other habitation in sight.

'Not long – possibly not more than an hour.'

'Nobody heard anything?'

'The house has been empty most of the day. The family – there's his wife, and a boy and a girl in their teens – had all been out separately, but arrived home more or less at the same time, within the last hour. It was his daughter, young Amy, who found him. She was upstairs changing, and happened to look out of the window.'

'Strewth. Any thoughts so far, Abigail?'

'It seems he was in trouble financially, according to some letters in his pocket.' She thought back to her earlier conversation with Ellie, to Ellie's oblique, but what she now saw as loaded, references. 'I have the impression his marriage wasn't any too happy, either,' she said cautiously. To say so felt dangerously like gossiping about her friends, but that's how it was as a police officer. It was one of the reasons why you became cautious about making personal relationships, you didn't have any choice, when it came to the crunch. 'It's only hearsay, but I believe the source was reliable. I've met his wife a few times, she runs that business near the market, called Miller's Wife, with someone else I know, a woman called Ellie Redvers.' She hesitated. 'To be honest, Ellie's my source. I don't *know*, but I suspect she's been having an affair with Wishart.' It wasn't a pleasant thought, but if it was so, it might well have precipitated this situation. She made up her mind and took a deep breath. 'If my knowing her's any problem – '

Mayo raised an eyebrow. 'How well *do* you know her?'

'We haven't known each other long enough to have got close, not yet. I do know she's been having an affair, but I have to say, it's only my intuition that it was with Tim Wishart. We, er, we had lunch together at my place today.'

He took time to consider what she'd said, noting the slight strain in her voice. 'You asking to come off the case? Feel you're too close?'

'Not unless I'm instructed to. If not, there'll be no conflict of interest. I can cope.'

Requesting to be taken off a case was the last thing she needed, career-wise. Plus, a heavy case-load was just what her personal life needed at the moment. The less free time she had to brood, the better.

'Fair enough, I believe you.' But watch it, his eyes said. 'Well, what about him, then, Wishart, what did he do for a living?'

'He called himself a financier,' she answered, relieved to have got that out of the way. 'Also dealt in the property market, I think, but other than that, I don't yet know. I need to talk to his wife and family, if they're up to it, or at least with Sam Nash.'

'Sam and I are old sparring partners, in a manner of speaking. I'd like to come along with you and have a word or two with him before I leave you to get on with it,' he said, brisk once more. 'All right?'

The question was rhetorical, an offer Abigail couldn't refuse, nor was she expected to. Every inquiry was ultimately the Super's responsibility, and Mayo was unorthodox in his approach, choosing to be in on some cases more than was strictly necessary by the book. In this instance, Abigail saw his intervention might be useful. A previous acquaintance with Sam Nash, even if it was only through Sam's position as a past chairman of the police committee, could smooth down a few raised hackles. Though perhaps they met socially as well, for all Abigail knew.

In this last assumption she was wrong. The two men's acquaintance had arisen merely through Sam's service on various community liaison projects, and had never extended to social encounters. But Mayo knew a lot about Sam. He made it his business to learn as much as he could about anyone he was officially associated with, but Sam interested him, anyway.

The old man had a lot of popular support locally. A member of the town council, he was one of that rare breed who could be relied upon not to put his own interests first. There had been talk of him becoming Mayor at one time, but nothing had come of it. That kind of recognition wasn't the sort Sam went in for, but he was a force to be reckoned with, however you looked at it: a self-made man who had quietly but relentlessly built up a little empire, a man who cared enough about the town where he'd been born and bred to spend most of his leisure time on council business, and a good deal of his own money on public causes. He was a native of the Holden Hill side of the town, the scruffy end, which in parts still bore ugly scars and grim relics from the Industrial Revolution – the criss-cross of disused canals and redundant railway lines, the subterranean mine workings and claypits that had brought industry to Lavenstock. No one knew their local history better than Sam, or was keener in keeping its traditions alive, but he was also ruthless in his pursuit of a clean-up-and-sanitize campaign for the whole area. Sam didn't suffer fools gladly but then, neither did Mayo. He had rather a soft spot for the old man.

'Let's go and talk to him,' he said.

Sam was, for once, looking his age. He'd driven over as soon as he heard the news. He was alone in the big first-floor sitting-room that stretched from front to back of the house when they entered, a wiry, white-haired man of middle height. He turned from where he'd been standing by the window, with his hands in his pockets, looking out over the river.

The converted mill house was very simply furnished, with good, country pieces and colourful soft furnishings in a thrown-together look that nevertheless gave an effect that was far from haphazard. Mayo recognized the curtains as being the same pattern as those acquired in the recently enforced refurbishment of his own flat. He wondered if Lois French, Alex's sister and partner, had had a hand in the decorating of this, too, and concluded that it was more than possible. It definitely bore her stamp.

Sam waved them to sit down, explaining that Clare was still upstairs with Amy. The child had been hysterical, and Clare was staying with her until the sedative the doctor had given her took effect. Richie had shut himself in his room.

70

'Well, we can see them later,' Abigail said. 'As soon as Mrs Wishart feels able.'

Sam, however, was ready to talk. 'You won't get much sense out of Amy, poor child, Richie neither, for a while, but Clare will cope,' he said with grim pride, 'as she's coped with everything else.'

What he meant by this last was evident when he began to tell them what he knew about Wishart's activities. He made no bones about it, any distress he was feeling wasn't for his son-in-law. As far as Sam was concerned, he was wasting no tears on Tim Wishart. He'd always been a bad lot, he said contemptuously, never had any backbone. Typical that he'd simply opt out and leave others to sort out the rotten mess he'd left behind him. He stood up and went to kick down the logs on the big open fire, threw another on top, and with his hand resting on the mantel, watched the wood crackle and splutter as it caught.

He was obviously fiercely angry with Wishart, and yet ... He finds it hard to accept, Abigail thought, watching Sam narrowly as he resumed his seat, he can't believe Wishart had the guts to take his own life. One, at least, who'd find it easier to believe in murder.

'I hope you'll keep this as quiet as possible, for Clare's sake,' he said eventually, his heavy brows beetling, stress bringing out his Black Country accent. 'She's had a lot to put up with, for too long, she doesn't need this.'

'We'll do our best,' Mayo assured him, 'but it's not easy, things will inevitably come out.'

Sam laughed shortly. 'There'll be plenty, you can rest assured on that. Don't let his so-called popularity fool you. There's always been summat, as long as ever I've known him ... women, gambling – '

'Yes. Letters in his pocket suggest he was deeply in debt.'

'That's what I meant about a mess. He's gambled away more money than most people have ever laid hands on, wasn't particular how he got hold of it, neither. But he's been lucky, somebody else always there to carry the can. Until the Lloyd's fiasco. He was one of those Names, you know, and it damn near finished him off. I blame that mother of his, if she'd taken a firm hand with him when he was young – well, any road, that's water under the bridge.'

71

'Where was his office? In Lavenstock?'

'No, he worked from here.'

'What about staff? A secretary?'

Sam made a face. 'Not any more.'

'We shall require Mrs Wishart's permission to go through his papers – '

'What for? I'd hardly have thought you'd need to bother her with that.'

'That's all right, Dad,' said another voice, 'they can get on with it whenever they want.'

They all turned to see Clare, looking like a ghost, with her pale hair and no vestige of colour in her cheeks. She was in control but she seemed to Abigail to have shrunk, physically, as she went to sit by her father. 'Amy's asleep,' she told him. They sat together, without touching, but the effect of solidarity between them was overwhelming.

It seemed to be a relief to Clare that she'd already met Abigail, knew, at least slightly, the sort of person who'd be probing into the details of their lives. She was accepting the necessity of this, unlike some people, who found the additional burden to their grief hard to take. Yes, she admitted, she knew her husband had had money worries, but she hadn't realized they were preying on his mind enough for him to have taken his life. 'In fact, it was only last night that he asked me for money. I wish – God, I just *wish* I hadn't refused.'

'Clare!' Sam said. 'You mustn't blame yourself for what he's done.'

'How can I not?' she returned in a low voice.

Abigail exchanged glances with Mayo and said, 'I feel I should warn you, there's a possibility it might not have been suicide.'

'An accident!' Clare's relief was palpable.

'I'm sorry, I'm afraid that's not very likely, either.'

'Then . . . I don't understand.'

Abigail's explanation was followed by a long, painful silence. She didn't rush things, giving them time to assimilate the news, seeing the dawning comprehension on their faces. 'I realize how shocked and upset you must be, but there are things we need to know. Do you feel up to answering questions? I can leave it for the moment if you don't.'

But not if she'd any choice, she wouldn't. It was often the best time to talk to bereaved relatives, before the facts had sunk in, before they realized what it was all going to mean, and their lips became sealed as the consequences of what they might say occurred to them. Whether Clare was aware of this or not, she stiffened.

'What sort of questions?' Sam asked.

'Anything that might help us establish a reason for his death.'

'But I've already told you!' Clare exclaimed. 'He was in deep waters, financially. Though how that ...' She was unable to finish.

'Apart from money worries, had there been any other trouble lately?'

Sam made a small protesting movement, but quickly checked it and sat back, his hand covering his mouth. Clare reached out and touched his knee gently, briefly. She was sitting upright on the edge of the sofa, without any support, but suddenly she began to tremble. Sam stood up abruptly, and went out of the room.

'I suppose you mean women,' Clare finally answered Abigail's question. 'There could have been, there usually was. Our marriage was – wasn't – '

Sam returned with a heavy, crystal glass in his hand, containing what looked like brandy. 'Drink this.' Clare shook her head, but he insisted and she took a tiny sip. 'All of it,' Sam instructed.

When she'd drained the glass, she sat quietly for a moment. Its contents seemed to give her courage, for a faint warmth crept into her cheeks. 'I'd appreciate some time before I answer any more questions. It's been a shock,' she said to Abigail.

'I understand. I don't want to distress you further just now, but we shall need to talk to you again, and your children. May we call round tomorrow?'

'Of course. I shall be here. There'll be things to do, things I have to see to.' She gestured vaguely.

'You yourself run a successful business, Mrs Wishart?' Mayo asked, as they stood up to leave. 'Was your husband part of it?'

She answered with a quietly spoken negative, but the expression in her eyes was fiercely defensive. The impression left was that Wishart wouldn't have been allowed to dip a toe into the water.

At that moment a car was heard to draw up on the gravel outside. A glance through the front window showed Ellie Redvers's dark blue Fiat. She could be heard speaking to the uniformed constable on the door, then light footsteps tapped across the wide, bare floorboards in the hall.

She stood poised in the doorway like a ballet dancer, her head with its cap of short, dark hair slightly to one side, her brown eyes wide and stricken, a vulnerable, thin, Audrey Hepburn look-alike. During the few hours which had passed since they'd parted, Abigail realized that she'd lost none of her talent for dramatizing a situation.

She looked at no one except Clare, who had stood up. Something was being said between them. Clare knows about Ellie and Tim, Abigail thought, and Ellie knows she knows. They kept eye contact until the silence became almost painful, until at last the tension snapped. Ellie's eyes brimmed and then Clare held out her arms wide while Ellie skimmed across the floor and into them. The two women hugged each other wordlessly.

Now what had all that been about? Abigail wondered. A natural generosity of spirit in Clare? If so, wasn't it a somewhat unnatural generosity in the circumstances? Or had it been a show of solidarity, necessary for some reason – for the benefit of the police, perhaps? Collusion was the word that came to mind.

Maybe, of course, Clare was heaping coals of fire. There were more ways of killing a pig than slitting its throat. More ways of Clare punishing her husband's mistress than cold-shouldering her. She looked at Clare with more interest.

John Fairmile, Wishart's shooting companion, had heard the shot which had killed Wishart.

They had been shooting on his land, just the two of them, and had parted at about half-past three.

'Where was this?' asked Carmody.

'By the stepping stones in the valley. I came home by way of the top barley field, Tim crossed the river and took the short cut through the woods to Clacks.' It would, he said, have taken Tim no more than fifteen minutes to get home, himself rather less. Home to Fairmile was the farmhouse not more than a quarter of a mile from Clacks Mill, a comfortable, pleasantly untidy place with children's books and toys much in evidence in the big, family living-room.

They'd had a disappointing day, he went on, the light had been bad and the bag was consequently poor. Fairmile had rubbed down his golden retriever then routinely cleaned his own twelve-bore before returning it to the locked case where it was kept. It had been a raw day and he was cold when he got in, so he'd poured the scotch he'd promised himself and taken it upstairs with him to drink while preparing to shower and change.

'All this would have taken you some time?' Carmody asked.

'Twenty minutes, half an hour maybe, hard to say. Could've been more. I took my time, listened to the messages on the answerphone and so on, put a casserole in the oven. My wife's taken the children away for a few days to her mother's and she left it ready, with instructions to leave it on for three hours.'

The savoury smell permeated the room, drifting in from the kitchen. Carmody's mouth watered. It would be some time before he ate, and he'd be lucky if it was a ham sandwich. 'At what point did you hear the shot?'

'When I was rubbing Rosie down – it must have been about ten to four by then, I guess.'

'You're sure it was the sound of a shotgun?'

'Can't mistake it, heard enough in my time.'

'Were you surprised to hear it?'

Fairmile was a pleasant-faced young man with a ruddy, outdoors complexion and an easy manner, who'd been badly shaken by the news of Wishart's death. 'Didn't give it much thought. I suppose it went through my mind that Tim had decided to take a pot at something else, but I can't honestly remember that it did. Could've been someone else out shooting, anyway, though we hadn't heard anything, and the light was fading by then.'

'Did you know Mr Wishart well?'

'Only as neighbours. We shot together, we were in the same gun club, and we've exchanged hospitality. But we hadn't much in common, apart from a bit of sport.'

Carmody listened carefully. Not a lot of love lost there, he thought. No obvious signs of animosity, as such, but not bosom friends, by any means.

'Penny – my wife – knows Clare a bit better, perhaps. They occasionally have coffee together, and Clare's offered to look after the children once or twice. They're boys, seven and nine, bit of a handful, you know what they are at that age,' he added with pride.

Yes, indeed, agreed Carmody with feeling, a family man himself, though his lot were now grown up and thank God he didn't have to live through that stage any more. 'What sort of mood would you say he was in?'

'Tim? Not depressed, not *that* depressed, anyway, I wouldn't have thought.' Fairmile broke off and made his way to the drinks table in the corner. 'What can I offer you? Nothing? Sure?' He hesitated, raised his shoulders, then poured himself a small amount of whisky, adding water. 'Look,' he said, as he came back, 'I don't think I'm breaking any confidences, seeing the poor bugger's dead, but he was trying to touch me for a loan. He was out of luck, I'm afraid, it's all I can do to keep my end up, here. I'd have liked to help him, but I've my own family to consider. I hope to God it wasn't that tipped him over the edge.'

'Shouldn't worry about it. Takes more than that as a rule, sir.' Carmody flipped his notebook shut and uncoiled his length from the depths of the easy chair. 'Thank you for your help.'

'Sorry I couldn't do more.'

'There's just one thing – '

Fairmile didn't look any too pleased when he heard that his guns would have to be taken away and examined.

7

Wishart, too, had owned several guns.

'And all present and correct, all locked up, only for the one he had with him,' Carmody reported, having checked Wishart's gun-cupboard on his return from his interview with Fairmile.

They had reassembled round the back of the house while the business of the removal of Tim Wishart's remains took place: Mayo, Abigail and Carmody. The ambulance with the body of the man into whose personal affairs they were now about to be plunged had departed, and the three of them were once more overlooking the place where the tragedy had occurred, their faces an uncertain blur in the murky light.

It was growing late. Any further poking around here tonight would be counter-productive. Abigail hunched herself into her jacket, preoccupied with thoughts of the routine procedures which needed to be initiated.

'Murder it is, then?' she said.

'That's my gut feeling, yes. We need a firm result from the PM, and to see what turns up here, but we can't afford to discount the Prof's opinion, until we know otherwise.'

Neither of the others seemed inclined to disagree with Mayo. Accident seemed highly unlikely, and the idea of Wishart as a suicide candidate had fast lost ground.

Mayo stood relaxed, hands in his pockets, but anyone who knew him might have read a hidden urgency behind his prosaic remarks, have sensed the tension, and perhaps the flicker of excitement, which the beginning of a murder case always brought. Abigail, at any rate, with the same sort of keyed-up feeling, glanced quickly at him as he added, 'Anything strike you, so far?'

'Yes. He was facing the wrong direction. If he was on his way home when he was shot, you'd have expected him to be either lying on his front with his head to the house, or on his back, feet forwards.'

'Instead of which, he was slumped against the handrail of the bridge, facing the other way, having fallen back with his head towards the house.'

'So for some reason he turned back towards the woods and was shot from there.'

'Stacks, doesn't it? Less risky for the killer to hide there, waiting for Wishart, than hanging around near the house. It's what I'd have done if I'd been him. The path comes alongside the river, and what with the way it turns, and the trees limiting his vision, Wishart wouldn't be a good target until he was on the bridge, with his back to the woods.'

'How very un-British.'

Abigail's remark was flippant in a way Mayo understood: it was even getting to him, too – this foggy, eerie night, reminders of mortality – and he was a natural sceptic. 'By fyre and fleet and candlelight, May Christe receive thy soule.' The ancient dirge for the dead dredged itself up from somewhere in his memory, making his skin crawl. He gave himself a mental shake. For Pete's sake!

'Bad form would have been the least of his worries,' he said, very dry. 'And shooting him in the back wouldn't be an option, anyway, if it was meant to look like suicide. If. Or did that idea only come to him afterwards? Whichever way, something made Wishart turn round to have got the full blast in his face.'

Silence fell, broken only by the chug-chug of the SOCOs' emergency lighting generator. Carmody stamped his frozen feet. It was bitterly cold, and the thick, curdling mist had got into the marrow of his bones. He was hungry enough to eat a horse. 'Like the killer shouting to him, maybe?' he suggested.

'Right. Ballistics isn't my field, but I know there's a chance that if we can get hold of the cartridge, we can eliminate the probability of it having been fired from his own gun.'

Any search, however, would have to be left until the daylight hours of tomorrow. Darkness had fallen by now, and this, combining with the fog, had made the night as thick as a bag. The locus had been taped off and sealed, some of the arc lights switched off, a couple of luckless PCs put on guard, fore and aft, and that would have to be it for tonight.

'Mind you,' Abigail said, without much conviction, 'he could simply have surprised someone who'd no reason to be in the woods, heard a noise, turned to investigate, and the person panicked.'

Possible, just. Mayo turned to Carmody. 'Find out who these woods belong to, if there's any poaching goes on, and where there's access, other than over this bridge, will you, Ted? Put Pete Deeley on to it. Better still, get Scotty up off his backside – he lives around here, doesn't he?'

'Next village on.' Carmody privately speculated that if any poaching *was* going on, DC Scott was unlikely to know of it – officially, anyway. It might, of course, have meant nothing that at the last CID whip round for a Christmas raffle, Scotty had chipped in with a brace of pheasant, or it might not. But . . . his wife Susan had a brother who had the born countryman's attitude as to what rightly belonged to whom.

The sergeant went to have a word with the duty constables, to inform them that they still had a long time before they would be relieved, and Abigail and Mayo walked round to the front of the house to where their cars were parked. Mayo slid into his seat, wound the window down and leaned out to speak to Abigail. 'I'll see you back at the station, as and when. Keep me informed.' He looked at his watch. 'Give me a couple of hours, I've some personal business to attend to.'

Keep me informed, Abigail thought as she watched him drive off. Since this was routine as far as they were both concerned, and scarcely warranted a mention, it meant: 'I'm keeping a particular eye on this case.' Hell and damnation. For several reasons she wanted this investigation to be hers alone, to work it in her own way. She could handle it. But it definitely had 'Handle with Care' stamped all over it: when he heard that it was murder, if murder it was, then Sam Nash wasn't going to be satisfied with anything less than a thorough inquiry, however unpleasant were the things likely to creep out from under upturned stones. It was becoming clear that Wishart had led a far from blameless life, and already the case had a whiff of things unsavoury. If Mayo wanted to take full charge, he took full responsibility, too. So be it.

Carmody appeared from the back of the house, sketched a farewell salute as he sloped off to where his own car was parked and left at speed, in urgent need of sustenance, if she knew Carmody. Come to think of it, she felt peckish herself, now that her stomach had settled. Hot soup. A whisky before bed wouldn't come amiss, either.

A couple of hours, Mayo had said? Personal business, at the crucial beginning of a murder investigation? *Mayo?* She didn't believe it.

Freesias. The favourite flower, favourite scent of Alex Jones, ex-police sergeant, their scent almost shutting out the antiseptic smell. Freesias. Not merely a metric five in a slim, cellophane cone, but fifty at least – oh, how extravagant! Gil Mayo's native Yorkshire caution overcome by his natural generosity. They almost made up for being in hospital. Almost. Self-deception is easy when the alternative is something that can't be borne.

A little miscarriage, they said. Nearly as ridiculous as a little bit pregnant. 'Wiser not to try again, Ms Jones. Your previous history, your – accident . . .' Looking at the long scar of the gunshot wound. 'Your age.'

Loss and shock were the same whatever your age. Never mind that you hadn't dreamed you were pregnant before being rushed in. Shattering, that. And in a way, the loss was greater, as if you'd been cheated, never having had the joy of knowing, not even for a moment.

A bit off-colour for a few weeks, she'd told Mayo, nothing more, and then this. What a thing! Promise not to tell anyone, except Lois. Blowing her nose hard. Sister says if I'm a good girl and buck up I'll be in the pink and back in harness in two ticks. All right for her.

She felt so – so feckless. She should have managed things better. Had she, subliminally, let it happen? She was capable of that, if the need arose. But there was no question of it in this case, no necessity, either. *She* was the half of the partnership who was hanging back from commitment. Had it been up to Mayo, he'd have made an honest woman of her long since. Given her all the babies she wanted.

It was too late, now. The perfume of the freesias filled the room as she turned her head into the pillow and softly wept.

Abigail's hand was already on the door handle of her car when she noticed, in the circle of light from the lamps outside the front door, someone sitting hunched over the wheel of Wishart's off-road vehicle, which hadn't yet been removed from the front of the house.

'Hello,' she said, walking across and speaking through the open window. 'I'm Detective Inspector Moon. And you must be Richie.'

'Richard,' corrected the youth truculently, looking down at her. 'It's only my family who still call me that.' He added, 'I was only going to put this in the garage, not drive it away, though I *could*. I've passed my test. First time.'

He was about seventeen, she guessed, with a young, unformed, but nonetheless intelligent face, and with the promise of character evident in a determined chin.

'Mind if I ask you a few questions?'

'Why?' He shot her a look smouldering with resentment, from under thick eyebrows. 'Why can't you leave us alone? Isn't it bad enough that my father's just been shot?'

Abigail saw the misery in his eyes, and heard the tremor in his adolescent, as yet not entirely dependable, voice, and liked what she had to do no better than he did. 'It won't take long,' she said gently. 'What time did you get back home this afternoon?'

'I don't know. Ask my mother, she'll know. She always checks me in, especially when she's allowed me to use her car.'

'Where had you been?'

'Playing in an inter-school basketball match this morning. Then some of us went into Lavenstock for a coffee and a burger.'

'Who won?' Abigail asked with a smile.

'We didn't, but what does that matter?'

She ignored the rudeness. 'If your mother was at home, it must have been after half-past three. So what else were you doing in town?'

'We went down to the market, that stall where you can get computer games and tapes cheap, and hung around a bit. You know.'

Abigail nodded. She knew all the spots where the youth of the town hung out, and what went on when they did. Horsing about round the back of Tesco's, kicking Coke cans in the space designated for motorbikes in the Hill Street car-park, smoking outside the bus station caff and other, less salubrious places. And that was the least of it.

'After you came home, you didn't hear the sound of the shot, or any other sound for that matter?'

He hunched further over the steering wheel, his bony young shoulder blades showing through his thin shirt. He had no coat with him but didn't seem aware of the cold. 'No,' he said, his voice thick. He avoided looking at her, and she knew he was desperately fighting off tears. 'I put my new tape on as soon as I got in.'

'Right, then, that's it,' she said, snapping her notebook shut. 'Thanks for your help, Richard.'

His head jerked up. 'Is that all?'

'For now, yes. We'll probably need to have another chat, later.'

She left him sitting in the car and drove off thoughtfully.

Wasn't it odd – very odd – that Richie had used the phrase

'been shot'? Wouldn't it have been much more natural to have said 'shot himself'? Or, if that had been too painful, 'that my father's just died'?

Sybil Wishart had been drinking, though it was barely ten o'clock when Clare arrived at her flat in Edgbaston the next morning.

Clare didn't feel prepared to criticize her for that, not when her only son had just died, so suddenly and horribly. And it was no secret that Sibyl was drinking steadily these days. The only difference today was that she didn't trouble to conceal the near-empty vodka bottle, or make the effort to pretend that her speech wasn't slurred.

She was dressed as carefully as usual, out of habit, Clare supposed. How long would it be before alcohol got the better of her and habit began to slip, before standards no longer seemed to matter? She'd always been a good-looking woman, who dressed expensively, and today was no exception: a cashmere jersey over a silk shirt and a good, well-cut skirt, with a gold chain and gold-and-pearl ear-rings. She'd have been better advised to do without the make-up, but Sybil would as soon appear naked as without it; her mascara had smudged with tears and left her eyes looking bruised, her lipstick had been carelessly applied, as if her hand had trembled, so that her mouth looked like a bloodstained gash. She lolled, uncharacteristically, against the cushions of the slippery satin-covered sofa, one of the remnants of palmier days with which the flat was furnished.

When the thought of having to tell Sybil that her son was dead occurred to Clare, her first thought had been no, not me, that's too much to ask! and she'd cravenly allowed Sam to take over that task, as well as taking care of so much more. It hadn't, perhaps, been the best of ideas.

Sam had asked Mary Bellamy to go with him, a sensible decision, it had seemed, since Mary's training as a nurse had taught her how to deal with bereaved relatives. Together they'd driven over to Edgbaston, where Sybil had this flat in a quiet, tree-lined road. She'd been so distraught on hearing the news that Mary had offered to stay the night, but even in her distress Sybil had managed to show affront at being expected to accept support from a stranger and had, not very graciously, refused.

In the end, they'd sought out the woman who lived in the next flat, who'd obligingly come in and slept in the spare room, though she'd been unable to stay today.

Little as she welcomed the idea, Clare felt it was her duty to try and persuade Sybil to come and stay at Clacks Mill, at least for the time being. She was Tim's mother, after all, and facing the loss of the son she'd doted on must be utterly devastating to her. She was seventy, and hitting the bottle, and really mustn't be left alone.

However, Sybil's first words disposed of this idea. 'You needn't have come,' she said. 'Rula will be here any moment.'

'Sybil, of course I had to come and see you!' Clare said in distress, but she couldn't hide her relief.

Rula – Muriel Brinsley – was Sybil's closest friend. One of the few who still bothered with Sybil. The two women had known each other all their lives and there existed a strong bond between them, unaffected by their constant falling out and making up. It was a pity she lived so far away. But Rula, though unmarried and with no encumbrances, had steadfastly resisted all Sybil's entreaties to come and live permanently with her, and who wouldn't sympathize? Small and eccentric, but eminently sensible, she declared roundly that if Sybil wanted a dogsbody, she'd better get herself a paid companion. But when circumstances warranted it, she could always be relied on. She had, Sybil said, set off from Scarborough at the crack of dawn in the black Rover they all called Rula's Hearse, which was so old it was practically a vintage model by now. Hopefully, she would arrive in one piece. She could barely see over the top of the steering wheel and charted a middle course down any road whatsoever, refusing to be intimidated into driving at anything more than a steady forty; more by good luck than anything else, she'd never yet had an accident.

Good old Rula. Her sterling presence here could be guaranteed to keep Sybil reasonably sober, if nothing else. 'I don't know why I didn't think of her before.'

'I've told her she can't bring that animal with her!' Sybil warned. 'Nor that painting muck!'

She was presumably referring to Rula's bad-tempered Yorkshire terrier, and her watercolours, which she dashed off at great speed, later to sell in her own small gift shop. She disparaged herself as 'merely a talented amateur', but the paintings were always quickly snapped up by holiday-makers as pleasant souvenirs of their fortnight by the sea, and she didn't sell herself short, either. She had her head screwed on, and Clare was certain she would ignore both Sybil's injunctions, but didn't think it prudent to comment.

An awkward silence ensued, while she wondered, torn between sympathy and exasperation, what else she could say to comfort the old woman, a silence which Sybil broke by saying, 'I suppose you're satisfied now!'

The malevolence shook Clare. There had never been any love lost between the two of them, but dislike had never been overtly expressed, either. She looked at the older woman's lined face and the discontented droop of her mouth, the glassy eyes, and read pain there. She tried to put herself in her mother-in-law's place. How would she feel if Richie ... God, no, that way madness lies. She said gently, 'Don't let's quarrel now, of all times. We're both in the same boat.'

'How dare you? Presume to know how I feel?' Sybil burst out. 'Don't think I don't know you were behind all his problems! He was right not to trust you.' She looked sly. 'It was his mother he turned to when he needed someone to trust.'

She wasn't really responsible. 'Don't say anything you'll be sorry for, Sybil.'

Sybil ignored this. 'I know Tim wasn't perfect – but my God, he'd a lot to put up with, married to little Miss Daddy's Girl!'

'Sybil – '

'And what's all this nonsense about him being murdered?'

'The police aren't absolutely sure, yet, but it looks as though he couldn't have shot himself.'

'Shot himself? What are you talking about? Of course he didn't shoot himself! He'd never have done *that*, not to me! It was an accident. It had to be an accident!'

With a shaking hand, Sybil pushed aside the untouched coffee that Clare had made, reached for the vodka and sloshed a whopping amount into her glass. She downed half of it and then began to cry.

'Oh, Sybil.' No way, Claire could see, was Sybil going to accept that her son had been murdered – but even less could she let herself believe that history was repeating itself, that Tim had died the same way as his father, by his own hand. Leaving Sibyl alone, to cope.

Clare wished for the courage to take the old woman into her arms and comfort her. But never in her life having received from her mother-in-law anything more than a dry peck on the cheek, she realized how impossible this was, how bizarre and embarrassing they would both find it. Any effort she made would only be greeted with repulsion.

She sat miserably dropping panaceas into an uneasy silence until Sybil's eyelids began to droop. Anaesthetized by alcohol, she started to nod, and finally fell heavily asleep, a blessing perhaps, since Clare guessed she hadn't slept much the night before. She lifted the old woman's feet up on to the sofa, covered her with a rug and left her until Rula, who had her own key, should arrive. Even at Rula's pace, it wouldn't be long now before she got here.

'Chap called Harry Leicester owns the shooting rights on that land,' Barry Scott said after those who'd been roped in for Mayo's first briefing had watched the video the SOCOs had made.

Clacks land, he pointed out on the map of the area now attached to the wall, was a few rough acres, more or less in the shape of a quadrant, bordered on its three sides, firstly by the river, beyond which was Fairmile's farm and the woods owned by Harry Leicester, then by the lane and lastly, on the third side, by the curve of the road.

'A bit of poaching goes on, specially around Christmas,' Scott said, 'but as long as it's not too bad, Leicester turns a blind eye. "No trespassing" signs all over the place, but there'd be no problem getting in. If you think it's worth fighting your way through the gaps in the hedge, that is. I wouldn't do it for a pension.'

Carmody could believe it. Scotty was a slummocky type, not one of CID's finest. 'I drove past on the main road last night,' he remarked, 'but I didn't see anywhere much where you could leave a car, not without ending up in the ditch.'

'You wouldn't, Sarge, not in the dark, but there's one or two places where you *could* pull in, at a pinch.'

'He wouldn't want to risk being seen walking far along the road, carrying a shotgun,' Abigail commented. 'Or his car being recognized, either. The road borders the woods for less than a mile before the houses start. But there's no reason why anyone shouldn't approach from the other direction, across Fairmile's land, is there?'

'No problem, as far as I can see,' Scott agreed.

Mayo took up where he'd left off. He was almost finished. 'You've already been given a summary by Inspector Moon of what we know so far and an outline of how I want this inquiry to proceed. All the usual lines will be pursued. With special attention to the victim's business affairs, which were apparently decidedly rocky, to say the least. That will give us some substance to work on. He also seems to have had a wide-ranging circle of acquaintances, and he was a regular Jack-the-lad with the ladies by all accounts as well. So we'll try the golf club, his gun club. Ask around, talk to anyone who knew him, especially anybody who had access to shotguns, naturally. We need to know what he was like, what sort of chap he was, from people less subjective than his family. His mother, Mrs Sybil Wishart, has already been on to the Chief Constable, wanting it all hushed up,' he finished drily, to the accompaniment of a few ironically exchanged glances, 'so don't go putting any size twelves in, but don't let it intimidate you, either. That about wraps it up, as far as I'm concerned. We'll meet at six to compare findings. Meanwhile, I'll leave you to DI Moon. Thank you, all of you, and good luck.'

A uniformed PC intercepted Mayo at the door, handing him a note. He read it and came back to the front of the room, raising his voice above the hum of talk. 'Before I go . . . We've just had word from the support team, who've been out at the mill house for some time, making a fingertip search on the far side of the bridge. They've now found a cartridge case. But that's no good unless we find the gun that shot it and even then we may not be able to match it. Finding the gun's a priority. As you know, it looks well-nigh impossible, at this stage, that Wishart himself could have fired the shot that killed him. We shall learn more from the post-mortem, and we shouldn't have long to wait. The Prof's agreed to do it later this morning – Inspector Moon will be there, right?' He turned to Abigail for confirmation.

Abigail would, unfortunately. Post-mortems, like migraines, were supposed to become bearable if you taught yourself to stand aside from it, as though it was happening to someone else. That was the theory, at any rate. Only, like migraines, they didn't. So what couldn't be cured must be endured, as somebody's granny had undoubtedly once said. Timpson-Ludgate was going on holiday the following day and had magnanimously agreed to oblige with an autopsy before he went. 'Nothing like leaving the decks clear,' he'd announced blandly, 'and you know how I always like to oblige with an early result.' Abigail thanked him, while cynically reflecting that it was more likely that he didn't want anyone else horning in on something that was likely to prove more interesting than the usual routine: ordinary stuff, like road pile-ups, overdoses, industrial accidents, old folk dying of hypothermia.

Abigail wound up the meeting after Mayo had left. 'I've no more to add, except to say that we're going to solve this one, right? Inspector Atkins will allocate. By the way, George,' she said, turning to Atkins in the hubbub of general departure, 'has anybody made an appointment yet for me to see that friend – associate, whatever – of Wishart's?'

'Tony Pardoe,' Atkins supplied as she paused to scan her notes for the name. 'He's agreed an appointment for this afternoon, if that suits you.'

'Pardoe, that's right.'

Her own most pressing task was to trace back the dead man's recent movements, over and above the scanty information Clare had been able to supply. Clare had furnished them with details of Wishart's activities, as far as she had known them, during the last week, plus a list of his closest associates, and Pardoe's name had featured in both, so he'd seemed to be a promising start.

'This afternoon's OK, I'm going back to see the family this morning. I'll look in on Farrar. He's there already and he should have made some headway into Wishart's records and computer files by now.'

It was no use having somebody like Farrar on the strength if you didn't make use of them. The ambitious DC had responded eagerly to the task allotted to him. He saw his computer-literacy as a possible advancement to the promotion that perpetually evaded him and was keen to demonstrate his skills whenever he could. It was unfortunate that he got on Abigail's nerves. On most people's. Despite – or perhaps because of – the fact that he was so damned efficient. It was no use to remind him that promotion depended on more than efficiency and the ability to pass exams, he never listened, Farrar would always be his own worst enemy. It was beginning to look as though he was basically unpromotable. Abigail sighed. Her thoughts, where Farrar was concerned, were likely to be uncharitable.

When Clare arrived back home after leaving Sybil, she found a message on the pad in the hall to say that Tony Pardoe had telephoned. It had been taken down by Amy, who'd added a long row of kisses at the bottom. Clare didn't immediately return the call. Instead, she sat in the kitchen drinking the mug of coffee which Richie insisted on making for her, feeling overwhelmed by her children's unprecedented solicitousness in the midst of their own world turned upside down, and by the residue of sadness and despair the conversation with Sybil had caused. She couldn't imagine why she'd allowed the old woman's unfair accusations to upset her so much, but they undoubtedly had.

There was always guilt, for things done and not done, when anyone died, she knew that, especially when the death had been as sudden and horrible as Tim's. God knows, she blamed herself as much as Tim for the failure of their marriage. But ... *Miss Daddy's Girl!* The childish taunt rankled. It wasn't fair of Sybil to try and smirch her relationship with Sam. Sam would do anything for her, that was true, and she loved him deeply, but she had never let it override her duty to Tim.

And let's face it, duty had been all that was left, at the end.

That terrible thought almost brought the tears which so far she hadn't been able to shed, but not quite. There was still a hard, painful lump, lodged somewhere near her breast-bone. She must pull herself together, there were chores she ought to tackle. Balance her bank account for instance. It was not likely to be as healthy as she would have liked, in view of the fact that she was going to have to be entirely responsible for Richie and Amy from now on. She wished she knew the extent of Tim's debts, because she was determined to honour them, every last one, no matter what they amounted to. He'd really screwed them all up, Tim.

She faced the horrendous prospect of his creditors baying at the door, and just the thought of it gave her a headache. Then she recalled with relief that the police had all his papers, that terrifyingly competent young policeman was still occupying the study, so she couldn't get at them yet, anyway.

She didn't really want to have to speak to Tony Pardoe, either. He'd been a close friend of Tim's since their schooldays and, later, one of his business pals, but Clare had never been easy with friends like Tony, whose conversation began and ended with money-making and, failing that, sailing, skiing, making more money and other related topics. His wife, Marianne, with her passion for horseflesh, was worse, if anything.

Get it over and done with. She gulped down the rest of her coffee, then dialled Pardoe's ex-directory number, relieved that it was neither his alarming secretary nor Marianne, but Pardoe himself who answered.

'Clare. What can I say?'

Not able to find a ready reply to this unanswerable question, she at first remained silent, then stumbled out her thanks for the call. 'Are you all right?' Tony went on. 'I mean, is there anybody with you? Would you like me or Marianne to come round?'

God forbid!

'That's good of you, Tony, but I have the children, and my father will be here again, later,' she said quickly, endeavouring to put some warmth into her voice. He was being kind, she really ought to try. He sounded relieved.

'Bloody awful business, this. I know Tim was in deep – I know he was up to the neck in it – but nothing's *that* bad. I'd never have thought that of old Tim.'

'The police don't think he shot himself, Tony.'

There was a silence on the line, Tony readjusting himself to what he didn't want to hear. 'An accident?'

'No, not an accident, either.'

Another silence. 'Jee-sus,' he said after a minute. 'Are they sure?'

'They didn't commit themselves, there has to be a post-mortem and all that, but I'd say they were pretty certain.'

'This is one hell of a mess, Clare. What's he been up to, getting himself done in?' Sensitive to the last, Tony didn't seem to realize he might have expressed himself better.

'I don't know. I only know his life was in a pretty bad mess.'

'I'm sorry, Clare, this must be rotten for you,' he said belatedly. Then, 'What *about* you? He did provide for you?' His tone sharpened. 'He's left *something*, I suppose?'

That meant Tim had owed him money, too. Just how much, she didn't want to know, not at this stage of the proceedings, at any rate.

'Don't worry about me, Tony,' she said, deliberately not taking that up. 'I shall be OK.' It wouldn't hurt Pardoe to stay on the hook for a while. But she thanked him sincerely for calling. 'Yes, yes, I will let you know if there's anything you can do, I promise.'

8

Just before lunch Abigail, with Jenny Platt by her side, pulled up in front of Clacks Mill.

This morning the old three-storey house, looming under the leaden skies, revealed in the car lights, proved no less dismal than it had the previous night. It was utilitarian in shape, a solid block of brick and timber construction, partly weatherboarded, with a pantiled mansard roof over the top two storeys, shining damply in the murky, overhung morning. To one side stood a shaggy cedar with long, forlornly drooping arms, as if mourning in sympathy with its occupants, on the other was the defunct mill wheel.

The rain was holding off, but only just. This everlastingly miserable weather was beginning to feel as though it might go on for ever. 'Makes you understand the Swedes, doesn't it?' Abigail remarked to Jenny as she killed the engine.

Her spirits hadn't been uplifted, either, by having spent the last hour in the mortuary, attending T-L's post-mortem. She had, however, been rewarded by receiving confirmation of his original hypothesis: that the shot which killed Wishart had certainly come from a distance of several feet. This would have to be backed up by forensic and ballistic tests, but it was firm enough to rule out suicide or accident, and to justify calling on the full resources of a murder inquiry team. The time of death, based on the temperature of the body when it was found, had been estimated at between three thirty and four, near enough to mesh with the time of the shot Fairmile had heard.

Opening her door, Jenny jerked her head in the direction of one of the lighted front rooms, where a figure could be seen crouched over a flickering computer screen. 'Hard at it, already, by the looks of things,' she remarked with a grin. 'Trust our Keith.'

They walked down towards the lighted room and Jenny tapped on the french window. The tall, handsome DC, surrounded by files and papers and computer print-outs, busily flicking through the computer, jumped a mile, then came sheepishly to the window to let them in, smoothing his blond hair self-consciously.

'Are you winning?' Abigail asked.

'Not likely!' Farrar looked sourly at the screen and gestured to the files and papers. 'This is not why I became a detective! This whole bloomin' lot's a shambles. Business and personal stuff, all mixed up. It's more than I can get to grips with.'

'And here was I, thinking you liked nothing better, you and your computers.'

He looked offended and said stiffly, 'Oh, I've no problem with the technology, ma'am, it's the financial shenanigans I can't cope with.' He had enough trouble balancing his own books, with a wife who spent money as though there was no tomorrow.

'That's not what you're here for,' she said sharply. It was unlike Farrar to admit to being outclassed, but the financial side would be handled by the experts, anyway. They'd be moving in soon to sort that out, which he knew well enough. His brief was simply to produce a list of the victim's business associates, and any other incidental information he could glean by the way, but that was a routine task, obviously too mundane for someone of his potential. She fought the impulse to snap, but didn't succeed. 'You keep your mind on what you were told to do, never mind trying to sort out the high finance, that clear? Forget anything else, except where it touches on his personal life, that should keep you busy enough.'

'That's what I've been trying to do,' he complained, looking hurt, the reproof sliding off him. 'Sort the wheat from the chaff. I'm getting down to the dross now, the stuff he just shoved in drawers and forgot about.'

'Sort of thing we all do from time to time,' Jenny commented.

Farrar's look said, 'Not me,' and Abigail could believe it. 'Keep at it, Keith,' she said coldly. 'We'll look in again before we leave.' They left the way they'd come in.

'One day, I'll tell him – ' she began, as they crossed the forecourt to enter the house in a more orthodox fashion through the front door, then amended what she was going to say, recollecting it was young Jenny she was speaking to. 'What's the matter with him? He looks down in the mouth.'

'Poor lad, he's having problems at home. They've been trying for a baby for yonks and Sandra's just been told it's unlikely they'll ever succeed. She's giving him a hard time.'

Abigail, who liked children, as long as they weren't hers – not yet, at any rate – didn't ask how Jenny had acquired this information. Young as she was, Jenny had a sympathetic ear that encouraged people to confide in her. She was developing skills in that direction which would bear watching. No doubt the information she'd just imparted explained a lot about Farrar, Abigail thought, though it didn't account for everything: he was, as Mayo said, a cocky bastard, it did no harm to put him down occasionally. But she'd better beware of letting him become a major problem.

Abigail had chosen to bring Jenny with her to Clacks, having had a gut feeling that Clare Wishart responded more easily to women than to men.

She was all the more surprised, therefore, to find with her a man who was introduced as David Neale – quiet, bespectacled, bankerish-looking, a man who, it appeared, lived up to his looks and did indeed deal with the finances at Miller's Wife. He had a warm smile, a firm handshake. A trustworthy man.

Clare was pale and subdued, the dark, finely drawn brows emphasizing her pallor, but she was bearing up and appeared to have come to some quiet accommodation with herself about her loss. She and Neale were drinking coffee in a small sitting-room off the hall which, like the large room where they'd sat yesterday, overlooked the back of the house but not, Abigail noted, the bridge. She saw Jenny looking somewhat disconcerted by the toughened glass panel set into the wall, so that the millstream could be seen rushing down into the race; how could you live with that dizzying reminder of ceaseless movement, that continual sound of water underneath the house?

Neale immediately offered to leave them alone when he learned who the visitors were, but Clare's murmured request begged him to stay. He gave a slight nod and settled back in his chair, following her departure with his eyes when she went to fetch fresh coffee.

A silence ensued. Neale coughed. 'Damnable business, this,' he remarked, in a pleasant Scottish burr. 'Such a tragedy, getting killed with one's own gun!'

'Dangerous things in the wrong hands, shotguns,' Jenny said neutrally.

'I imagine so, though they're not something I'm familiar with. Not with my eyesight,' he added.

Abigail had known excellent marksmen who had worn spectacles. Wasn't that the point of wearing them – to correct imperfect vision? But images of the pleasant and correct Mr Neale in casual country wear, potting birds or rabbits, weren't easy to conjure up. She smiled at him and let Jenny carry on with the small talk . . . How well had Neale known Wishart? she was asking. Scarcely at all, it appeared, they'd only met when Tim had popped into Miller's Wife and Neale happened to be on the scene at the time.

'My wife recently died and was ill for some time before that. It didn't leave much opportunity for socializing,' he offered briefly.

Jenny nodded sympathetically and consulted her notes. 'Mrs Wishart tells us you drove her home yesterday afternoon.'

'Yes, I did.'

'She can't remember exactly what time you arrived . . . maybe you can tell us more precisely?'

'She went with me to look over a house that's for sale. We'd had traffic problems on the way back and it was getting late. It was three thirty exactly when we got here, so I turned round straight away. I had an appointment at four o'clock that I was anxious not to miss.'

'Who was that with?'

'A boy called Damien Rogers. I help out at the Old Chapel sports and social centre, and he'd promised to meet me there. But he didn't turn up,' he said, putting his hand into his pocket with the automatic gesture of the habitual smoker, fumbling around and seeming surprised to find himself empty-handed when he brought it out.

Intercepting the look which passed between Abigail and Jenny, he blinked behind his glasses, fingering his tie. 'Have I said anything I shouldn't?'

Abigail said, 'I'm sorry to have to tell you that Damien died during Friday night. As the result of a drugs overdose.'

Several seconds crept by. 'We are talking about the same Damien Rogers? The one who lives on the Somerville Estate?'

After a few more words, there seemed to be no doubt that they were.

'Why had you arranged to meet Damien, Mr Neale?'

Neale passed a hand across his face. 'I knew he was taking drugs. So many of them are, I don't have to tell you that. Damien ... he'd take anything he could get hold of, he'd begun shoplifting to pay for his habit ... I wanted to talk with him, to persuade him to get some help. I wasn't surprised when he didn't turn up. In fact, I'd have been surprised if he had. I believe he only promised – well, to appease me. His parents weren't aware of what was going on, and I'd warned him I must tell them if he wouldn't try to kick the habit.'

'Are you a professional drugs counsellor, Mr Neale?'

'Not as such. I merely try to help.'

Abigail decided not to say what she thought. A threat to tell the parents was unlikely to be effective, but Neale was no doubt sincere, a decent man, genuinely shocked. It would do no good at this stage to tell him that, earnest and well-meaning as they were, non-professional attempts such as his were more likely to hinder than help. She would bear in mind that Neale could be a possibly useful contact as far as the drugs scene was concerned, however.

'Do you have any idea where Damien was getting his supplies?' she asked, more in hope than expectation, and of course, Neale hadn't.

At that point, Clare came back, bringing more cups and a fresh pot of coffee, and the conversation was abandoned, to be resumed later, if necessary. 'Amy has something to tell you,' she said, pouring coffee.

'Fine, if she's up to it.'

'Oh, I think so. She'll cope with all this, never fear. Not immediately but, for sixteen, she's amazingly strong. It's Richie I'm worried about.'

'He's taking it badly?'

'He won't speak to anybody, though I don't think it's entirely because of – what's happened. He came home very upset the night before, Friday night, and won't say why.'

'A tiff with a girlfriend, maybe, teenage moods?' Neale offered diffidently. 'Something like that?'

'I expect you're right.' Clare directed a distracted, grateful smile at him. She was about to fetch Amy, when Abigail detained her.

'Before you go, I think you should know that we've had the results of the post-mortem on your husband.'

'Oh.' Clare sat down again.

There was no way of wrapping this one up. In so many words, Abigail told her that it had been confirmed that there were now grounds for going ahead and treating the case as a suspicious death. 'Which means, of course, that we don't think it was either accidental or self-inflicted, and that someone else was involved.'

'Murder, in fact,' Clare said tonelessly.

'Clare – ' Neale began as she briefly closed her eyes.

'It's all right, it's what we were expecting, after what the inspector said before.' She took a deep, steadying breath. 'In a funny sort of way, it's a relief. At least he didn't do it because I refused to help him. He had money worries, as I've told you, and he'd been depressed about them – but whatever they were, I didn't want to believe he would take his own life because of them. And he knew enough about guns not to be careless with them.' There was a silence. 'Well, maybe that makes what Amy has to say all the more important. I'll ask her to come down.'

When, in a few moments, mother and daughter were sitting side by side on the sofa, Abigail was struck by the strong resemblance between them, the same pale skin, the same silvery hair. Today, Amy had one side tucked back behind her ear. The big, loose top she wore over her jeans, covering her from her chin to her fingertips, was roomy enough to encompass two of her. Her slight, immature figure drooped inside it, but youth was kind to her: her dewy-complexioned face showed no signs of recent weeping, until speaking of the tragedy brought tears which brimmed, and threatened to spill over. Her chin trembled. It was a square, very determined little chin.

'I've remembered something that Mum thinks might be important,' she began in a soft, barely audible voice when she'd blinked the tears back, then stopped and bit her lip, looking at her mother, who nodded encouragement.

'Take your time, Amy, there's no rush,' Abigail assured her. Amy swallowed hard several times, looked down at her small, clenched hands and eventually was able to begin. 'Well, one night last week . . . a man came to the house to see my father.'

'Which night was that?'

'I can't remember. Thursday, I think.'

'It must have been Thursday,' Clare intervened. 'Daddy wasn't home on Wednesday, and you were in the games room with your friends all Friday evening.'

'Oh yes. Well, I didn't know he was there, this man, until I went into Daddy's study. My friend, Katie, had just rung to say she'd got tickets for the Scorpions' concert next week in Hurstfield and I went in to ask him if he would take us.'

'We think, whoever this man was, he must have just come in through the side french window,' Clare put in. 'Tim was alone in the study not fifteen minutes before, when I went in for a stamp – '

'And I'd been on the telephone in the hall for ages, talking to Katie, so he couldn't have come in through the front door without me seeing him,' Amy added.

'So what happened?'

'When I opened the study door this man was standing by the fireplace. Then Daddy got up from his desk and came to see what I wanted. He stood in front of me so that I couldn't go into the room. He was looking really, really cross and told me to go away, he didn't want to be disturbed. He banged the door behind me. Wow. I was so mad at him! Well, *I'd* done nothing wrong, had I?' Tears threatened again, but after a moment she went on in an anguished little voice, 'The thing is, I – well, I went back to talk to Katie, and I heard Daddy yelling – and then, everything went quiet again. I was there in the hall for quite a while, but the man didn't come out that way.'

'Would you recognize him again?'

She played with a gold signet ring on her little finger. 'I'm – I'm not sure, I only got a glimpse. I might.'

'Can you describe him?'

'Well . . . hair brushed back, sort of greasy.'

'Do you happen to remember how he was dressed?'

'I don't know. Black, I think, but I can't be sure. It was dark-coloured, anyway. Bomber jacket and black jeans. Trainers.'

It would be. The universal uniform. 'You heard your father shouting – what about the other man? Did you get any idea of what they were quarrelling about?'

Amy looked uncertain, then shook her head.

'It was probably about money,' Clare said flatly.

'You didn't hear the other man at all? Not even the odd word?'

'No,' Amy whispered. In the ensuing silence, she looked at her feet. The untucked-back side of her hair curved down and hid her face.

'Is there anything else you haven't told me, Amy?'

The girl looked up, flicking her hair over her shoulder with the back of her hand. 'No! No, why should there be?'

'I just wondered. If you do remember anything, you will let me know, won't you?'

She nodded, her eyes sliding away. Clare intervened, slipping her arm around Amy's shoulders. 'So maybe you should be looking for this man.' She held Amy's head against her shoulder, and the girl began to weep again as they left.

As the front door closed behind them, Abigail told Jenny, 'This is one for you, right up your street. Get cracking on this mysterious stranger, see if we can't track him down.'

Jenny looked resigned, but cheered up with the remark that at least it was something definite to work on. 'And in that case, maybe I'd better see if Wonder Boy's come up with any names I can start with.'

'There's a mailing list and an address book over there,' Farrar answered Jenny's request when they went back into the study, clearly having found something which was making him more cheerful. 'And you might care to take a look at this, ma'am.'

He held up a sheet of crumpled paper. Unlike the DC, who was his usual smooth, unruffled self, despite his trying morning, the paper looked tired and creased, as if it had been around a long time. It read as though a twelve-year-old with a taste for bad B-movies had written it. Printed in ill-shaped block capitals with a black felt-tip, on cheap lined paper, without heading or signature, the message on it began baldly: 'I told you you'd hear from me again. Look forward to hearing from me, as long as you live. You're a bastard, and you'll pay for what you've done. Leopards don't change their spots and I know what you're up to now, so watch it.'

Abigail wondered whether anyone was expected to take it seriously. 'Where did you find this?'

'With a lot of throw-out stuff. I nearly did throw it away.'

It was so dog-eared, anyone else might not even have read it. But that was where Farrar came into his own. Whatever else, he was alert and thorough, and rarely missed a trick. Abigail studied the paper for a minute or two. It looked like a crude threat of future blackmail. By whom? Wishart himself, maybe doodling with a rough draft that he'd had second thoughts about sending out? On account of the purple prose, if nothing else.

'It could be someone playing the fool, but on the other hand . . . We'll have it tested for prints, anyway. Well done, Keith.'

The DC flushed at the praise which he always felt he deserved, but rarely received. 'If blackmail was the game, he was on to a dead loss as far as Wishart was concerned,' he added, unable to resist going further. 'Doesn't appear to be anything in the kitty, though I suppose we'll only know for certain when we gain access to his bank accounts. Funny thing is, he hadn't been pulling his horns in lately. I'd be surprised if that Discovery does more than fifteen miles to the gallon, for one thing. Maybe his wife was subsidizing him, of course, or his mother.'

'Not his mother, from what I've heard,' Abigail said.

'Well, he'd also paid off a lot of his bills recently – to the tune of about forty thousand quid.'

'What? From a man who was supposed to be on his beam ends, that's not bad going.' She decided to overlook the fact that Farrar had once more strayed outside his province.

'Could be what cleared him out, though he'd borrowed money to do it. From a company called Neptune Holdings.'

'That doesn't make sense.'

'Maybe it does, at the low rate of interest he was paying. Wish I was only paying that on my mortgage. Still . . .'

She became thoughtful. 'Have you got that photo, Jenny? Let Keith have a look at it and see if he recognizes it.'

Jenny handed Farrar a photograph of Tim Wishart which Clare had given them, giving it another glance and raising her eyebrows as she did so. It was a good likeness, Clare had assured them, which had been taken at some all-male function or other, when he'd been standing with a group of other men in dinner jackets. He was holding a glass, caught smiling and half-turned to the camera, and Abigail, taking it back from Farrar as he shook his head, was immediately aware of the charm of the man, some sexual charisma which was apparent even in a casual photo.

'Handsome devil, wasn't he?'

'If you like the type.' Jenny screwed up her pretty face. 'Me, I wouldn't trust him as far as I could throw him.'

Which happened to coincide exactly with how Abigail felt.

Would she ever see daylight again?

Lying here in the dark, she was so cold, despite the blanket. The sick headache was worse, and her stomach was tight with gnawing hunger. He hadn't been back for two days.

At least, she thought it was two days, it could have been more, or less. By now, she was thoroughly confused and knew she'd lost all track of time. She'd tried to keep tally of the hours by the distant clock she could hear, though sometimes, however hard she kept her ears strained, she missed the strikes of one hour, or even two, and despite herself, she kept falling asleep, or rather, into some sort of torpor. Perhaps he'd put something in her food.

Had there been two lots of daylight hours, or three? She couldn't remember. Daylight was, in any case, merely the difference between pitch black and a rather lesser black, when a faint chink of light crept in through some sort of shutter fixed to the outside of the window.

The window was high on the wall, far above her reach. She'd

thought of trying to break it by throwing something at it, hoping her shouts might then be heard through the chink, but she'd never heard anyone passing outside to shout to, and in any case, he'd see the window was broken when he came, and might move her to somewhere else. Or get rid of her altogether. The idea had soon died, anyway, for lack of anything to throw. He'd taken her shoes away and it wasn't possible to throw the water container: it was too big – the sort of plastic thing campers used, with a tap to draw off the water. There were paper cups, and she vaguely remembered him topping it up on his last visit, but the water was flat and stale-tasting by now.

Her thoughts were still disconnected and confused. Try as she would, she couldn't remember who she was, or what had gone before the time when she'd woken up in this place. Perhaps that was due to what she guessed must have been a blow on her head: she had this persistent headache, and the first time he'd come, he'd explored her skull with probing fingers, which had hurt, but he must have been satisfied to find that she wasn't bleeding, or anything like that.

What she clung to was the one thing she was sure of ... the certain fact that she'd met her captor before, though how she knew that was another of the things she couldn't work out. She'd no visual clues to go on, except glimpses of him when he came and left, before and after he blindfolded her, and fastened her to the bed, while he performed the necessary tasks. She submitted passively, having learned that it was useless to struggle, though she sensed a rough kindness in his actions. He wore a black wool balaclava with holes only for eyes and nostrils, and he was dressed head to foot in a black, baggy track suit and black wool gloves. He never spoke to her, or answered when she spoke to him.

So what was it that made up the sum of one's knowledge about a person? Their size, the way they moved, their general shape – and their smell. Every time he came near her, she tried, like an animal, to distinguish his personal scent, his own essential, chemical secretion, or to discern some aftershave, perhaps, or the scent of the soap he'd used to wash his hands; but he always had food with him, which masked any other smell.

Until now, he hadn't starved her, which had given her a faint hope that he meant to keep her alive. Each time he came, he brought food, a scant meal only, but enough to keep her going. Though once it had been a feast of fish and chips, hot and greasy, which she'd crammed into her mouth with her fingers. The memory made her salivate.

So far, her most intimate personal needs had been taken care of, and somehow, she hated that more than anything, hated him for the concession of tampons and toilet rolls. There was an Elsan in one corner. She'd thought about throwing that at him, too, when he came in, but she knew she hadn't the strength. She still felt woozy every time she moved.

When he arrived he used a low-powered flashlight, and she'd seen that her prison had just the one arched window, set high in the wall, and a heavy wooden door which opened outwards. Though he'd taken her shoes away, and the flagstones on the floor were damply cold, she was able to get up and move gingerly around when he wasn't there, and she thought, by counting her paces round the room, that it must be about twenty feet square. It was very high. At first, she'd shouted until she was hoarse, but her voice had been lost in the space above her. Perhaps it was in some part of a church.

She lay, tense and half-frozen on the narrow camp bed, willing her memory to return, striving for anything that might give her a clue as to who he was, though this was probably the wrong thing to do. Think of something else, and it would come back of its own accord. That's what you were told to do when something evaded your memory, wasn't it? Useless advice in this context. What else was there to think of, except the horror of her situation and the ever-nagging question of who she really was?

Why didn't he come?

She kept thinking of him as 'he' but now a new thought came to her: her captor might just as easily have been a woman.

9

'Make it snappy, Ted. I get the impression from his secretary – sorry, his PA – that Mr Pardoe doesn't appreciate being kept waiting.'

They were speeding towards the outer fringes of the county, having left Jenny Platt to begin working her way through Wishart's other known associates in the search for his as yet nameless visitor, the man with whom he'd quarrelled on Thursday night, while other team members were making themselves unpopular by knocking on doors, interrupting after-Sunday-lunch snoozes and *The Antiques Roadshow* to inquire about sightings of unfamiliar cars parked around the approaches to Clacks Wood on Saturday afternoon.

'Secretary works Sundays, does she?'

Carmody was sitting clamped to the steering wheel, looking trussed as an oven-ready chicken, despite having shoved the seat back as far as it would go to accommodate his long legs. A pale sun emerged every now and then to give hope that some day the weather would get back to normal but gloom had settled on Carmody's basset-hound face. He was being very Liverpool-Irish. The presence of the mega-rich (which Mr Pardoe was reported to be) tended to bring this out, but any doubts Abigail felt about the wisdom of taking him along with her were assuage by reminders of his basic good sense. He was shrewd and dependable, there was no one she'd rather work with. She ignored his proddings.

'I wondered about that, too.'

Cool and crisp as a Granny Smith apple, Pardoe's assistant had informed Abigail over the telephone that she was lucky to find him with half an hour to spare. She herself would, unfortunately, have gone home by then, she didn't normally work over the weekends at all, this one being an exception because Mr Pardoe had a specially important business project which he couldn't complete without her assistance. But she would make sure Mr Pardoe kept the time free, leave a note to remind him. Abigail wondered about men like Mr Pardoe, apparently incapable of functioning without some capable woman at their beck and call, organizing their lives for them.

The man in question lived in some style, in a mock-Georgian house, almost big enough to qualify as a mansion. It was set in several acres, some of it woodland, and built on top of a hill, making a large statement that was visible for miles before you reached it, even on a day like this. Stone gateposts topped with lions rampant announced the entrance to Norton House. Startled pheasants lumbered away from the car as it wound up the drive through stands of beech and oak. The trees opened out on to a wide gravelled parking space before a flagged stone terrace and a porticoed front entrance flanked by pots blazing with winter-flowering pansies. Carmody muttered something bolshie under his breath.

They crunched towards the front door.

By this time Abigail was prepared for nothing less than a butler, but Pardoe's wife answered the door herself and led the way into her husband's study. She was a tall woman, thin, flat as an ironing-board, the skinny sweater and narrow trousers drawing attention to the sparseness of her figure. She carried an unspoken air of disapproval with her like a protest banner. Abigail put her in her late forties, though her skin aged her, having the tanned, leathery appearance of having seen too much sun.

She walked them across an immense hall, where they warily skirted oriental rugs spread in dangerous isolation on the mirror-finished floor. Enigmatic modern paintings sent cryptic messages from the walls. Through open doors, opulent set-piece rooms could be glimpsed.

Pardoe, informally dressed, rose from his desk and shook hands. A warm, deliberately sincere handshake. He, too, had been in the sun, though he was less tanned than weatherbeaten; he was very dark, with a blue chin and heavy eyebrows, but there seemed little else left of any Cornish origins, other than his name. He was a big man who moved with a leisurely grace and had watchful, pale blue eyes. He and his wife seemed an ill-assorted pair, but who could account for love?

'Sit down, make yourselves comfortable. How can I help?'

'Just a few words, sir. We shan't keep you long,' Abigail said, bearing in mind the spirit of his PA's warning, if not the letter. When they'd entered the room, he'd swung round from a computer screen which blinked mesmerizingly in the middle of a desk littered with papers, so presumably he was at least capable of operating that without her help, in order to manipulate the affairs which had doubtless created and maintained this lifestyle.

'We're looking into Mr Wishart's business affairs,' she began. 'We need to talk to people who knew him, to try and establish a reason for his death.'

'Then it's true? I spoke to Clare this morning and she told me ... Is it right that he's been murdered? Christ.'

'I see it's been a shock.'

'Well, it doesn't happen every day that a friend gets himself topped! Suicide – hell, I found *that* hard enough to believe at first.' He had a way of looking from under his heavy eyebrows. 'Though frankly, old Tim was a disaster waiting to happen. He'd been sliding down the slippery slope for some time. You know he was a Lloyd's Name?' Yes, said Abigail, they'd heard that. 'Lost a packet over it – but didn't we all?' His eyes involuntarily strayed to the winking screen, where columns of figures from the realms of fantasy appeared and disappeared. With difficulty, he tore his gaze away. 'Trouble was, he'd dug himself in too deep. Staked more than he should have, had a run of bad luck and didn't have the wherewithal when they came to call it in. In hock to his last pair of braces, he was, poor sod.'

'When did you last see him?' Carmody asked, his face wooden. Abigail sympathized with the feeling. It wasn't easy to shed tears for anyone who let themselves in for unlimited liability just to make a quick buck, pledging assets they didn't now possess.

'Saw him a couple of weeks ago. We took Nancy Norton over to Fécamp.' Pardoe's eyes went to an outsize, blown-up colour photograph prominent on the wall above his desk.

Carmody blinked. Abigail could see him adjusting, as she was, to the fact that Pardoe was speaking of his yacht, *Nancy Norton*, which, in the picture, was riding at anchor on a blue sea with a grinning crew holding champagne glasses up to the camera.

At that moment Mrs Pardoe brought them tea, served it and then left them to it. 'Housekeeper's day off,' she explained abruptly and unsmilingly. 'Lots to do.'

While she was pouring the tea, and Pardoe's eyes were straying compulsively back to the screen, his fingers towards the keyboard, as if unable to keep his mind off insoluble mysteries like futures and commodities and options, Abigail took the opportunity to study the room. It was big, approached through his assistant's office (pin-neat, custom-built limed oak, cherry pink soft furnishings and grey walls) whereas this room was a tip. Or ordered chaos, your viewpoint perhaps depending on whether you could imagine having to clean it or not. The contents of the overflowing bookshelves appeared to be mainly files and sailing manuals. Seafaring pictures occupying much of the wall space underlined that sailing was Pardoe's main leisure interest and maybe his other passion, the first being money, though a golf bag stuffed with clubs leaned in one corner, and there was a picture of him with his wife, taken on some sunlit ski-slope or other. The window overlooked a large paddock in which three beautiful horses grazed.

It became evident as they spoke that Wishart had shared the interest in sailing, though not, as Pardoe's next words showed, to the extent of owning his own yacht – or not now. 'Old Tim used to come out with me on *Nancy* whenever he could,' he was continuing. 'Had to sell his own boat when they began to tighten the screws.'

'Lovely vessel.' Was that the right word for a yacht, vessel? wondered Abigail, whose knowledge of all things appertaining to the sea was abysmal. 'Where do you keep it, Mr Pardoe?'

'She's moored on the south coast, near Gosport. We're about as far as you can get from the sea here, but I couldn't abide piddling about on reservoirs. *Nancy*'s a sea-going yacht. I like to get over to the other side when I can, though finding time's a real problem.'

'Long way to go for a bit of sailing,' Carmody said, his heart evidently bleeding for the problems of the very, very rich.

Pardoe smiled thinly, but Abigail shot a warning glance at the sergeant. Pardoe had sensed his antagonistic attitude and didn't like it. 'Not so far in a fast car,' he replied shortly. 'We can be down there in two or three hours, depending on traffic.'

'You and Mrs Pardoe?' she asked.

'No, whoever's crewing for me. Marianne has her horses, I have my boat, it works very well. Not too much proximity – know what I mean?' One suggestive eyebrow was raised, good humour restored. He smiled a white smile; his teeth had evidently been capped. The skin under his eyes looked a little puffy. He wore a royal blue cashmere sweater and his slacks were expensively tailored to fit a slightly expanding waistline. He seemed overly pleased with himself – didn't it ever occur to him that Marianne might enjoy the lack of proximity, too?

'You say it was a couple of weeks since you saw Mr Wishart?'
Abigail repeated. Pardoe nodded. 'Then we can take it you
weren't at the Lodge dinner in Birmingham on Wednesday?'

'Ah.' He sat back, elbows resting on his chair arms, and
steepled his fingers, pulling a rueful face. 'I've just gone and
dumped my old mate well and truly in the proverbial, haven't
I? Well, I suppose you'd have checked, anyway. Fact is, I didn't
know he was supposed to be there.'

'Have you any idea where he might have been?'

'Knowing old Tim, I'd say it's more than likely he'd a bit of
skirt somewhere – but don't ask me to name names. I don't
know any, and it'd have taken a better man than me to keep up
with them anyway.'

'You were close to Mr Wishart, personally and in business.
Can you give us the names of other friends or associates – and
maybe some who weren't so kindly disposed as yourself? You
knew, I assume, that he was deeply in debt – '

'Too right, he was! He owed me a packet, for one thing!'

'How much would that be?'

'Never mind how much. More than I can bloody well afford!'
His heavy face had reddened slightly, but he soon had himself
in control again, and came back smoothly, 'However, that's
water under the bridge, the price one has to pay for friendship. I
shan't press Clare for it.' He leaned back expansively. Was he
really so magnanimous, or had he exaggerated the implications
of the amount Wishart had owed him?

'Do you own a shotgun, Mr Pardoe?'

He blinked rapidly. 'I own several, why? Whoa there, just a
minute – what are you getting at? You surely don't believe . . .'

Neither police officer was moved by this, a stock reaction at
best: *Moi?* My best friend? Don't even *think* it!

'We shall need to examine them,' Carmody returned stoically.

'Check them by all means, but you won't find anything.'

Of course they wouldn't. It was a formality to be gone through,
no one with an atom of common sense – and Mr Tony Pardoe
wasn't short in the sharp wits department – was going to leave a
murder weapon hanging around. But he was rattled.

Abigail asked, 'Can you account for your movements yesterday? For the record,' she added, anticipating objections.

'As a matter of fact, I was finishing some important work with Camilla, my secretary.'

Camilla. Abigail could see her, tall, fair, Sloanish. The bossy voice over the telephone went with the image. Camilla had definitely sounded more than capable of lying in her teeth for her boss, if it came to the point where an alibi was needed for Tony Pardoe. At the moment there was no reason to suspect him of anything more than slipperiness.

He added, with a touch of malice, 'Most of the afternoon, I was waiting for a transatlantic phone call. It came at a quarter to four.'

Impassively, Abigail asked for details, which would certainly be checked. 'That's all for now, sir.' She slipped her notebook into her bag. 'Thank you for your time. Don't bother to see us out, we can find our own way.'

He looked distinctly alarmed at the very idea. 'No, no, my wife will do it.' He pinged a bell on his desk, as if for a servant. Before Marianne Pardoe promptly appeared, his hand was already stretching towards the computer keyboard.

As she left them at the front door, Mrs Pardoe said, 'Don't try too hard to get him. Whoever had the sense to kill Wishart, I mean. He did us all a favour. And I mean all. No one who knew Wishart would disagree.'

'Would you care to elaborate on that, Mrs Pardoe?'

'That's all that needs to be said,' she answered, the door almost closed. 'He was an out and out bastard, that's what he was. And good riddance.' She shut the door firmly in their faces. But not before Abigail had glimpsed a shine of tears on the weather-beaten cheeks.

'And what', said Abigail, 'd'you make of that?'

'What the lady said about Wishart goes for his mate Pardoe, too.' Carmody started the car. 'Slimy sod. He's not shedding any tears over Wishart, he's about as upset over him as I am. He'd have shot him in the face as soon as look at him. I'd trust next door's cat first. I'm not being prejudiced. Want me to go on?'

'Don't bother, I get the drift. You and me both, as it happens.'

They drove in silence towards the rampant lions at the gate of

Norton House. Carmody negotiated the turn into the main road. 'And maybe he *was* a good mate of "*old Tim's*", but he's fit to be tied about that money he owed him, never mind forget it.'

'I know. But enough to have killed him? And why? Because he felt there wasn't an earthly, as far as getting it back was concerned? Possible, but not what you'd call a compelling motive, is it? Unless it was a huge amount, which I doubt.'

'I dunno, blokes like him, they never miss a trick where money's concerned. It *hurts*, even to lose a brass farthing.'

'Try and find out just how much Wishart owed him. And any other dirt you can dig up about Pardoe. Can I leave that one with you?'

'It'll be my pleasure,' said Carmody.

The quietly authoritative professional exterior Mayo presented to the world hid a sometimes irascible impatience when results were not as quickly forthcoming as he thought they should be. By Tuesday, he was demanding to know what progress had been made in the Wishart affair.

He had authorized the press office to make a media statement that the death of Timothy Wishart was being treated as murder, with a further appeal for anyone who had information, or who had been in the vicinity at the time, to come forward. It was vital that the man who'd called at Clacks Mill on the previous Thursday evening should make himself known to the police, 'in order that he could be eliminated from inquiries'.

The first two or three days in a murder inquiry were paramount; after that the trail grew cold and the initial impetus was lost. Sometimes a case could drag on for months. Sometimes it was never solved.

Abigail, sifting through the reports which were beginning to stack up on her desk, devoutly hoped this was not going to be one of the last. A substantial amount of information about Wishart's business affairs had, in fact, already begun to filter through, but it was going to take longer than two days – more like two months, she thought pessimistically – to obtain a complete picture, due to the complexities of his affairs. From time to time he'd been involved in inquiries into financial irregularities, but nothing had come of them; and there'd been a money-laundering prosecution in 1994 from which he'd emerged without anything being proven.

But he'd dabbled in murky waters, and no doubt upset a lot of undesirable people in the process, and that was probably where the roots of his murder lay. A contract killing could not be ruled out. Hell's teeth! Abigail wanted to shut her eyes to this worst-case scenario: a professional hit man, who had no connection with his victim, the only surprise being that the shotgun hadn't been sawn-off, and fat chance of catching the perpetrator. It was increasingly unlikely that this was a domestic, but that didn't automatically let off the hook any person intimately connected with the dead man.

She ran through the names of the few who might be classed as suspects again. Sam Nash for one, pillar of the community though he might be, who'd hated Wishart pretty comprehensively, but who hadn't had the opportunity. As a director of Lavenstock United Football Club, he'd been in the directors' box with his fellow board members from the time the match began until he'd been summoned away by the telephone call which had told him of his son-in-law's death. Had it been possible for him to slip away unnoticed during that time? Unlikely, or not for the minimum thirty minutes he would have needed to get to Clacks Wood and back, plus lying in wait for Wishart. He'd have to be more closely questioned, however. Clare and his grandchildren were obviously the centre of his universe. Would he have been prepared to take such a final step to rid them of Tim? Abigail didn't doubt him capable of decisive – even ruthless – action. But murder was another thing.

Apart from Wishart's family, David Neale was the only other person known to have been in the vicinity, but he'd gone straight to the Centre after leaving Clare, his arrival at twenty to four had been confirmed by several witnesses, and his car had still been in the park until at least half-past five; his, and the one next to it, had been hemmed in by some woman who had (illicitly) parked her car in the Centre's car-park while she went shopping. It all seemed straightforward enough. Moreover, there was nothing to indicate why, as little more than an acquaintance, he should wish to murder Wishart. Unless Clare was a reason. Mere speculation, this, but Abigail had picked up something, from Neale's attitude – though what, it was hard to pinpoint.

Ellie Redvers admitted to being desperately unhappy in a relationship, almost certainly with Wishart, but Abigail herself had been with her until shortly before Wishart had been shot. And there was no way Abigail could realistically see her rushing off after their lunch meeting to find a gun and shoot him.

In fact, unless both Timpson-Ludgate had been substantially mistaken about the time of death, and Fairmile about the shot, none of them had had the opportunity. Except for Clare. The husband or wife was always the strongest suspect, and Clare had a prime motive in that Tim Wishart had been a faithless and unsatisfactory husband.

Abigail obscurely wanted it to be none of them. Pardoe excepted, who had his alibi, they were all people she liked. But these were brief thoughts, and dangerous. Personal likings had nothing to do with it, they only got in the way. She sighed and pushed her chair back. It was getting to her, this case. A nastiness was permeating through it.

Deeley breezed in from the humming incident room with a tray of coffee she'd asked for, a canteen doughnut she hadn't, and a further stack of reports. What she saw as the lack of progress was making her feel guilty. Guilt was an unproductive emotion, arousing compensating needs. She ate the doughnut and felt worse rather than better, finished her umpteenth cup of coffee, ran a hand through her hair. Slapped the case file closed and asked George Atkins, her fellow inspector in CID, if he could spare her a few moments, away from the incident room.

'Tell me about Wishart senior,' she asked, when they were alone, with no fear that she'd be disappointed. She liked George, despite the permanent reek of old tobacco about his person, though he knew better than to puff away at his evil pipe in the presence of either her or Mayo, both of whom waged a constant, if ultimately unsuccessful, war of attrition against it.

'Freddie Wishart? Oh, great character, Freddie.' The chair creaked under his weight as he lowered his backside on to it. 'This county lost the best cricketer we ever had when he went. And you couldn't have wished for a nicer chap, by all accounts.'

'What made him kill himself?'

Atkins blew his lips out. 'Who knows? But – like father, like son, I imagine. He had his financial problems, too, as I remember.' George had been doing his homework, and he added, giving her an old-fashioned look, 'You met his widow yet?'

'No, that's a pleasure to come.'

'Your pleasure rather than mine. Sybil Wishart's reputed to be a bitch, twenty-four carat. And likes her tipple nowadays, I hear.' He lifted his elbow, miming a drinking action. 'Brought a lot of money to the marriage but went through it, plus what Freddie had, like water, or that was the rumour. True or not, he died a bankrupt.'

'So Tim wouldn't have inherited anything through his father? Made his own money, did he?'

George smiled, the closed smile which had become habitual because of the pipe normally jammed between his teeth. 'Whatever he did make, he lost, so I'm reliably informed. If there's anything left for his wife and kids, it'll have been down to Sam Nash, I should think.'

'There wasn't much love lost there, George.'

'Ah, but Sam had his daughter to think of, didn't he?' He drank the last dregs of a pint mug of tea. 'Well, if that's it, I've work to do.'

'Thanks for the briefing, you're a wonder, George.' A vision of Milford Road nick without George's inexhaustible supply of local knowledge passed before her mind's eye. It didn't bear thinking about. He was less of an inspector than an institution. He was working steadily towards his retirement, due within the next year, and speculation was rife as to his successor, but this appeared to trouble Atkins not one bit. He plodded on in his usual phlegmatic way, competent, unspectacular, but more often than not confounding the computers with his memory.

'What are you going to do when you retire, George?'

Automatically, he pulled his pipe from his pocket, looked at it regretfully and held it with the bowl cupped in his palm, caressing it with his thumb. 'Might work in private security. I've had one or two offers.' He shrugged, not wanting to talk about it, and she knew he was as reluctant to go as Milford Road would be to lose him. He stood up and made for the door. 'I'd get a damn sight more money than I do now.'

As the door closed behind him she wondered if George had been one of the people Nick Spalding had approached.

111

She hadn't entirely forgotten her promises to Nick, and had put one or two things in motion, but other events had taken precedence over contacting him. She'd nothing of any significance to tell him, but now a new idea occurred to her. She thought rapidly. The last hour had been the only quiet oasis in a hectic day. She'd already planned what was left of it and there was no way she could reschedule, but a quick check with her diary told her she could squeeze in a few minutes with him on her way to see Ellie at Miller's Wife. A talk with Ellie was, she'd felt, overdue, and Ellie had agreed, albeit not very willingly, suggesting her workplace as a rendezvous.

She was lucky enough to find Nick at home when she rang.

While Abigail was making her way to meet Nick Spalding at one of the new coffee shops along Coronation Wharf, Mayo was squeaking down the hospital corridor, wishing he were anywhere else.

Gynaecological wards rendered him tongue-tied and had him falling over his own big feet; he was embarrassed by this mysterious world of women and their complaints, and ill-at-ease and angry at his own inadequacy. After all, he was no boy, no stranger to female ailments, he knew what it was all about. He'd been taken in minute detail, albeit unwillingly, through all the various uncomfortable stages of pregnancy with his wife, and the disease which had later killed her. He was aware of the trauma Alex must be facing, but he viewed the whole situation with male perplexity, able to understand with his mind but not really with his emotions.

'I've come to take you home, love.'

Alex was already dressed, nothing of her short, sharp ordeal evident except for a certain big-eyed wanness. Ready to leave, armed with a list of instructions and strong injunctions from the sister. Chocolates dispensed to the nurses, flowers and plants left to brighten the wards. Except for the freesias, slightly papery-looking now, some of their fragrance lost but not all, to be clasped in her arms all the way home, and stubbornly kept until they withered and their scent was just a memory.

10

Abigail walked to her meeting with Nick, reminding herself to make sure Mayo knew about it. It would raise her standing with him. A dedicated walker, he'd dragged her reluctantly around often enough. It was bound to be quicker than getting herself jammed into the traffic around the circuitous ring road, anyway.

The short cut through the Cornmarket and the old part of the town, via Butter Lane, meant passing Lois French's shop. As usual, Interiors was a feast for the eye, glowing from across the narrow street. Abigail wondered if Alex was truly happy in what she was doing. Interior decorating was about as far from the police as you could get. She was going along with it, but Abigail had lately detected a dangerous trace of wistfulness and nostalgia when she spoke of the old days.

Damn you, Nick, she thought, damn you for stirring it up. He could be manipulative. No one knew that better than Abigail, even when she'd been in love with him – or fancied she was. Yet how much was Alex likely to be influenced by Nick's persuasions? Cool, level-headed Alex, who was always in control?

The afternoon had deteriorated even more by the time she left Butter Lane and turned into Stockwell Street, parallel with the river. The street had gone upmarket during the recent redevelopments, or as upmarket as Lavenstock would take. There were now shops selling wine and cheese, one or two discriminating boutiques, even a hopeful new bookshop. But it was very quiet, no one else in sight, not much trade going on, and her footsteps rang with an uncanny, hollow reverberation.

She cut through Cat Lane, between the bookshop and the newly tarted-up Nag's Head, an alley with a notorious past and a not too unblemished present. Too narrow for comfort on a dark night, or at any time. Despite herself, she quickened her footsteps until she emerged on the embankment. She walked along with the collar of her raincoat turned up, her hands shoved deep in her pockets, moisture clinging to her eyelashes, and the drizzle making a halo around the streetlamps. It was already dark enough for a string of fairy lights, outside the Community Centre, to be reflected palely in the dark, oily surface of the water. It was dangerously high, the river.

Along the waterfront, the defunct old warehouse quays and landing stages, originally intended to serve the needs of the industrial traffic along the waterways, were vanishing in a plethora of patios and waterside gardens. Very soon, all the old buildings would be gone. In summer, the gardens blazed with flowers, and chairs and tables were set out in front of the ground-floor shops and cafés beneath the expensive, newly converted warehouse apartments, popular with young Birmingham city executives. The whole area, from river to canal, had been attractively landscaped. Overdone, some felt, prepared to argue the point at length. The last thing Ben had done before he left was finally to put an end to a hotly debated and ultimately tiresome correspondence on the subject in the columns of the *Advertiser*.

Nick was waiting for her at the Holly Tree, and immediately signalled the waiter. 'What will you have?' He looked terrible. He was nervy and on edge and his eyes glittered.

It was self-service here when they were busy, but you got more attention at times like this, when only another two tables were occupied. Hot chocolate, advised the waiter, who seemed inclined to chat. The dark, rich, frothy sort that was a speciality of the house, he said, adding in an aside that it was better than either the tea or coffee on offer, which would have to improve – though the almond gâteau was worth trying. He looked disappointed when Abigail, regretting the doughnut she'd eaten earlier, aware of too much caffeine already consumed, plumped for tea only. Nick ordered likewise. 'Any news?' he demanded as soon as their order had been placed on the table, getting rid of the talkative waiter with a dismissive nod of thanks.

Abigail watched the waiter reluctantly sidling away. A short, swarthy boy, who looked like a gypsy and spoke with a public school accent. She'd seen him around, but couldn't remember where.

'Nothing useful, Nick.'

One thing she could tell him was that she was fairly sure Roz hadn't embarked for Tuscany by air. She'd had inquiries made about airline tickets, and certainly Roz hadn't made any booking through any of the travel agents in the town. It was possible she'd booked direct, or she might have decided to drive, via the Channel tunnel, but when Abigail put this last suggestion forward, Nick dismissed it out of hand, stating categorically that Roz hated driving any distance and would do almost anything to avoid it.

Abigail sipped her tea in silence for a moment or two. 'Well, that's all I have. Sorry I haven't been able to do more. But I've had other things on my mind since then.'

'That chap who shot himself? The one in the papers?'

Wishart's death was naturally headline news locally, a scoop for the *Advertiser*. Ben had missed the most exciting thing to happen in Lavenstock for months. The Wishart name had been one of consequence in the area for generations, and details of the family history had filled the front page. Inevitably, comparisons had been drawn with his father's suicide. Nick would have seen the reports and guessed she'd be part of the investigation.

'You don't want to believe all you read in the papers.'

'How's that?'

'He didn't shoot himself.' There was no harm in telling him, it would soon be public knowledge. 'We've had the path report and we're treating it as murder.'

'Murder? Poor devil!' Nick stirred his tea with jerky, nervous movements, so that the liquid slopped into the saucer, lit a cigarette and took a long drag, drawing smoke into his lungs with suicidal recklessness, but it seemed to calm him.

'Funny how things turn out,' he said eventually, watching her through the smoke. 'All weekend I've been trying to remember where it was that Roz had worked, that temporary job she took, and then when I saw his name in the paper, Wishart, it clicked. That's the name of the woman who runs that place, isn't it, where I ran into you the other night?'

Where you were waiting for me, Abigail amended silently. And wondered at yet another chance happening. Or was it? With Nick, you could never be sure. The impact of what he'd said suddenly struck her.

'You mean *Roz* worked at Miller's Wife?' She'd long since ceased to be amazed by life's coincidences, but this *was* amazing. She'd given neither Ellie Redvers nor Clare Wishart, not to mention Nick and his wife, scarcely a thought for weeks, months, and now here they all were, crowding in on each other, like stars moving through space to form a cluster. And what about Miller's Wife? Events and conjunctions appeared to be stirring around that place, too.

She showed him Wishart's photo, handsome, arrogant ... 'Ever seen him before, Nick?'

'This is the victim – Wishart?'

'Yes.' She'd had hopes that he might have recognized the dead man from the photo. Several people at the station, besides George Atkins, had known him. His face had often featured in the local papers in connection with various events. Moreover, he was his father's son, and his father was remembered as popular sporting personalities always are. True, it was now some time since Nick had left Lavenstock, but Wishart had been around during his time here, and Nick had always had a facility for remembering faces, as well as for ferreting out and storing up information, not all of which he necessarily saw fit to pass on.

His response in this case was disappointingly negative. 'Can't say I've ever seen him.' She wasn't sure whether she believed him or not.

He stubbed his cigarette out, half-smoked. 'So that's it, then. We're no further forrard as far as Roz is concerned, and you've no more time to bother with it – understandable, but thanks anyway.'

'Just a minute, Nick, not so hasty. Listen to what I have to say.' She topped up her cup. 'As you know, there's a man we're looking for.'

Still looking for, she might have said. It shouldn't have taken so long to trace Wishart's visitor, not if he'd had a legitimate excuse for being at the mill, or even if he hadn't. Having sources, snouts you could rely on, was a matter of course in CID, but the criminal fraternity seemed to have been afflicted with a sudden, remarkable amnesia, even those with a previously one hundred per cent total recall.

But Nick, when he'd been in Lavenstock CID, had had his own methods, his own informants. She went on to describe the visitor whom Amy had seen, aware how meagre the detail was, though Nick, like every other detective, had often worked successfully on less. 'Maybe,' she suggested, carefully watching him, 'you could do some ferreting around.'

His face immediately darkened and he moved his hand in a violent sideways denial. 'Uh-oh. Not me. No way. I'm strictly non-operational nowadays.'

There was something over the top about his refusal, something too vehement that she didn't understand. She put a little more pressure on. 'The girl, Wishart's daughter, helped us with a photofit picture.' She fished the picture which had been compiled with Amy's help from her bag. It looked up from the table, side by side with Wishart's.

He shook his head. 'Don't know him. And still no deal.'

'Tit for tat, Nick.'

They eyed each other steadily. This was the sort of bargaining he understood, but she knew it was an offer he was about to refuse. She sighed. It had been worth a try, all the same.

But his hands, as he lit another cigarette, were not quite steady, and his answer, when it came, wasn't what she'd expected. 'Haven't much choice, have I, really? Roz is my wife. And I want her found.'

'Much more satisfaction in doing things by hand,' Ellie said, wielding a murderous-looking knife on a slippery-looking onion with the rapid nonchalance of the practised cook. 'Quicker, too, in the long run.'

She was looking sallow and drawn, Abigail thought, and too nervy to be safe with a knife like that in her hand. A white head-covering was swathed around her head, totally obscuring her hair. The soft fronds of her fringe normally concealed a forehead that now seemed large and rounded; beneath it, her brown eyes looked enormous, devouring her whole face. 'We don't make huge batches of anything, you see, we try to cater for a more individual market . . . I'm concocting a new sauce for venison, it can be such a dry meat if you're not careful – '

'Ellie – '

Ellie scraped the onions into hot oil before lowering the heat. 'I'd advise you to sit over there,' she said, waving her knife dangerously to where two or three stools were drawn up to a counter at the far end of the kitchen, 'otherwise your clothes will pong. *Nothing* is worse than fried onions.'

She went to wash her hands at a sink with a tap she could

operate with her elbow, like a hospital nurse. The gleaming kitchen had white paint, white surfaces and shining, stainless steel sinks and appliances, but its warm yellow walls cast reflections on the batteries of cooking utensils massed in ordered chaos on racks and shelves, or hanging from hooks, witness to the amount of serious cooking that went on here. Scrupulous hygiene would have to be followed, the premises would be subject to official inspections and regulations, but the abundance of paraphernalia gave it a warm and homely clutter that was comforting and appealing, rather than clinical.

Abigail went to sit on one of the stools, as she was bid. 'Ellie, I have to know this, officially, otherwise I wouldn't ask, but ... The man you were talking about the other day, when you came to lunch – it was Tim Wishart, wasn't it?'

Ellie turned abruptly and removed the skillet of gently sizzling onions from the ring. She picked up the knife she'd been using and stared at it, then put it into a dishwasher. 'Yes,' she said, returning to stand in the centre of the room, looking lost. 'How can I bear it?' she asked, closing her eyes.

'Come and sit here,' Abigail replied, taking charge of the situation, unsure of how deep this went with Ellie, bearing in mind her propensity to dramatize herself. 'We have to talk.'

'You can't *possibly* think any worse of me than I do myself!'

'Ellie, I'm not here to make judgements. I just want the facts. What I have to know is – did you see him after you left me?'

Even allowing for her state of mind on Saturday, it still didn't seem likely that she'd have made the attempt to see him. She would have known how he'd planned to spend his Saturday. On the other hand, armed with this knowledge, she could have waited for him in the woods ...

'You mean, did I tell him we were finished and did he kill himself because he was devastated? No, he didn't, because he didn't know. I didn't see him after I saw you, but it wouldn't have mattered enough to him if I had told him,' she said bitterly. 'He'd have been furious, but not desperate. Not enough to kill himself.'

She put her head in her hands.

Abigail noted that Clare didn't appear to have passed on the news that his death was now being looked on as murder. 'A cup of coffee would be nice,' she said eventually.

Ellie roused herself. 'I'm off coffee, as from today. I need to sleep, not keep awake,' she added with a touch of humour, though her voice trembled. But that's better, thought Abigail. She did look as though she needed to sleep, for a week maybe. She seemed emotionally wrung out. 'I'll make you some coffee, but I'll have tea.'

'Tea will do fine for me. I don't need any more coffee, either.' Nor tea, for that matter, but still.

The tea, unsurprisingly, was excellent. Earl Grey, the bergamot flavour enhanced by a sliver of lemon, and served in a thin, delicate cup. 'I don't really know why I came in today, there's no point,' Ellie said when they were sipping it. 'We're not expecting any deliveries, and with Clare not here, I could have shut the place up, but I need to cook when I'm upset, you know? I suppose it's a sort of therapy, and it's the only thing I'm any good at, anyway.' She was trying to avoid any more discussion of Tim. Abigail recognized the need to distance herself. 'And I'd some idea I could maybe get on with some ordering or checking stock or something like that, with Barbie gone.'

'Gone?'

'She's left. When I got back from having lunch with you, there was a message on my answerphone from her. She'd decided to leave. Just like that. And I'd only been speaking to her that morning.'

For no accountable reason that Abigail could think of, a sharp prickle of warning touched the back of her neck.

'Isn't that rather sudden?'

'Yes, but that seems to be our fate, they never stay long, the women who help us here . . . it's only menial work they do, not high on job satisfaction, or pay if it comes to that – and I told you, didn't I, that I thought she was under-employed? It appears she's been feeling that way herself, and thought it time to move on. She could have given us more notice, though. Ungrateful, I call it, to leave us in the lurch like this.'

Not so much ungrateful, Abigail thought, as questionable, in the circumstances. 'She certainly chose her time.'

Ellie shrugged. 'She'd no allegiance to us. We shall miss her, though,' she admitted, 'she'd turn her hand to anything. We shall have to replace her.'

Abigail was thinking of the last time she'd seen Barbie,

perhaps only the third or fourth time she'd ever seen her, in fact. Five days ago. Barbie, larger than life, a little bothered about the situation at Miller's Wife, but seemingly involved enough to want it to succeed. It was something that needed thinking about. Meanwhile, she had other questions to ask Ellie.

'Remember a woman called Roz Spalding? I believe she worked here for a while.'

Ellie immediately looked guarded. 'Of course I remember her, I've known Roz for years, that's how she came to work here. I offered her the job, as a matter of fact.'

'Tell me about her.'

'If it's that husband of hers – ' Ellie began.

'You know Nick, too?'

'Heard of him, and I'm not very impressed by *what* I've heard. She's a fool to have gone back to him, which was what she was intending to do when she left here.' Her eyes widened. 'There's nothing wrong, is there?'

'I hope not, but at the moment, we don't know where she is. She seems to have disappeared.'

'*Disappeared*? Roz? Disappeared, how?'

When Abigail had explained, Ellie said positively, 'I'll tell you what I think: I can see Roz taking off in the state she was in, but she would never have done anything stupid. She'd got past that stage, thank God.' She sipped her tea and said soberly, 'Poor Roz, she was devastated when she came here at first, that goes without saying. I can't think of anything worse to happen to anyone – I mean losing her child like that ... this job was just something to occupy her time, but she needed a supportive relationship, and I think we were able to give it.'

Miller's Wife induced the sort of sisterly solidarity that women were good at. But, working so closely together, it could also have generated the sort of hothouse atmosphere where passions and jealousies developed ... 'Did she ever meet Tim Wishart?'

'*Tim?* Why yes, he was never away from the place. He was hankering after an active share in the business, but Clare wasn't having any.' She watched Abigail thoughtfully. 'You're on the wrong tack there, though. Roz couldn't stand him, and vice versa.'

'Why?'

'Why?' Ellie seemed nonplussed. 'Why *do* people like or dislike each other? Chemistry? Or maybe she'd got wind of – ' She fiddled with her teaspoon. 'She's a straight down the line person, you know, a bit prim and proper.'

But she'd started to say something else entirely, Abigail thought as she finished her tea. 'Got wind of our relationship'? Or 'his reputation with women'? Maybe.

'What about Barbie? How did they get on, she and Tim, I mean?'

'Now, that's different. They had a very good rapport, as it happens. Friendly, joking, Barbie was good at that. Not sexual, of course – ' She stopped and stared at Abigail. 'Why am I saying *of course*? It's obvious now. She was chatting him up, letting him see she fancied him.'

'Was it likely? That he'd fancy her?'

'Remember what we were saying about her the other day – that she could've been very attractive if she'd bothered? Tim wouldn't have missed that – and he was nothing if not susceptible,' she added, sharp as one of the knives in the block in front of them, deliberately hurting herself. 'That could be why she left, couldn't it? There'd be no reason to stay on, now.' She suddenly pulled off the ugly head-covering and ran her hands through her soft, dark hair so that it feathered around her face in the familiar way as she shook her head. 'No, forget it, I'm being paranoid, I don't honestly think there was anything that serious.'

'She lived in the flat above the premises, didn't she?' Ellie nodded. 'Mind if I take a look around?'

'It's empty. The furniture's still there, such as it is, but she's taken all her own things.' She stared at Abigail. 'You can't believe there's anything *suspicious* about her leaving, surely? She hasn't run off with the takings, you know!'

'All the same . . .' People left their traces. And Abigail was more than intrigued by the suddenness of Barbie Nelson's departure.

Perhaps it wasn't the best moment, just now, to inform Ellie of the true facts of Wishart's death, but was there ever a best moment for that sort of thing? Ellie absorbed the news in silence. When she spoke, her voice shook, and her eyes were wide and frightened. 'My God, that's terrible, but Barbie wouldn't have done anything like that!'

121

'I'm not saying that, but I'd better have a look at the flat. You needn't come up with me, I'll find my way.'

Ellie didn't argue but produced a key from a key-cupboard on the wall. 'There's only David Neale's office on the same floor. His name's on the door, but he's not there.'

Abigail left her sitting on one of the stools, staring into space. It was natural that she should be upset at hearing how her lover had died, but Abigail noted with interest that she hadn't seemed to find it incredible.

The premises of Miller's Wife as a whole weren't large – the big kitchen which was the heart of the enterprise, with cold rooms and storerooms and a cloakroom behind, the shop in front with its tiny glassed-in cubicle where Barbie had kept check of the stores, typed the odd letter and filed invoices. At the top of the stairs on one side was the office normally occupied by David Neale, on the other Barbie's bed-sitter, plus a minuscule bathroom-cum-kitchen.

The accommodation was spartan, furnished only with essential pieces, so that it didn't take Abigail more than a few minutes to establish that Barbie had left nothing behind in the drawers and cupboards. The wardrobe, likewise, revealed nothing but a few wire hangers. Behind the bedroom door a large black plastic bin liner stood on the carpet, about a quarter full, its neck twisted into a knot. Abigail undid it and peered inside, then began working her way through layers of discarded tights, old cosmetic jars, an empty talc container, and a screwed-up sheet of newspaper which contained a miscellaneous assortment of debris of the kind suggesting that Barbie had decided to tidy out the scruffy contents of a handbag by shaking it out over the newspaper. Among several till receipts for small amounts, a wrapper from a Cadbury's Fruit & Nut bar, a broken comb, an empty paracetamol blister pack, a safety pin and four one-pence pieces, was what looked like a small folded newspaper clipping.

It was fraying on the folds, and very gently Abigail opened it up, to reveal a grainy photograph of a young man and a woman. The caption underneath read: 'Paul Matthews and his fiancée, Barbara Nelson.' It had been cut from the *Daily Telegraph*, August 22nd, two years previously.

Abigail perched on the edge of the bed, staring thoughtfully at the photo, trying to assess what it might mean. It wasn't until after she'd refolded it and slid it into her wallet that she noticed the knife.

It was on the small table by the bed, a razor-sharp, wicked-looking object, with a triangular blade of carbon steel, fastened into the black wooden handle with brass rivets. Identical to the one Ellie had been using to chop the onions.

'Yes, it's one of ours,' Ellie said, when Abigail, holding it gingerly with a handkerchief, took it downstairs to show her. 'One of those, look.'

There was in fact a whole battery of such knives in the kitchen, suitable for every possible function, ranged on various racks and blocks set down the middle of the long, central working surface, within easy reach of anyone working there. The knife found by Barbie's bed would have fitted exactly the empty space in one of the racks.

'By the bed?' Ellie repeated. 'Goodness. I suppose it might be a bit weird, being here on your own at night, but who'd have thought Barbie the type to be scared of intruders? It's more likely they'd have been scared of her.'

Abigail was beginning to have other ideas.

The knife looked surgically clean, but she wrapped it carefully and told Ellie she'd like to take it away. 'You're not needing the flat at the moment, are you?'

'Not unless we can get someone to replace Barbie immediately, someone who needs the flat. It's a good inducement. Why?'

'We'll need to take a proper look round. I'd like to have the door sealed up, just in case. Meanwhile, did Barbie leave a forwarding address? There must be money owing to her.'

'She said on the message she didn't know where she'd be, she'd let us know, and we could forward it.'

'Where did she live before she came here?'

Ellie spread her hands helplessly. 'We shall have the address somewhere, I'll have a look. Funny, but we never talked about her personal circumstances. She didn't give you much oppor-tunity, you know. She kept the conversation jokey, she'd fool around, make fun of her size ... I'm sorry, it's a rotten thing to say, but I only looked on her as a bit of a clown.'

The fate of fat people everywhere. Sad, but true, that nobody thought, or cared much, about what was going on inside.

11

Col was having one of his better days. He woke Jem with a mug of herbal tea, then squatted on the edge of the bed, by which name the lumpy mattress on the floor was dignified, talking until Jem was forced to sit up and drink the tea, though he hadn't wanted it. It was only eight o'clock and he could've slept until lunch time, if he hadn't been disturbed, seeing that he didn't need to show his face at the job any longer. He'd jacked it in, it was all too much of a hassle, getting there on time, working late . . .

But he drank the tea because he didn't want to upset Col, though he seemed rational this morning, or what passed for rational as far as he was concerned. It was sometimes hard to tell. He was vague at the best of times. He took the mug when Jem had finished the tea and began to potter about the room.

'Looking for something?' Jem asked at last, irritated, knowing that if it had been anyone else he'd just have told them to piss off and let him go back to sleep. But he was wary of upsetting Col.

'My library book.'

Col was moony and gentle-looking, and when he wore his glasses, half-way down his nose, he looked like the professor he could one day have been. He was a university drop-out, like Jem, which was where they'd met, only Col's drop out had been enforced, through his illness. He'd been reading PPE, and couldn't seem to get out of the habit of books. In spite of everything, he was never totally going to abandon the idea of returning and completing his degree course.

'Had your pills this morning?' Jem asked.

He'd assumed responsibility for Col ever since he'd been released from the psychiatric unit. His father, who was divorced and on top of that had multiple sclerosis, needed care himself, and a son with problems like that was a responsibility he couldn't undertake. His mother, who'd left them when Col was ten, didn't want to know.

'He can come and live here with us,' Luce had said at once. 'His poor dad, as if MS wasn't enough! Life's a right cow, sometimes.'

The MS apart, the two couldn't have lived together. Their temperaments were totally incompatible, to begin with, and the wasting disease had soured John Denby's already none too sweet disposition further. But at least he kept in touch, and occasionally sent some money, though he'd little enough to spare, so he must have been grateful to them all for befriending Col and giving him somewhere to stay. Fortunately, he'd never been able, in his condition, to get down to the Bagots and see how his son lived. Even Jem could see that might have finished him off.

'I said, have you had your pills?' he repeated when Col showed no intention of answering his question.

'Yeah,' he replied, so definitely that Jem knew he hadn't. Sometimes, he would admit to the necessity for his medicine, but at other times, when he was feeling well and co-ordinated, he would angrily reject any idea that he needed treatment.

'You have to keep up with them, you know that.'

'And *you* know how I feel about pumping drugs into my body, I've told you often enough.' This was true, he wouldn't touch anything if he could help it, he was very puritanical in some ways, and he desperately needed to believe he could be well without constant medication. He stirred an amorphous pile of clothing on the floor with his foot and screwed his face up. 'I want to talk to Luce.'

'So do I. Morgan says she told him to get them out – Ginge and his woman – but I think it's just Morgan who wants it.'

'Oh, he does, does he?' Col scowled. 'Well, he won't get my co-operation. They're asking for trouble – Ginge, anyway, but that's up to him. I wouldn't want anything – well, nasty – to happen to anyone else. One thing leads to another, before you know where you are.'

He wandered to the window, opened it and leaned out, squinting along the mist-shrouded river's length. The smell of the river rushed in, cold and damp and heavy, with a hint of decay. Jem shivered exaggeratedly and slid down between the grimy blankets and stained pillows. Col pulled the casement closed.

'Water level's down,' he remarked. It had gone down in the

cellar, too, as Jem had found out on his inspection last night. 'We shan't be flooded.'

Jem's only reply was a grunt, and Col mooched around the room, hands in pockets, lifting things up and dropping them.

'Did Luce lend it you – my library book, I mean? I can't find it anywhere and I think it's overdue.'

'Ring her and ask her,' Jem said from under the bedclothes.

'We don't know her number.' He added doubtfully, 'I suppose I could try directory enquiries, but we don't know her mother's address, either.'

It would be simple enough for him to find out by asking Morgan, but he wouldn't, of course, he never spoke to Morgan if he could avoid it.

Jem gave up the attempt to get back to sleep and sat up. 'Forget it. It wouldn't be a good idea, the way her mother feels about us,' he warned. And Morgan wouldn't like anyone else trying to contact Luce, either. Especially Col. There was a lot of tension between those two. Mainly, thought Jem, with some perception, because Morgan knew that during his lucid times, Col could always win in an argument and had better ideas than he did about almost everything, and that the others listened to him. Morgan didn't like that. And when Morgan didn't like anything, he could act very, very weird. Jem often wondered if he wasn't madder than Col.

'*We* need her here, as well,' Col was muttering in his self-communing, introverted voice. 'It's too quiet without her.'

Luce was a great talker. She'd rattle away to anybody. Hind legs of donkeys flew around in all directions when she was about. Sometimes, you wanted to tell her to give her tongue a rest, but he knew what Col meant. He, too, missed the sound of her voice and the sight of her slim, quick figure and her cropped blonde head. 'You know Luce. Her mum gets on her nerves, but she wouldn't leave her in the lurch.'

She rebelled against society in general but, like Jem, she had this feeling of responsibility to people, even to the family she reputedly despised. Until the advent of Ginge and Sheena, the house had been clean, no drugs . . . apart from the odd spliff, but that didn't count. She even made Col, when he was in a condition to do so, go home once in a while to visit – though apart from

126

the bit of stuff he took his father, for medicinal reasons, to help his condition, that did neither of them much good.

Col's own condition was unpredictable, that was his problem. One day, happy and full of excited, intelligent ideas, the next in a black, faraway mood. When he was like this, he had a compulsion to go for long tramps, walking the streets or going further out into the country, sometimes coming back soaking wet, as he had the other afternoon. But Col never seemed to notice things like that. His dad, before his illness, had been a gamekeeper and he'd been brought up in the country. Col could have got them an occasional rabbit for the pot, he said, if they hadn't all decided to go vegetarian. At the thought of skinning a rabbit, Jem, the one who would have had to cook it, turned green.

The knife had been sent down to the lab, though what she was expecting it to reveal, if anything, Abigail wasn't sure. Meanwhile, she'd showed the newspaper clipping to Barry Scott, with instructions to obtain a copy, pronto. 'And the text that accompanied it, all the relevant data.'

'Right, ma'am,' said Scott, an idle so-and-so if his interest wasn't caught, but on the ball when it was. In this case it was, and very shortly he'd come up with a faxed copy of the newspaper report which had accompanied the photograph. This was an account of the last day of a trial at the Old Bailey, two years previously, when Mr Justice Orpington had sentenced a young man named Paul Matthews to seven years' imprisonment. Scott had also obtained the earlier reports, which traced the case back to its beginnings and led up to the sentencing.

Matthews had been a young City whizz kid, the financial brains of an investment company set up specifically to advise on pension schemes. Pensioners had fallen over themselves to invest their savings on the strength of wild promises. When the venture had crashed, Matthews had been the one to take the rap, while two of his fellow directors, also accused, namely Timothy Wishart and Anthony Pardoe, having engaged first-class lawyers to defend them, had been exonerated on a technicality, getting off with little more than a wigging and their futures and fortunes still intact.

There was a silence when Mayo had finished reading the last report, which told how Matthews, six months later, had hanged himself in prison. An open prison, this had been, since his was a white-collar crime and he hadn't been deemed a dangerous criminal. But he hadn't been able to take even that degree of incarceration, or perhaps it was the shame and disgrace that had got to him, and the fact that all the blame had been laid at his door.

'You're sure it's the same woman?' Mayo tapped the newspaper photo. 'This is the Barbie Nelson you know?'

'Couldn't mistake her. She's a bit slimmer in the photo, better dressed, and she must be wearing contact lenses, but it's her, I'd swear.'

He went to stand at the window, hands in pockets, a favourite position. He could see little besides the bulk of the Town Hall, but knew every inch of what lay beyond it, and most of the criminal activity that went on there. 'So what do you make of it?' he asked, over his shoulder.

Lowering skies were again the order of the day, and Abigail could see his desk-light reflected in the dark window. His office was one floor nearer to God than hers, but he had the same view of the same damned pigeons, a row of them now huddled together on the parapet. She thought about the wood pigeons cooing on the bare branches at Clacks Mill, and Wishart's body slumped on the bridge. 'If a man can use a shotgun, so can a woman.'

'Revenge? OK, but why Wishart? She might just as easily have picked on Pardoe.'

'Except that Pardoe's a different kettle of fish – but who knows? He might have been next on her list. I think Barbie Nelson took the job with Miller's Wife deliberately, with something of that idea in mind, not just by chance.'

The way he folded his arms across his chest and looked steadily at her showed he wasn't entirely convinced. Though he'd long since ceased to be surprised by the unlikely, incredible things people did all the time, solid facts were what he preferred to work with.

'Especially when put together with that letter in Wishart's desk,' Abigail said. 'If we take it seriously, it must constitute a prelude to some sort of blackmail, sooner or later.'

'There's nothing to support her having sent it.'

'The trial report alone shows pretty conclusively that she had a big grudge against Wishart, no better motive for finishing him off, in fact.' She hesitated, wondering if his mood was receptive enough to go further – but Mayo, give him his due, always listened. Even if he didn't always act upon what he heard.

'Go on.'

'Ellie Redvers says they were friendly – Barbie and Wishart, I mean. He was nothing if not susceptible and she was a very sexy lady, take my word for it. You mightn't have thought it at first sight, and this photo doesn't give much indication of it, but – '

'Oh, I don't know,' Mayo said with a grin. 'Big, buxom, beautiful.'

'Well, you see what I mean, then. The idea being to get friendly enough with him to be in a position where she could kill him.'

'And that's where the knife comes in? Mm.' Mayo pushed out his lips. *Another* weapon which could have killed Wishart, as well as the gun which had actually done so? The gun that hadn't yet turned up, though a ballistics report was on his desk saying that Wishart's own gun had definitely not been the one which killed him. Along with a frustratingly inconclusive SOCO report which revealed how little evidence had been turned up at the crime scene. Nothing more than some scuffed footprints under the trees near where the cartridge case had been found. 'So what made her change her mind, then?'

Abigail frowned, worried. 'It's a bit obvious, keeping a knife by the bedside if you intended to stab your lover with it – though I suppose your lover wouldn't think of it being meant for that!'

'One person can tell us. What are we doing about finding her?'

'Barbie gave a Nottingham address when she started at Miller's Wife. I'm sending Carmody and Platt up there tomorrow.'

She shut her notebook. Should she mention Spalding and the part she'd induced him to play? In the end, because of the involvement of Roz with Miller's Wife which had now arisen, she decided she'd better come clean.

'Spalding, eh?' he asked, after listening to what she had to say.

The non-committal answer didn't reveal whether Nick's return to Lavenstock was news to Mayo. It might have been deliberately kept from him, here at the station, it didn't always do to let it be known upstairs what was known lower down. But in a quiet way, there wasn't much he wasn't wise to, when it came to his own patch. Abigail had always wondered how much Mayo had known, or suspected, of her own affair with Nick. But if he had heard about Nick's return, he was keeping the knowledge to himself, which was also possible.

'Spalding's genuinely worried about his wife, and I'm beginning to think he might have cause. Two missing women, Roz and now Barbie, I don't like it.'

'Both apparently missing of their own accord,' he reminded her. 'As far as we know.'

'Yes.'

But there was a network surrounding the case, too many lives touching, spinning off one another, with Tim Wishart at the centre of the web. 'And all of them connected in some way with Miller's Wife,' she added. 'Or with Tim Wishart, which amounts to the same thing. According to Ellie, he was always in and out, it's that sort of place, free and easy . . . people casually dropping in.'

Coincidences happened. Barbie Nelson wouldn't be the first woman to have a secret life. 'Have they reopened for business yet?'

'Not yet. This affair has knocked them all for six.'

Still, it seemed to Abigail that Miller's Wife was more than just a means of livelihood to the women who worked there. It was a committed lifestyle, and one through which they received succour and support from each other. And even more than that . . .

'On second thoughts, it probably won't be long before they do open again.' She explained her reasons for thinking so. 'And whatever it is, there's something definitely needs watching down there.'

Abigail had been right to suspect that Mayo knew about ex-DC Nick Spalding's arrival back in Lavenstock. He'd first spotted him on one of his regular prowls around the town, a habit started when he was new to the area and needed to learn all he could about it, and to see it in all its moods. Continued because a town, like life, is always changing.

Spalding hadn't been aware that he'd been spotted entering a public house, or that, later, he was being studied from one of its quiet corners. If Mayo didn't choose to reveal himself when he was watching someone – especially someone like Nick Spalding, whom he'd always known to be devious, a man who played his own, not always above-board, games – then the one being watched never knew.

More quiet observance and unobtrusive detective work, second nature to him, had revealed to Mayo the source of his disquiet about the man, a worry that was too close to home to be comfortable.

It was almost back to normal, that night. Alex home, and Mayo cooking the supper, ineptly, falling over the cat and cursing the noisy parrot. 'Like a damn zoo in here,' he grumbled, trying to bring liver, bacon and onions, mashed potato and greens all to fruition at the same time. Perhaps he should teach himself to cook properly. All you had to do was follow a good recipe, if you could read you could cook. He'd just never bothered, having always been catered for by excellent women: his mother, his wife, and then his daughter, whose passion in life was cooking – who, in fact, had made it her career. Alex's meals were not up to their standards. Good, plain food, cooked well but without a trace of imagination, until it came to the pudding stage. She had a sweet tooth and her idea of a gourmet meal was cheesecake and coffee.

Moses, the old grey cat who'd heartlessly abandoned his true owner, Mayo's landlady, and had somehow taken up occasional residence here since Alex had moved in, smelled the liver and twined himself round his legs in an ecstasy of optimism. 'Move over, Mosh, can't you,' he said irritably, rescuing the bacon before it turned to leather.

Later, after they'd eaten, he threw himself into a chair, watching Alex sort through a portfolio of watercolours, more worn out by his labours in the kitchen than by a hard day's police work. As always, music played in the background. But it was Alex's choice, not his, tonight he was being accommodating and trying not to wince at Lloyd Webber. Music – though she was learning through association – wouldn't ever be important to her, not in the way it was to him. She still needed to sew, or knit, anything

131

to keep her awake during the more esoteric reaches of Britten or Wagner or Michael Tippett. She felt it wasn't polite to fall asleep. He had a new recording of *Orfeo* which he thought she would like, but the Monteverdi might have been too tender, too moving even for him that night.

She was holding up a small, intense watercolour in front of her, judgingly, squinting at it. 'What do you think?'

'It's great. Hockney, eat your heart out.'

'Thanks, but no need to overdo it!'

'I mean it, I like it.' Painting was something she'd taken up lately, and she had been astonished to find how well she could do it. Only last week she'd come in from her evening class, her face alight with achievement, having been praised for some work she'd done, confirmation that two other paintings which had recently graced the walls at Interiors and almost immediately been sold were not a fluke.

Mayo watched her going minutely through the folder, making one or two pencil notes. After a while, she closed it and sat fiddling with the pencil, staring into the gas flames. He wondered what she was thinking.

'How about some coffee?' he asked, levering himself up.

'Relax, I'll make it. It's time Bert went to bed, anyway.'

He forced himself to sit back. He was trying hard not to act over-protective, in a way that she might see as both patronizing and irritating.

She threw the cover over the parrot's cage as she went into the kitchen. Bert was invariably soothed by music almost as much as Mayo was. Apart from the odd squawk, he'd been quiet during the last hour, but now it had finished, he was starting the chuntering and muttering that was a prelude to making his presence really felt, herringboning his feet back and forth along his perch. Now, he fell abruptly silent. His age was uncertain. Julie, Mayo's daughter, when she'd departed for foreign shores and left him in her father's care, hadn't a clue how old he was: he might have been ten, or a hundred, for all either of them knew. But however long he'd lived, Bert had never learned to connect the sudden advent of night with his raucous outbursts.

When Alex came back and sat in her favourite position, curled on the hearthrug near his chair, Mayo told her about Spalding's return, and about his missing wife, cautiously, because Spalding

132

was a delicate subject. 'I met his wife once, briefly, in connection with the Flowerdew murder. Roz, wasn't it?'

'I've met her, too,' Alex said. 'She's bought things at Interiors, nice woman. I'm so sorry about the child.'

Briefly, he cursed himself. But it was she who'd mentioned the child, and they couldn't sidestep for ever, they'd agreed on that, talked it over lovingly and sensibly. He had to learn not to feel he was walking on eggshells all the time.

'Home so soon?' he had asked the ward sister.

'Good gracious, yes. We're not an invalid, are we?'

No, and we're not a bloody mental defective, either, he'd silently riposted at the time, not knowing that now he was casting the occasional concerned glance towards the top of Alex's head, until at last, with that amazing empathy she'd always shown, she looked up at him and said, 'Stop looking so worried, Gil. It happens all the time. Just one of those things.'

A phrase he hated, and a magnificent understatement, he knew. He reached out and touched her hair sadly. Being Alex, she would have to come to terms in her own way.

'It's only that I feel so damned incompetent,' she said, with a laugh that almost convinced him. 'Mortified. But I have the rest of my life to live. I'm going in to work tomorrow.'

Work, now, was it? The word was encouraging. Before, it had always been 'I shall be in the shop' or 'down at Interiors'. As if what she did at Interiors couldn't be important. Not classed as real work. She saw it as inherently frivolous and, being a basically serious-minded person, unlike her sister who held the controlling interest in the business, it worried her from time to time.

He knew better than to ask her if such an early return was wise, and merely commented, 'Don't overdo it. Sister said you had to be careful.'

'Sister can take a running jump,' said Alex forcefully, with the first real smile she'd shown for days.

'And Nick Spalding? You haven't changed your mind?'

'Him, too. But I told you that ages ago, didn't I?'

He'd accepted her decision easily at the time. Only too relieved that it was Spalding she'd been seeing when he had, basely, suspected the return into her life of the troublesome Liam, her ex-lover. It was only later that he began to have his doubts about whether she'd been absolutely certain of her decision, aware of the animation that lit her when he discussed his cases with her. Police work had once been her life, after all.

'I'm still of the same mind,' she said, 'I wouldn't be happy working with someone I couldn't...'

'Couldn't what?'

'Trust, I think I was going to say. What Abigail ever saw in him I don't know.'

'DI Moon isn't so enamoured of him now. She thinks there's some funny business going on.'

Alex said, ever so casually, 'Want me to have a word with him and see what I can find out?'

He was right. She'd by no means got police work out of her system. Would she ever? He was beginning to doubt it.

'Keep out of it,' he answered, more forcibly than he intended. 'If Spalding is mixed up in anything dodgy, I don't want you involved.'

'If that's what you want,' she said. 'Far be it from me.'

12

Captivity. Birds in cages, lions in zoos, hostages in cells.

Fleeting impressions, the only images that punctuated her seamless days, that floated in and out of her subconscious, whether she was asleep or awake, or in that trance-like state that was neither, since she had nothing else, no past, no sense of self with which to create pictures in her mind. She couldn't envisage the past because there wasn't one, only that terrifying blank.

Until the day she woke from a dream that wasn't filled with the disordered, elusive, nightmare images which usually woke her, sweating and panicky, but with laughter and happiness. It had been a lovely summer's day in the dream and she was a child again, roly-polying with her sister down a grassy slope to the picnic place. Her mother had spread a cloth in a field filled with buttercups and daisies, where they'd had tea. Hardboiled eggs and sardine sandwiches – and Coke to drink, which their mother didn't usually allow because she said it would rot their teeth.

The dream slid away and she fought against wakefulness, not able to bear the ending of happiness, but it was a useless struggle, and she opened her eyes to the same dank and dismal cell – but this time, the despair wasn't total. The dream hadn't slipped away entirely from her.

And something else had changed ... whatever it was, it had loosened the knot of fear and hopelessness. It took her a moment to realize that something real had stepped from out of her memory, at last. A mother, a sister. *Were* they real, or images sent to torment her, part of the continuing nightmare of being here?

Time wore on. And then, not with any sudden revelation but quite quietly, the clouds parted and she knew who she was. She tested it by saying the name out loud and it sounded true and familiar, and her heart leapt to her throat with hope.

Her joy was short-lived. Her own name, and her sister's, were there in the remnants of the dream, solid reassurance, but everything else remained tantalizingly on the edge of consciousness, slipping away when she tried to grasp it. Yet, as the time passed, awareness kept coming back to her in brief flashes, some of it not yet meaning anything to her. She felt frustrated and confused, as though she held all the separate pieces of a broken wireless set and didn't know how to begin putting them together.

Yet it was in one of those small epiphanies that it came to her who her captor was.

The shock was total. At first she thought that lack of food and light was making her hallucinate, that it was another of those terrible, inescapable nightmares. But it was the one solid fact, apart from her identity, that she knew was certain. The sense of betrayal made the fact of her imprisonment even more incredible.

He was sick, of course, he had to be, but that didn't explain why he was doing this to her. To teach you a lesson, he'd said. They were the last words she remembered hearing.

It had been a long, long time since she'd had food or water brought to her, but she didn't seem to be hungry any more, and the stomach cramps which had beset her had gone. There was still water left, since she'd instinctively been careful with it. She

135

tried to master her lethargy and plan what she would say and do when her captor next came.

If.

She found that she was able to let the horror of that 'if' wash over her: she'd become accustomed to fear and it no longer had the same power to terrorize. She simply thought that it would be the final irony, now that her memory had returned, if he never did come back.

It had been a long and exhausting day and Abigail dropped into bed like a log. She fell into a heavy sleep, punctuated by confused and vaguely frightening dreams, as soon as her head touched the pillow, and then woke suddenly and fearfully with her head ringing, or was it her head?

No, it was the telephone. She stretched her hand out for it, answering blearily. For a moment, what she was hearing didn't make sense, and then it did, horribly.

The desk sergeant gave her the details with a question in his voice that she answered with one of her own. 'Why me?'

'He mentioned your name.'

'All right, I'll be there. Quick as I can.'

It was two twenty-five by her bedside clock as she switched off the bedroom light.

His body was wired up to frightening-looking machines, tubes and plastic bags, blood plasma, a saline drip. Electronic bleeps sounded and an oscilloscope traced a jagged line on a monitor screen. His arms and shoulders were bare and his head was swathed in bandages that completely covered his hair and part of his jaw. He was unrecognizable as Nick, almost unrecognizable as a human being.

'You can sit there if you want,' offered a staff nurse called Storey, by the name badge on her chest, indicating a chair by the bed, 'but there's no point, really. He won't come round for ages yet.'

'He is going to come round?'

The dark-blue uniformed nurse gave her a guarded look.

'I'm the police,' Abigail said, bringing out her warrant card. 'Inspector Moon.'

'Oh.' She looked confused. 'He asked for Abigail, before he passed out, and they said – '

'I'm a friend as well. He used to be a policeman.'

The eyes assessed her professionally. 'I'm sorry. He's very ill. Ruptured spleen, kidneys badly damaged, his jaw and his skull fractured, plus several broken ribs, and knife wounds. The depressed fracture of the skull is the worst – '

'They really meant it, didn't they?' Abigail's mouth twisted.

'I'd say so.' A bleeper went in the nurse's pocket. 'Sorry, I have to go. There's one of your lot here already, gone to find some coffee I think, he'll be able to give you details when he gets back.'

She whisked out and Abigail followed her into the corridor and sat on one of the uncomfortable moulded plastic chairs to wait, cold to her core despite the overheated hospital temperature. It was a young uniformed constable named Spellman who arrived a few minutes later, armed with a plastic beaker of coffee and a cellophane-wrapped pack of sandwiches. His ears red, he put them down on the window sill. The DI! He'd be for it, leaving his post for nosh while on duty. He should've let one of the orderlies bring him something later, but he was young, perpetually hungry.

'Go ahead, don't let your drink get cold, eat your sandwiches.'

He looked relieved. 'Can I get you something, ma'am? There's only cheese and onion, though.'

'No thanks, not at the moment. Where did they find him, Andy?'

Gratified that she'd remembered his name, the young PC took a sip of coffee and began to tear at the cellophane while he told her that Nick had been picked up by the river. 'Outside one of these old warehouses, about midnight. A couple had been celebrating their anniversary at that new place, the Holly Tree. They were walking back to their car when they nearly fell over him. Lucky they did. Doctor says he'd have been a goner if it had been any later.'

His eyes were speculative as he gave her the information. He obviously knew that Nick had asked for her, and was wondering why, but he was a very new recruit and would know nothing of Nick having once worked at Milford Road, or of their affair. Few did. They'd been very discreet. Even so, someone there had known that she was the 'Abigail' Nick had asked for. It would soon be all around the station. She didn't enlighten Spellman.

'I'd like to be told immediately he comes round. It seems it's going to be some time yet, so I'm going back to the station. Get back to his bedside as soon as they'll let you.'

Cheese and onion fumes mingled with the antiseptic hospital smells and followed her as she walked down the corridor.

She drove straight back to the station and carried a drink from the dispenser in the CID room back to her office. She drank it piping hot and though she couldn't have told anyone whether it was tea, coffee, chocolate or hot water, she felt slightly warmer after it.

She thought about the disaster her decision to ask Nick for help had turned out to be. That her request was a direct cause of what had happened to him, she couldn't have much doubt. By asking around about Wishart's anonymous visitor, he'd put himself in the front line for a horrendous and vicious attack. No mere opportunist mugging, but done with deliberate intent, which lent even more weight to the theory that there were connections between Wishart's mystery visitor and his death. It was A1 priority to talk to Nick as soon as he was able. She would get someone more experienced than Spellman to sit by his bedside, ready for when he came round.

The grave face of Staff Nurse Storey flashed before her mind's eye, and her heart gave a nasty downward plunge. His attackers hadn't intended him coming out of this situation alive, and even though he had, it seemed doubtful if he'd stay alive much longer.

Mayo was told as soon as he arrived at the station. He asked her to come up to his office and then sat in silence for a while after he'd listened to what she had to tell him, thinking about it.

'I'm taking you off the case, Abigail.'

'No! You can't.'

His eyebrows shot up.

'I have to stay with it!'

'You know as well as I do that personal involvement is the last thing we want on any case, never mind one like this is turning out to be.'

'I'm not personally involved, not in the way you mean. But it *was* my fault that Nick was roped in and I want to see it through. No,' she said levelly, pre-empting any attempt to interrupt, determined not to weaken her case by showing emotion, 'I knew what I asked him to do might be risky, but I'm not breast-beating. He's had enough experience to know what's what. After all, he could have said no.'

His expression stayed impassive and the necessity to try and make him see got the better of caution. She spoke heatedly. 'But I'd be lying if I said I didn't feel responsible – I am, and it's damn stupid for me not to follow it through – you absolutely *must* let me stay with it!'

'Abigail, don't shout at me.'

She bit her lips when she saw the warning flash in his eyes. 'I'm sorry, I shouldn't have said that.' He wasn't one to insist on protocol but he wouldn't stand for anyone stepping over the mark, whoever they were. She was way out of line with this, and his frosty silence told her so, but at least he hadn't called her 'Inspector'.

She sat contemplating the carpet. The lights were on in his office. Curtains of fine rain swept across the windows. A patrol car with its siren going left the car-park outside. At last Mayo spoke.

'I'm not at all sure that I'm doing the right thing, but all right, you can stay on the case. On one proviso – that you go home and get yourself a couple of hours' sleep before you do anything else. You look done in. No, no argument, it's not an option, it's a bloody order! And think yourself lucky I'm such a soft touch.'

By nine thirty Carmody and Jenny Platt were half-way to Nottingham. It was three hours since Carmody's breakfast, and his stomach was growling. 'Want a coffee?' he asked Jenny.

'I wouldn't say no.'

He peeled off down the slip road at the next services. They took their drinks to a seat by the window and watched the three lanes of traffic shooting past without pause, like a shoal of rainbow fish.

News of the attack on Nick Spalding had run through the station like a hot knife through butter, and the fact that Abigail had been to his bedside had raised more than a few eyebrows.

'He was before my time,' Carmody said. 'Before I was transferred here, but you'd remember him, wouldn't you, Jen?'

'Mm. I'd just made CID. But he left soon after.' She drank some of her coffee. 'Wouldn't say I knew him, though. I don't think anybody did, really.' She looked as though she wanted to say something else, but evidently thought better of it.

Nobody except DI Moon, thought Carmody, supplying to himself what Jenny hadn't said, knowing why she hadn't. Solidarity, that was it. Abigail was the only other woman in CID. Besides, she was their boss. Carmody knew all this well enough and, since he'd been teamed up with Abigail long enough to have his own loyalties, he didn't press the point. 'His condition sounds serious, from what I've heard,' he said.

'Yeah. And the funny thing is, his wife's disappeared.'

'Whose wife?'

'Spalding's, of course.'

'Buggered off, you mean?'

'The DI didn't seem to think so, but she sent me to do a bit of poking around. No joy, though.'

Was there reason, Jenny wondered, to believe all this was the cause of Abigail's present mood? She wasn't normally a moody person – what you saw, with Abigail, was what you got, and that was a good-humoured, friendly relationship with those working with her, though anyone who dubbed her as a pushover would be seriously underestimating her, to say the least. Jenny, for one, certainly wouldn't. She'd be hard put to it to say just what was wrong with Abigail these last few days, but she certainly wasn't herself. The way she'd snubbed Farrar, for instance, the other morning at Clacks Mill when for once he hadn't really deserved it, and she'd been pretty sharp with Jenny herself once or twice. Jenny shrugged off the feeling of something out of synch. Put it down to PMT she wouldn't. That was the usual male assumption, an attitude she despised.

'When you say funny,' Carmody was saying, 'you mean you think this mugging had something to do with his wife disappearing?'

'I didn't say that. More likely Nick poking his nose in where it wasn't appreciated. You know he's going to set up a PI business in Hurstfield?'

'Not for some time, he isn't. If at all now, poor sod. Finished? Come on then, on our way. I feel better after that,' Carmody said, having despatched the couple of large sticky buns that had accompanied his coffee, and wondering what Jenny knew that she was keeping to herself.

An order, Abigail repeated, as she closed her front door behind her. One you didn't disobey if you valued your job. But reluctant as she was to admit it, the way she felt, Mayo could be right, and maybe she *would* feel better if she went to bed and made up on the sleep shortfall. You could learn to do without sleep but it was tough, if you were the sort who needed your eight hours to function properly. And even before last night, when she'd caught three hours' sleep at most, she'd been losing out, and was beginning to wonder if it was Sunday, Monday or Christmas Day when her alarm woke her. But she didn't give much for her chances of sleeping now, with her brain leaping around like a salmon caught on the line.

She did an unprecedented thing in the middle of the day, and poured herself a slug of whisky, albeit a cautious one. Might just help her to relax, but there was no point in overdoing it.

She slumped into a chair and tried to think sleep, but that was easier said than done. The picture of Nick plugged into the life-support machine wouldn't leave her mind. She'd listened to the local radio on the way home and heard a news flash to the effect that a man, identified as ex-Detective Constable Nicholas Spalding, had been discovered late last night near Cat Lane, having been viciously attacked, almost certainly by more than one person. The police were appealing to anyone who might have witnessed the attack, or seen anything suspicious, to come forward. It was routine procedure, just going through the motions. The only witnesses who were going to come forward had already done so – the couple who'd found him – at Abigail's guess, only minutes before he would have ended up in the river.

The whisky had been a rotten idea. Rather than being anaesthetized, she felt more alert than ever. Maybe if she lay down properly, it would work and she'd zonk out for a few hours. She had her foot on the bottom stair when there was a knock on the door. What now? Hardly anyone came out here to the cottage. She dithered for a moment, then gave in and opened it. Two females, one very tall, one short and round. Jehovah's Witnesses, anxious to share their knowledge of the Bible with her.

'Sorry, but you'll have to go and share it with someone else,' she snapped, and shut the door firmly on their determined, smiling faces.

She felt immediately better for it, then ashamed. She was tempted to call them back and offer them explanations, plus tea and a slice of her mother's date, cinnamon and walnut cake that she'd been heroically saving for Ben, who wouldn't be needing it now. But common sense reasserted itself when they turned back to smile and wave at her from the gate, *knowing* she'd be watching them, chirpy as crickets, forgiving, smug, self-righteous. They'd probably smelt the whisky on her breath.

Which had had the very opposite effect of what she'd intended. Sleep? Forget it.

With a sigh, she tipped what was left of the scotch down the sink, made herself a triple-strength coffee, threw her coat on again, and drove back to the hospital. This could be counted as personal, not professional, involvement.

Nick hadn't yet come round, Andy Spellman told her. The PC was sitting in the corridor, reading a paperback western. 'They've shunted me out here,' he said, breathing onion fumes over her as he added, 'there's someone else in with him, now.'

'Doctors?'

'No, ma'am, I think it's his wife.'

The address they were looking for was the one Barbie had given when applying for the job.

They reached Nottingham and drove through some fairly solidly affluent suburbs until they came to a maze of small streets. The house they wanted was in a small brick-built terrace called Florence Street. The next was Edith, and the one next to that Violet, no doubt a tribute from the Edwardian builder to his female relations.

'How much d'you bet we don't find her here?' Carmody asked as he banged on the door.

'No takers.'

If Barbie Nelson had indeed been the one to shoot Wishart, the chances of finding her at the one address they had for her were not high. It was a starting point, that was all.

The woman who opened the door was a solid, heavily made-up lady who wore highly coloured clothes and the sort of swept-down spectacles which looked as though they had been put on upside down, by mistake. She received their introduction with some hostility, annoyed at having been interrupted in her intention to go out shopping for groceries. 'We're right out of everything,' she complained in a gravelly, gin-and-cigarettes voice. 'Had flu, like everyone else, and I'm due back at work tomorrow.' But when they told her that their business concerned Barbie Nelson, the hostility subsided somewhat and she stood back to let them in.

'Phyllis, somebody at the door!' called a querulous voice from the back regions of the house, as they stepped over the threshold.

'It's all right, Mother, I'm seeing to it!'

The shout echoed down the hall and then, lowering her voice and timing the start of their visit by a glance at her wrist-watch, she announced, 'I can give you ten minutes. I really have to go out and I can't leave my mother for long.'

Her name was Phyllis Whitelaw and she worked in the local job centre. She had a strong face, pepper and salt hair which she wore tightly permed.

The sitting-room was cold, stuffy and furnished in the same spirit as she had dressed herself: with no inherent sense of style, she'd tried to find it in strong and not always complementary patterns and colours, in a patently unsuccessful attempt to update the old-fashioned furnishings. It was a room evidently not often used. It smelled of stale tobacco and mothballs.

'Looking for Barbie, you say? Sorry, but she's not here,' she told them, lighting a cigarette.

It seemed that Barbie, who had worked with her at the job centre, had lodged with her for about a year before leaving to take the job at Miller's Wife. 'She left her flat in Birmingham and came here after that terrible business about Paul, told me she was trying to get over it in a new place. I did hope it might have become permanent, staying here with us, she was good company.' The woman's red-lipsticked mouth drooped at the corners, her heavily pencilled eyebrows followed the line of her spectacles so that her whole expression was very nearly as mournful as Carmody's. She was single and obviously on the verge of retirement, and her disappointed tone suggested a loneliness she probably wouldn't have admitted to.

'Phyllis! You get them Jaffa Cakes?' screeched the old voice again.

The daughter rolled up her eyes. 'Haven't gone yet, Mother! I won't go without letting you know.' She looked at her watch again, squinting through a plume of smoke. 'I was sorry when Barbie went, but she was wasting her talents working at the job centre. I missed her though, she used to make me laugh.'

Jenny felt sympathy for her. She'd have put money on it there weren't many laughs now in Phyllis Whitelaw's life.

'What do you mean, wasting her talents?'

'Well, she was a qualified accountant, wasn't she? She only took the job with us until she could find something better. A pity her new job was so far away, but she wrote and said how happy she was there, how pleased they were with her running their finances. They're going to miss her if she *has* left.' She squashed out the cigarette, while Carmody and Jenny exchanged looks at what was news to them regarding Barbie's position at Miller's Wife. 'But that's not like her, you know. She wouldn't just go and leave them in the lurch.'

The sound of pots and pans being banged about in the kitchen made her look apprehensively at her watch again. Jenny glanced at Carmody and they stood up.

'Thank you for your help, Miss Whitelaw.'

'She's not in any trouble, is she? Sorry, silly question, you wouldn't be here if she wasn't. But I hope it's not serious?'

'I hope not, too.'

When they had asked her at first if she knew where Barbie was, she'd said she couldn't help them, but as she opened the front door for them, she suddenly changed her mind. 'I can give you her father's address. She might just have gone there.'

It was in Herefordshire, which meant that they weren't going to get there that day. They thanked Miss Whitelaw once more for her help. They'd barely reached the end of the street before they saw her emerge from the house with a shopping bag on a trolley.

Abigail stood in the doorway of the small ward and looked towards the woman seated by Nick's bedside. It was Roz, all right.

They had only ever met once before, and that briefly, but Abigail was unlikely to have forgotten her. It had been during a case in which her sister, Sophie, had been largely involved, when Abigail had been a mere sergeant, and their meeting had been one of the reasons why Abigail had finally decided her dwindling affair with Nick must cease.

It had all been more complicated than that, of course, affairs usually were, and more difficult to end than it seemed in retrospect, and it had uncovered a ruthlessness in herself she hadn't liked to admit to; but there had never been any doubts that she'd done the right thing, as far as both her career and her personal life went.

As for Nick, and Roz, and the child who'd since died – well, it had been all set to work out for them, and might have done, who could tell? She'd done what she could. Though a marriage which had never been very stable from the start hadn't really stood much chance, she had to admit.

Roz, the cool, very together lady that Abigail remembered, was looking distraught. She couldn't touch Nick but her hand was laid on the coverlet, her face ravaged as she gazed at him. She looked at Abigail without recognition.

'DI Moon,' Abigail said, automatically producing her warrant card.

For an instant, the tiny room held a boding stillness like the eye of a storm, and then Roz rearranged her face and said coldly, 'Is this a personal visit, or are you here in an official capacity?' She wasn't going to make it easy for Abigail.

Abigail was saved by footsteps outside, and voices, and then two doctors came in, followed by a young woman in a white coat wheeling an instrument trolley, with Staff Nurse Storey bringing up the rear. One of the doctors went to the bedside and looked down gravely at the patient without saying anything.

'I'm afraid we shall have to ask you both to leave for a while,' the nurse told them. 'We're going to do a few tests. Why not go and get yourselves some lunch? We shall be some time here.'

Out in the corridor, Abigail said, 'Maybe we should do as she suggests? I'd like to talk to you, if you're willing. PC Spellman can fetch you if necessary.'

Spellman said, 'Sure,' and after a moment, Roz nodded and they moved off together.

Roz toyed with a salad as she said, 'All right, you don't have to try and convince me. I know it was all over between you, long since, and I know you were the one to finish it. I've nothing against you now, not really. For Michael's sake I was grateful to you for what you did, but getting back together with Nick was never a permanent solution. We're a no go area, the two of us.'

'Was that why you decided to go away?' Against all expectations, Abigail was finding herself liking this woman who'd been little more than a name, a presence, a source of guilt, to her for so long.

'Partly. It was just that I suddenly had to get away from everybody and everything, get my head straight as they say. I told Nick I was going to Tuscany, it was the first place I thought of, anywhere to stop him coming after me. But then I realized there was no need to go far, I remembered my sister was in Egypt, her house was empty, so I went to stay there, didn't answer the phone or the door. I had plenty of books and the TV and radio for company, and Sophie keeps enough food in the freezers for a siege. When I heard the news about Nick, on the radio, I came over straight away.'

'He was very worried about you – genuinely. You left your own fridge full of food, for one thing – '

'I know, I remembered later. Nothing I could do, then.'

'And one shoe by the door.'

'*A shoe?*

'Black suede, strappy.'

'Oh, that! A buckle came off one. I picked the pair up to have it mended, then saw it was daft to take both, so I left the other in the hall. I'd forgotten all about it. You don't mean he thought . . .'

Her glance fell to her plate. She appeared to be struggling against tears.

'He thought all sorts of things. He asked me to help find you.'

Abigail explained, as briefly as she could, what had passed between her and Nick. 'What's puzzled me is why he was so reluctant to try and find you himself.'

Roz speared a piece of tomato, stared at it, then laid down her fork. 'It might have been because of Miller's Wife – at least because of Tim Wishart.'

Abigail stared at her. Was Roz going to say that she and Wishart had had something going? That Nick had been jealous?

'Could you tell me about it?'

It was some time before Roz was able to find the words. 'It's difficult for me to say this, but . . . Have you any idea why Nick left the police?'

'Not really. Except that I wasn't surprised. He never really fitted in, you know.'

'It wasn't that. He'd started gambling, heavily, and he was deeply in debt. He'd been taking money from Wishart to pay off what he owed, and he was afraid it would all come out.'

'*What*? Tim Wishart lent Nick money?'

'I don't think it was meant to be repaid.'

Abigail was stunned on both counts. Nick had never, to her certain knowledge, been either a gambler, or a grafter. But he *had* needed capital to start up as a private eye. So, rather than take money from Roz, especially in the state their marriage was in at the time, he'd taken it from Wishart. It made sense, in a cockeyed sort of way, if you knew Nick, and his stubborn, macho pride. But –

'What had Wishart to hide?' she asked sharply.

'I don't know. I didn't know what had been going on until after Nick had left the police, I swear, not until I went to work at Miller's Wife, in fact. Working there was only something to fill the time for me, I didn't want to commit myself to anything seriously, but Nick went spare when he heard, practically ordered me to leave. Naturally, I refused, why shouldn't I work there? In the end, it all came out, and he warned me that it was dangerous for me to stay there. Wishart was always around Miller's Wife, and he associated with some nasty types. There could be trouble for both of us if he found out who I was, that I was Nick's wife, he'd think I'd been sent to – well, spy on him, I suppose.'

'*Spy* on him? What was he up to, then?'

'I honestly have no idea.'

Abigail was beginning to understand Nick's worries when Roz disappeared, his reluctance to start asking his own questions about her anywhere around Wishart. But he *had* asked questions – after Wishart had been removed from the scene. When there'd been no more danger to himself. She didn't say this, because the follow-up was that Nick himself had had a very strong motive for Wishart's removal.

13

When Abigail rang the hospital the next morning the news was the same as it had been the night before – no change.

'Does that mean he's come round from the anaesthetic or not?'

'Are you a relative?'

'Inspector Moon, Lavenstock CID.'

'He's not conscious, but your man is still here at his bedside.'

When did being unconscious turn into being in a coma?

This time Jenny drove, while Carmody held the map on his knees.

An hour out of Lavenstock and they were off the motorway, into the rich, red Herefordshire countryside, lush in summer, attractive even on a dull, cold, heavy February day. They might have been in another country. That's what it felt like, foreign country, with the wild Welsh on the other side of the blue mountains. There'd been hoary old jokes about passports before they left the station.

Jenny was full of memories of when she used to come here for holidays with her family, better in retrospect than they'd been in reality. 'Can't think why I haven't been back to this neck of the woods for so long. All that history! They used to make raids on this part of the country from Wales. Offa's Dyke, Owen Glendower.'

The twisting roads of the border marches were quiet enough today, a wonder after the densely trafficked conurbation left behind. Carmody settled comfortably into his seat as she competently negotiated a sharp bend. 'You should've been a teacher, Jen.'

Jenny flushed. 'I nearly was, once.'

'What happened?'

'Didn't have the brains for it, for all those A levels.'

'From what I've seen of my kids' teachers, brains aren't mandatory.'

Jenny grinned. 'Well, maybe it was the patience I didn't have. Anyway, once the idea of the police grabbed me, that was it.'

'Big deal.'

'Come on, I don't believe you think it's so bad, either.'

'Yeah, well, I lost my starry-eyed look a long time since – and I do believe we're nearly there,' Carmody said, as they approached a quiet town with a profusion of black and white timbered houses along the main road.

The address which Phyllis Whitelaw had scribbled down for them turned out to be set back from the main thoroughfare, a very far cry from the one she herself lived in. It was a tall, brick-built house in a Queen Anne terrace, with gleaming windows, a handsome, glossy black door and shiny brass door furniture. A sizeable property, it was now divided into two flats.

Their visit was unheralded, but they were counting on the effectiveness of surprise tactics to offset any possible waste of time. Luck was with them. When Carmody pressed the bell for Commander H.R.J.Nelson, in the ground-floor flat, it was answered by a middle-aged woman with a flowered, wrap-around pinny and a voluble Welsh accent.

'Barbie? Afraid she's gone in to Kington to do some shopping. Be back in time to get her father's lunch, though. Least, I hope so, I've to get home and see to my old man's food. He'd starve rather than get it himself,' she added with a chuckle. 'Would you like to see her father? He's up today, in the conservatory, feeling much better, he is.'

She took them through the house and into a built-on, heated conservatory overlooking a walled garden, where an old man was dozing over the *Telegraph* in an upright padded cane chair. His eyes flew open as they came in, a tall, distinguished-looking man, wearing a yellow sweater over a checked shirt, twill trousers and highly polished leather slippers.

The woman announced, 'Some people here to see you, Commander.'

He put the paper aside before attempting to rise stiffly.

'Please don't get up,' Jenny said, and Carmody explained who they were, and that it was his daughter they'd come to see.

The old man sat up straighter, looked from one to the other, sizing them up. 'Better wait for her, then. Shouldn't be long. If you've come all this way, you'd like some refreshment. You can oblige, Mrs Sanderson?' he asked of the woman who had lingered in the background, clearly having anticipated the request.

'That I can. Coffee or tea?'

'Tea! Good God, they want something stronger than tea!'

'I don't suppose they do, and neither do you, if you're going to take any notice of the doctor.' Her smile made rosy apples of her cheeks, but her eyes were unrelenting.

'Chance'd be a fine thing,' he muttered, casting a longing look at the bottles ranged on a side table. When Jenny said coffee would be lovely, he cast his eyes to heaven. Mrs Sanderson beamed and bustled off, and when they were settled in chairs opposite the old man, he said, 'Know it's Barbara you've come to see, but can I be of any help?'

Jenny exchanged a swift glance with Carmody. The commander had high spots of colour on both cheekbones, his eyes were bright, and he had the drawn look of someone recently ill. He smiled, noting the hesitation. It was quite something, that smile, she thought he must have been a knockout in his younger days, in his naval uniform.

'I'm not an invalid, y'know, never mind all this claptrap.' His gesture took in the bottles of pills by his chair. 'Damn nuisance, that's all – though I thought I was about to cash in my chips, I can tell you, when they carted me off. Needn't have bothered, of course, fuss about nothing, right as rain in an hour or two. They're going to give me a decoke, blow through m'tubes. Something called an angioplasty.'

'When did it happen?' Jenny asked sympathetically.

'Last Saturday lunch time. Just doing the crossword and keeled over like a bloody pack of cards – if you'll excuse me, miss.'

Mrs Sanderson came back with a laden tray; her idea of refreshments was anyone else's idea of a substantial lunch. There were hot sausage rolls and sandwiches besides coffee and chocolate biscuits, and not until she had seen the visitors supplied to her satisfaction did she leave them again, informing her employer that it was time she was on her way, she'd prepared the veg for lunch. 'See you Monday, then.'

The commander left the subject of Barbie in abeyance while they ate – the sausage rolls were home-made, with country butcher's sausagemeat, Jenny decided appreciatively – and returned to the preoccupation of his own collapse which, despite his pooh-poohing, had evidently shaken him a lot. 'At least it brought Barbara home, it's a lonely life for me since her mother died. Nothing to do but write my damned memoirs. Well, I suppose it passes the time.' He waved to a table in one corner of the conservatory, neatly stacked with papers and a portable typewriter. 'Had an interesting life in the navy, never made admiral though, despite the name.' He paused to let them see the joke, but didn't wait for a laugh; the humour of it had evidently worn thin with familiarity, even for himself. Jenny smiled, all the same. 'Been all over the world,' he went on. 'Barbara thought the book a good idea.' The commander himself sounded depressed at the notion, and the papers didn't appear to have been disturbed that morning, at least. One more ex-service memoir would hardly set the publishing world on fire with enthusiasm, but Jenny could see that wasn't the point. As long as it kept a lonely old man occupied.

He said suddenly, 'The police are no strangers to this house-hold, y'know. And m'daughter and I don't have any secrets from each other. No need to take my word, of course, and if you want to wait until she gets here, I've no objections. But I might be able to help.'

His bluff manner didn't deceive. He had a shrewd assessment of what was to come, Carmody thought. He wiped the flakes of pastry from his fingers and reached into his inside pocket for the photocopy of the newspaper article and the picture of Barbie, which he handed to Nelson. 'What can you tell us about that case?'

The paper was steady in the old man's hand. He gave it a cursory glance – it was evidently not new to him – then passed it back. 'Thought that's what you must be here for. Well, the details of the story were common knowledge. It was in all the papers, *ad nauseam*. I assume that's not what you want to know.'

'You know that Tim Wishart is dead?'

An unreadable expression crossed the old man's face. 'Paul Matthews is dead, too.'

'You say you and your daughter have no secrets from each other. So presumably you know that the firm she went to work for in Lavenstock is owned by Wishart's wife?'

'Wishart's wife?'

He hadn't known that, at any rate. It had caught him off balance, but he quickly recovered and added gamely, 'That's a coincidence. Barbara and Wishart never met, you know, during the case.' He stared out of the window, where bluetits were trapezing to and fro, pecking on an almost empty wire mesh container. 'Bird-feeder needs filling again – damn squirrels,' he said. 'Come and pinch the nuts, bite through the mesh, greedy little buggers.' He turned away. 'She went through a rotten time after Paul was sentenced, y'know. Due to be married within a month of that, all the plans made. And then, when he took his own life in prison . . . my poor girl . . . she went to pieces. Never be any justice until people realize it's the victims who pay the penalty . . . there were times, I tell you, when I hated those two men, Wishart and Pardoe. No excuses for Paul, what he did was wrong, but they were no less guilty, and he was left to take the punishment. I can't be sorry one of them, at least, is dead. She went through a long depression, and lost her job. Since then – '

A kitchen pinger on the table beside him startled them all with a shrill noise. 'Blasted pills,' he muttered, 'wouldn't remember to take them, otherwise.' He took two with a glass of water, making a performance of it, grumbling about the necessity. 'Still,' he said, putting the glass back on the table with very careful precision, 'one thing this little how-d'ye-do of mine's done, it's brought m'daughter back home, as I say.'

As if she'd been waiting in the wings for the right moment to enter, Barbie Nelson herself at that moment came into the room.

To Jenny, who'd never met her before, she came as something

of a surprise. This wasn't the carefree girl pictured in the newspaper photograph, nor the one she'd imagined from the DI's description; she'd expected a quite different personality from the tall, rather severe-looking young woman who now entered, dressed in a well-cut skirt and heavy silk shirt. Expensive clothes, cleverly designed especially with big women in mind. She'd abandoned the heavy spectacles, revealing rather lovely, lustrous dark eyes, and the way she was now wearing her smoothly brushed dark brown hair, swept back from her forehead, showed off her creamy skin. Jenny, whose short, curly hair and pretty, round, pink-cheeked face forever denied her the elegance she longed for, looked down at her neat jacket and pleated skirt and sighed in despair.

If she was surprised to see the visitors, Barbie didn't show it. She said hello and then walked over to her father and kissed him before turning inquiringly to the others, a smile still on her face. The smile did a lot to change Jenny's initial impression of her severity. Could this be the sort of woman who'd deliberately shot a man in the face at close range? She did, in fact, look rather jolly. But appearances counted for nothing, as her next words showed.

'So, he's copped it at last, has he?'

'If you're talking about Tim Wishart, yes.'

'Somebody's shown some sense then. Given the bastard what he deserves.'

Not all women had been suckers for Wishart's charm, Carmody thought. This was the second who'd thought him a bastard. The commander made a small sound. He looked suddenly very tired.

'Sorry, Dad.' Barbie reached a hand out to his. 'You don't want to hear this.' To the others she said, 'Come into the kitchen while I get the lunch going.'

'Barbara – '

'It's better,' she said gently. 'I'll tell you everything later, I promise, but I'd rather you didn't hear this way.'

Her quiet, reasonable tone had its effect. 'Well, if you must. Don't think I'm really up to any more at the moment, if the truth be told.'

*

'He's right,' she said, when they were in the neat, well-appointed kitchen, where she made no attempt to start on the lunch, but sat with them at the table. 'My father's right. I wouldn't have come home if he hadn't collapsed on Saturday. Not permanently. I can't be glad for him that he did have that attack, but you don't always see things straight until you're shocked into it. When I got that telephone call, I suddenly saw myself through his eyes, and I thought, what am I messing about at? What am I doing here? So . . .' She shrugged and spread her hands. 'I came home.'

'And what *had* you been doing there, Miss Nelson?' Carmody asked. 'Apart from writing anonymous letters?'

A tide of colour swept across her face and neck. 'Oh God, he didn't throw them away, then! That was stupid, infantile. I only sent a couple, don't know why I sent any . . . except that it seemed to get rid of some of my frustration. I wanted to make him see, to prick his conscience. That's a laugh! He wouldn't have recognized his conscience if it had jumped up and bitten him. But I couldn't accept that he could just get away, scot free, while Paul was – dead. It was a case of lashing out, I was just so *angry* . . . I don't suppose you can understand that, people like you.'

'Like us?'

'Oh, you know, always so – together. You never see or hear of a policeman, or woman, freaked out.'

Jenny thought of PC Willens, an officer she'd once seen go berserk over a driver half asleep at the traffic lights – road rage, they were now calling it – but kept silent. Carmody, who'd seen more than that in his time, the force having its share of neurotics, just as anywhere else, with enough pressure to make the most stable personality lose both their balance and their sense of perspective, not to mention their temper, said nothing either. 'How come you were able to get a job with Miller's Wife?' he asked instead.

'I took the *Advertiser*, the local paper, for months. Just to keep tabs on him. When I saw the advert for someone to work there I grabbed it, it was the nearest I could get to him – and it turned out to be a good move, he was always around the place, one way or another.'

'Did you intend to kill him, Miss Nelson?'

She didn't answer immediately, tracing the grain of the woodwork on the table with her fingernail. After a moment, she looked up. 'I don't know what I intended. I felt as though I *could* have killed him, when Paul died. Perhaps I did mean it, I think I was a little bit out of my mind, you know? There was the idea of revenge, yes, but in a half-baked way – those silly notes ... Then, when I met him, and saw how susceptible he was to women – I thought, this is it. If I could get close enough, I thought, I could hurt him, the way he'd hurt me ...'

'Was that why you kept the knife by your bed?'

There was a slight pause. 'Didn't I put it back? I must have forgotten. I used to take it upstairs with me at first because – it was a bit eerie being on those premises alone at night, until you got used to it.'

'At first? You took it up later, intending to kill Tim Wishart with it?'

'I didn't have to, did I? Somebody else did it for me.'

Jenny looked at her and suddenly thought: she'll need watching, this one. For all her apparent frankness, there was something secretive about her, something unstable that would always surface. No one who wasn't slightly mad could have contemplated such actions. Jenny found no difficulty in accepting Barbie's story and could quite easily imagine it played out to its first intended conclusion, had it not been for her father's collapse. There was genuine love and concern there, she thought, and it might have been what had saved her.

Carmody was asking, 'What time did you leave Lavenstock on Saturday afternoon?'

'I didn't notice the time. I had the telephone call from Mrs Sanderson to tell me about my father and I just rushed off. About two o'clock, it must have been.'

'Mrs Redvers has told us that her answering machine recorded a message from you at two forty.'

'Then it must have been later than I thought, mustn't it? I was very upset and confused. I wasn't really thinking straight. I went straight to the hospital. They'll tell you what time I got there.'

'Why didn't you tell her the truth about why you'd so suddenly decided to leave? Or leave an address?'

Barbie watched Jenny taking it all down in her notebook, in her careful, schoolgirlish hand.

'I didn't – I *don't* – want to have anything more to do with any of them. I'm not proud of what happened, but it's over and done with. I just want to be left alone to live my life and forget it.'

'It's not as simple as that, Miss Nelson,' Jenny said, looking up.

There was another silence.

Carmody said, 'I noticed a shotgun propped up in the conservatory.'

'It's my father's, he takes pots at the squirrels and the magpies that pinch food from his bird-feeder. He never hits anything, just scares them off.'

'What about you, Miss Nelson? Do you shoot?'

'No, Sergeant, I don't. Not birds, or vermin. Not even Timothy Wishart.'

14

The investigation appeared to have reached a temporary impasse; Mayo felt the team deserved a break, and overtime figures being what they were, only the necessary few were kept working over the weekend.

Abigail contemplated the logjam of papers that confronted her when she opened her office door on Monday morning, pointing at her like some accusing finger of fate. A thing the general public didn't appreciate when they complained of lack of progress in a murder inquiry was that other criminals didn't take a holiday, out of respect; their activities still went on, all demanding that some time, at least, be allotted to them. She'd become adept at sorting the wheat from the chaff, those which clamoured for immediate attention from those which could sit in the in-tray. She was feeling mopey and sad about her own personal circumstances, missing Ben like hell and angry with herself for allowing it, and the only antidote she knew was work, even when she didn't feel like it. Work left no time for introspection, and it didn't now.

She was soon deeply immersed in the details of a fire-raiser who had apparently had a grudge against comprehensive schools, then with an inquiry over a house very nearly demolished by a gas explosion, whose owners were claiming that thieves had looted what was left of their possessions. How low could you get, they were asking? The one she picked up next made that look like one for the birds: a child, a boy of eleven, had just died from solvent abuse. A first timer, he'd over-used an aerosol can which had literally frozen his throat muscles.

This was a bloody awful job, sometimes.

It was while she was telling herself that railing at it got you nowhere that the call from the hospital came. Nick had died without regaining consciouness.

All impetus drained from her. She sat at her desk with her head in her hands, numb with shock and sorrow, unprepared, though she'd been expecting it. She wished she could cry, but the tears formed into a hard knot in her throat as images of the first weeks of their love affair, before it had all gone sour, of the gradually increasing guilt, the feelings of grubbiness that had overtaken her and in the end forced her to cut loose, swam through her mind. Images of Roz, doubly bereaved, followed, and wouldn't be dismissed.

After a while the telephone roused her. She took a big swallow from the coffee that had grown cold on her desk, then dealt with the call, which necessitated several follow-ons. Fifteen minutes later, when she put the phone down, she was calm. She sat thinking for a moment, looking at the subconscious doodles she'd made while telephoning. A previously blank page had got itself covered with jotted names, facts, queries, all of them factors in the Wishart case. She stared at the random scribblings, seeking connections, drawing lines between them until she had a spider-gram of balloons and boxes with arrows and loops leading from one to the other. Somehow, if she fiddled with it long enough, the names and facts should shuffle themselves around until a coherent pattern emerged. That was the theory, anyway.

She put her pencil down, linked her hands behind her head, watched the pigeons and thought about Marianne Pardoe, the only one who didn't seem to fit in anywhere, unable to forget the tears coursing down the leathery cheeks. She looked again at her scribblings.

At the moment, what she had was Tim Wishart, at the centre of the web – who, according to Roz, had been involved in some shady business, about which he'd paid Nick to keep his mouth shut. A nice little fiddle that was turning out to be, though still being investigated: Wishart funnelling suspect monies into the system via Pardoe, buying imaginary shares in Neptune Holdings, borrowing it back at a laughable rate to pay off his debts.

She could understand now Nick's reluctance to make his own inquiries about Roz's disappearance. The backhanders from Wishart had stopped when he'd left the force, if not before, or so he'd told Roz, but what he knew must always have presented a threat to Wishart.

If Roz had never gone to work for Miller's Wife, there might have been a different story to tell, but she had, and for her own safety, Nick had been forced to tell her the truth about his previous involvement with Wishart. He'd urged her to leave before Wishart found out who she was and saw her as a threat to whatever dodgy activity he was up to. Which indicated that he'd still been carrying on with it at that time, and probably was until his death.

She looked for a long time at the link between Wishart and his Thursday night visitor – X, in her doodles. The moment Nick had started asking questions about X, his death warrant had been sealed.

And she thought back to when she'd spoken to Amy, and the impression she'd had that the girl was keeping something back.

Amy wasn't to know that it was no coincidence that the detective inspector should pull up behind her and offer her a lift as she got off the school bus.

Abigail had waited in a side lane until the bus hove into view. She followed it as it trundled along the narrow, winding road and drew up at the bus stop at the end of Clacks Mill Lane. She saw Amy get off, wave to someone on the bus and set off down the lane. She followed and as she drew level with the girl, burdened with her bulging school bag and a violin case, slid the window down. 'I was just coming along to your house. Want a lift with your gear? Hop in, then.'

'Oh, hi!' Amy hopped in and sat with her school bag at her feet, her violin across her knees, awkwardly pulling her seat belt across. 'You should've come later if you want to see my mother. She's back at work. I think it's too soon, but she needs to have something else to think about,' she said, sounding like a concerned parent.

'I was told your grandfather would be here.' Abigail didn't say that it was Amy she needed to talk to, and that she'd deliberately chosen this particular time, when she'd learned Sam would be present, since Amy was under the age when she could have questioned her, alone.

'He's been here every day since ... He says he doesn't want us to be on our own, but we have to be, sometime, don't we?'

'Perhaps not just yet, though. And maybe he's feeling down, too.'

'Not Gramps! He didn't like Daddy much, in fact I don't think he's sorry he's dead.' Another very adult perception, stated without emotion, as though it were a fact of life for which no one was to blame. 'He's sorry for *us*, that's all. But he doesn't need to make a fuss.'

'Maybe he has a point, though.'

'What do you mean? You think somebody is going to come and shoot us, as well?' Suddenly, behind the coolness, a dart of fear showed. She was just a rather scared girl, after all.

'Unlikely, Amy. But it's not good to be alone just now.'

Abigail suddenly felt she was speaking for herself too, as, briefly, unbidden, Ben sprang to mind. Ben, who wouldn't be around much any more to take the pressure off with his good humour and common sense, or to make love to her after some sordid case, so that the world seemed normal and good, after all ... Oh blast, why had *that* crisis come at this particular point in her life? When she was up to the eyes in an investigation in which she now had a very personal stake, never mind what she'd said to Mayo? One thing at a time she could have coped with, the two together ... I don't need this, she thought.

Amy went upstairs to discard her school uniform the moment they got in, only taking a second or two to show Abigail into the kitchen where her grandfather was. 'Look who's here, Gramps,' she announced, planting a kiss on his cheek before flying upstairs.

Sam was preparing food, sautéing mushrooms, garlic and onions. 'The kids are always like starving hyenas when they get in from school, especially Richie, so they eat straight away.' He threw a shrewd glance at Abigail as he added tomatoes, basil and pine nuts. 'Why don't you join us? You look as though you could do with a break, young lady.'

Abigail was tempted. She realized her last meal had been breakfast, and that had been only a cup of coffee. Supper the night before had been a toasted sandwich. She hesitated only briefly, but why not? 'Well, if you're sure there's enough? It smells wonderful.' Her mouth was already watering.

'You're very welcome, though I warn you, it's vegetarian, because of Amy. She's going through that phase, but I don't object to a meatless meal, and Richie eats anything that's going.' He dumped what looked like enough pasta for ten into boiling water, put another plate into the oven of the slow-burning stove to warm, and began to grate cheese. 'He should be here in a few minutes, we shan't have long to wait. Before he does, before Amy comes down, tell me what you've found out.'

She was only too aware how little there was to tell. The events uppermost in her mind – Nick's death, Barbie's disappearance – were not ones likely to bring him any comfort, even had she felt able to speak about them yet. She took refuge in police-speak, and told him they were continuing with inquiries. He glanced sharply at her, but said nothing more, and at that moment, Amy came back in and began to set the table.

In figure-hugging jeans and her big sweater, she was at once less young and more vulnerable. She kept glancing sideways at Abigail as if expecting to be interrogated at any moment. But Abigail was waiting to talk to her until after they'd eaten. The front door opened and banged shut. 'That's Richie,' Amy said, quick with relief.

If Richie was surprised to see who the other guest at table was he didn't show it. When the meal was ready, he fell on it with a gusto Abigail felt like emulating. 'This is very good,' she told Sam appreciatively.

'If Mum ever needs somebody to take over at Miller's Wife, Gramps is the man,' Richie said, with a grin that revealed the likeable lad he was. He seemed to have lost his former truculence, although, like Amy, he cast wary glances at her from time to time.

Abigail waited until she'd cleared her plate before asking, 'Can we go over what you told me again, Amy? About the man who came here on Thursday night to see your father.'

'I told you everything I knew.' Amy had made a poor attempt at her meal, and was now poking her fork about in what was left of the congealing food.

'I was wondering if maybe you'd remembered anything more, anything that might help us to find him.'

The girl sat hunched on a kitchen stool, her legs entwined around the supports like a contortionist. She put her fork down and began to play with the ring on her middle finger instead, gazing at it with deep concentration.

'Amy?'

'Well, I'm not sure, but I *might've* remembered where I'd seen him before.'

Ah. When anyone finally admitted they *might* have remembered, it meant they surely had. 'Where was that?'

'When I saw him in the study, I thought maybe I'd seen him before, but he looked kind of different. Then I remembered. I'm sorry I didn't say, but I thought he'd come to tell Daddy – ' She broke off and looked at her brother, who was concentrating fiercely on mopping up the last drops of sauce with a piece of bread. 'Is it OK, Rich?'

'I can't stop you,' he mumbled, without looking up.

'Well, then. I thought he'd come to tell about Richie, and I didn't want to get Rich into trouble,' said Amy, in her reproving, carrying little voice. Then she burst out, 'Did he kill my father?'

'It's possible. And that he killed someone else, or helped to.'

She recoiled as if someone had slapped her across the face, and her eyes became huge. She looked like a little girl again who desperately wanted her daddy. Sam said, 'All right, m'duck, take it easy.'

'Please explain what you mean,' Abigail said. 'Start right at the beginning. Or you can tell me, Rich.'

'She started it, she can carry on,' Richie said gracelessly. 'OK, I'm sorry, Amy, sorry, but – '

'Oh, shut up, Rich!'

It took further encouragement, but at last, Amy made a halting start. 'A couple of weeks ago, I saw this man. Talking to Richie, up by the market. The gang I was with said he was bad news, he was a pusher, you know, he was selling stuff . . . they said you can get anything you want from him, you know? I told Richie he

161

was out of his mind, messing with things like that, but he wouldn't listen.'

Richie suddenly pushed his empty plate away, and now he was as pale as Amy. 'It wasn't me he'd been getting stuff for, you plankhead!' he shouted. 'It was for Nicola Blake. I told him to leave her alone, or I'd go to the police. He didn't like that and he – he asked me where I thought *he* was getting it from. I told him I'd no idea and I didn't bloody care. But he told me, anyway.'

His voice came out in a harsh croak. 'He said it was my dad, my dad was supplying hard drugs. I didn't believe him.' He jumped up from the table and threw himself into the basket chair by the Aga, burying his head in the cushion, thumping it with his fist. 'It's not true! Dad wouldn't do that, he wouldn't be such a wanker – '

Oh, but it was more than likely, Abigail thought, recalling the blown-up photo of *Nancy Norton*'s crew: Pardoe, Wishart...! She felt as Giotto must have done when he drew his perfect circle. It was beautiful. For a few moments, anyway, before questions began to make the circle look pear-shaped.

Sam was looking thunderstruck at this latest evidence of his son-in-law's depravity, of his own grandchildren's alarming familiarity with the adolescent world of drug-taking he read about in the newspapers. Abigail was sorry for him. It was always a shock to relatives to find out how much their children knew about the big, dark world outside.

'What's this dealer's name?' she asked, but that was going too far. It scared them, and rightly so. You didn't mess around where drugs were concerned. Look where interference had got Nick. That was a thought to choke on, though even harder to take was the fact that he'd been willing to be bought for keeping schtum about this in the first place. Nobody knew better than a policeman – even an ex-policeman – the havoc and horror drugs could wreak in young lives. But analysing Nick's actions would have to wait until she was in a frame of mind to see them in a more compassionate light.

'Would you recognize him again?' Brother and sister exchanged glances, then nodded. 'And where can I find him?' she asked Richie.

'Dunno.'

'Nicola Blake, who is she?'

'Just a girl I know.'

'Where does she contact him?'

'He contacts her.'

'You realize I shall need to see her?'

He went very red. 'She won't tell you anything.'

'Never mind, we'll find him.'

Richie capitulated suddenly. 'His name's Morgan,' he said, without looking at his sister.

Back in her car, Abigail rang Skellen on her mobile phone.

'Frank, I think it would be a good idea if you came into the station.' She gave the Drugs Squad inspector a quick run-through of what she'd just learned. 'Looks as though we've got him!'

There was silence at the other end of the line, then a few mutters. He didn't sound as excited as he ought to have done. 'Did you hear me? His name's Morgan.'

'I heard,' Skellen said. 'Morgan William Finch, known to all as just Morgan, like a bloody bishop. He lives at the Bagots. He's a low-life we've been trying to nail down for yonks.'

Skellen was worse than Mayo, when it came to taking the wind out of your sails. 'So now you've got him – and his supplier.'

'What use is *he*, dead?' Skellen sounded morose. 'You can back this up?'

'Not yet. We need to talk to this Morgan. It's odds on he killed Spalding, too – or had him killed, which comes to the same thing.'

'OK, be with you in half an hour.'

'So Wishart picked the drugs up when he went on these sailing trips – and Morgan did the dealing?' Mayo asked. 'Where did they meet? What linked them?'

Skellen said, 'Wishart was hardly a major league trafficker. NCIS has nothing on him, nor has anyone else, he must've been small beer, whichever way you twist it. Obviously, he got the great idea of peddling dope to get himself out of a financial hole, is my guess, starting with a few snorts of coke for his mates, maybe. It happens.'

Abigail had questions of her own. 'Well, OK, selling a few grams of coke to his cronies wouldn't be a problem, but anything else, finding a dealer, say – that'd be a different ball game, wouldn't it? As you say, he was no professional.'

'Hell, that's no problem. A word in somebody's ear, pubs, clubs – it'd go round like wildfire.' Skellen shrugged. 'But he was playing at it, in professional terms, although I'm not saying it would have stopped at that, once he'd got used to the idea of easy money. But that sort of amateur operation, dabbling, that's what brings trouble.'

'It brought him trouble,' Abigail said.

'Right. Organized traffickers aren't keen, somehow, on the idea of anybody horning in on their operations! No second chances there. Zap out the competition, just like that. I'd go for that rather than this idea of Morgan – a dealer killing his supplier. No way.' Skellen pushed out his lips. 'If it had been the other way round, now, for fear Morgan would rat on him . . .'

'Where does Pardoe fit into this?' Abigail asked. 'He had to have known what was going on, on his own boat.'

'If he did, he'll deny it, and who can prove it?'

'He'll have difficulty in explaining Neptune Holdings,' Mayo said, with satisfaction. He wasn't surprised to learn that Pardoe had been under investigation for some time. He now had on his desk a detailed report of the Neptune and other companies which Pardoe had set up to launder money illegally entering the system.

He explained: 'Basically, it worked something like this: Pardoe lends Wishart the original money to buy the drugs, taking his cut, of course, then sets up the company to launder the profits – making a non-existent loan to explain the cash Wishart has suddenly come by – '

'The interest being his cut for setting it up, of course,' Abigail said. She thought about it for a moment. 'Wishart was owing Pardoe when he was killed. He wouldn't say how much, but I'd say it was no mean sum.'

'Well, the lad had recently cleaned himself out paying off his creditors, you say. He'd have needed more money for his last consignment – presumably he did a repeat deal with Pardoe – but since he was killed before he'd any chance to sell, Pardoe lost out. He won't be acting the old pal again so easily, I'll bet, seeing Wishart's little enterprise finally fouled things up for him.'

Abigail doodled around with her pencil. Nick's murder, and Wishart's. The violent manner of Nick's death was the penalty for interfering in the dangerous world of drugs; Wishart's own death, too, could be explained in the same way. Except that something about Wishart's murder didn't fit.

Skellen wasn't looking too satisfied on his part, either. Supplier and dealer might have been identified, but the link with the source was gone. He had lines of weariness etched on his face, but he seemed resigned. In his job, it was one step forward, two back. He leaned back and said, 'All right, I guess we'll have to pull Morgan in now – and the rest of them down at the Bagots.'

Mayo's hand was half-way to the telephone to issue the necessary orders, when Skellen stopped him. 'First thing tomorrow'd be better. More likely they'll all be there. Surprise 'em out of their beauty sleep.'

This time, Mayo didn't object. 'I'll be guided by you.'

Skellen, after all, Abigail thought, had a feel for this sort of operation. He did what he was best at, what he believed in, it was why he'd chosen to remain with the Drugs Squad when he could have moved on, and up. He had his own motivations. She suddenly remembered the rumour that Skellen's own son had OD'd on heroin, and believed it.

15

The raid was a doddle, after all.

'In and out as soon as possible,' was the instruction from the beefy uniformed sergeant in charge of the half-dozen lads and lasses from the divisional support team. Skellen and Sergeant Tillotson were armed with a drugs warrant to search the premises, plus a black labrador bitch called Ebony and a hydraulic pump to bust the door open, which in the end wasn't needed.

The old front door of number six, the Bagots, wasn't even locked, and the occupants, five of them in all, four young men and a girl, strewn around the various rooms, were too befuddled with sleep or otherwise to put up much of a resistance. There was more danger, as Skellen later said, in breathing the air, which smelled as if something had been dug up that had been left underground for a long, long time.

Nevertheless, although the house was taken apart, the results were not overwhelming. No more than a negligible quantity of cannabis, plus a gram of heroin and some needles, recovered from the bedroom the ginger-haired Scot and his girl shared. Skellen forbore to say 'I told you so.' He hadn't allowed himself to hope they'd get lucky enough to find a safe house for the handover of drugs, so he wasn't disappointed.

'You squatting here?' inquired Tillotson, as he prised Jem out of the kitchen and rolled his eyes at the mushrooms on the ceiling.

Jem was indignant. He protested that the house belonged legally to Luce, that it had been left to her by her grandfather.

'Well, bully for Luce, whoever she is! She won't be so chuffed, mate, when she's done for allowing her premises to be used.'

Jem said, 'Luce isn't like that, she – '

'Save it. Save it for Mr Mayo. He likes fairy stories.'

The lot of them were bundled into the van and taken across to Milford Road station.

The redheaded Scot with track marks all the way up both arms was dealt with first: Jimmy McKeogh, the one they called Ginge, who lived there with his girl, Sheena. 'Ge' offa ma back,' he ground out in a Glasgow accent that was thicker than his skinny, undernourished frame. 'I havenae done nothin' but – '

'Shut up and answer the questions,' Skellen said. 'We've already charged you with possession. You know you can get big time for that. Good for seven years, anyway. Life, maybe, if we can prove intent to supply.'

McKeogh's skin turned a sickly greenish colour under the harsh fluorescent lights of the interview room as he protested he'd never in his life done any dealing ... He was shaking, he badly needed his next hit.

'Who's your dealer, then? Morgan, is it?'

He looked stubborn, with a stubbornness and distrust of the police born out of the Glasgow tenements. And scared. 'Are you crazy? Expecting me to grass? I'm no' ready tae die yet!' At the rate he was travelling, he was likely to be disappointed, said Skellen's glance. They went on questioning him, but he wouldn't be moved. Not yet; maybe later, when he was desperate enough.

His partner, Sheena Grant, was brought in. 'Won't get much out of her,' Farrar, who'd booked her in, warned. 'Not stoned, not at the moment anyway, but she's all the same on another planet.'

A small girl with a cloud of dark hair, she had an innocent, heart-shaped face and a sweet, lost, spaced-out smile ... What made her feel she *needed* drugs when being like this was her natural condition? Not over-bright, perhaps, a simple, pretty girl who seemed to inhabit a world of her own, just having an inborn reluctance to be part of the human race.

Farrar was right, as usual. It was no use questioning her, she only smiled.

The 999 had come in just before midnight. Two old ladies had been burgled, one had been attacked with a knife and was in a serious condition. The attacker had escaped. The injured woman was taken to hospital, with two uniformed police officers following the wailing ambulance in the hopes of a statement. They arrived just too late. Sybil Wishart had died a few minutes before.

WPC Carol Busfield, who had eventually brought Rula home from the hospital, was sitting with her when Carmody arrived at Sybil's Edgbaston flat the next morning, and was immediately despatched to make tea by the old lady. She raised an eyebrow at Carmody, but smiled placidly and did as she was bid. A steady lass.

Miss Brinsley was not above five foot tall, with a small monkey face equipped with outsize spectacles, behind which a pair of sharp eyes gleamed. Her iron-grey hair was cut in a no-nonsense fashion. She was dressed in a plaid skirt and jumper, sensible shoes, and the only sign that anything untoward had happened was that her hands shook slightly as she soothed in her arms the bad-tempered, elderly Yorkshire terrier who'd gone for Carmody's ankles as he entered, and was still glaring out at him from under its blond fringe.

The old lady studied Carmody's big, doleful face for several moments and evidently decided he would do. 'Sit down and listen to what I have to say, then,' she commanded.

Size had nothing to do with it, he thought, amused, towering fifteen inches above her. She indicated a slippery satin chair and took the opposite one herself.

'It was Tyke who woke me,' she said, 'didn't you, my clever darling?'

If Tyke had kept quiet maybe the burglar would have got what he wanted and gone away without having to resort to violence, but Carmody didn't intend to upset his mistress by saying so.

Hearing his name, the terrier started up his shrill barking again. 'He's quite harmless,' Miss Brinsley reassured the big detective, 'just upset, he'll be quiet in a minute.'

The dog did presently shut up, but continued to glare at Carmody, looking as if it would like to bite. The feeling was mutual. Carmody, sliding his behind back to get a better grip on the satin seat, averted his gaze. 'If you could just tell me what happened, ma'am.'

Tyke had wakened her, she repeated, with a proud pat on her darling's head. She'd immediately been aware of someone moving about in the flat. At first, she had thought it was Sybil, but when she went out into the corridor, she'd heard her – well, snoring. Her friend had been a little – how shall we put it? under the weather – before she went to bed. Pissed, silently amended Carmody, who'd boned up on Sybil with George Atkins before he came.

Rula had managed to waken her. The noise seemed to be coming from the kitchen-diner, and since the only telephone was in the sitting-room, they'd gone in there together to try and ring the police.

But the intruder had come out of the adjoining kitchen just as they got into the room – and then, all hell had been let loose. The dog had bitten the burglar on the ankle, Sybil had gone for his face with her nails, and Rula had picked up a silver candlestick and hit him on the head. 'He was wearing one of those woolly caps, however,' she said regretfully, 'so I'm afraid that didn't do much good.' But the burglar had panicked and got out of the flat as quick as he could. Not, however, without consequences. During the struggle, he'd pulled a knife and stabbed poor Sybil.

Bloody hell, thought Carmody. Who wouldn't have panicked, after an attack like that? They were gutsy, these old girls – and lucky, too, that only one of them had been knifed.

'He'll be well marked, then. He'll have a dog bite and scratches on his face, probably a lump on his head.'

'Yes,' she agreed with a satisfaction that soon died. 'If you find him, that is.' She had no more faith in the police than many more. Her face was suddenly drained of animation. She looked what she was, an old lady who had suffered terrible shock and bereavement. She said, her voice shaking a little, 'I've known Sybil for seventy years, ever since we were born. Our mothers were bosom friends and I suppose we were, too. When you think, it might just as easily have been me.' She blew her nose with determination. 'Well, that's enough of that. I'm fortunate it wasn't. And I've just thought of something. I can draw his face for you.'

'You can?'

She trotted away and came back with a sketchpad and pencils, and with a few sure, swift strokes produced what she swore was a passable likeness of the intruder. It was a competent sketch, showing a lean face with good bones, only marred by the villainous expression she'd chosen to depict. It was a face Carmody had seen a thousand times in one form or another: looking down from police station walls, identikit pictures, mug-shots of criminals . . .

'Will it help?' the resourceful old lady was asking eagerly.

'Yes, ma'am, I'm sure it will.' She had signed it with a professional flourish. Rula Brinsley. R-U-L-A, not Ruler, then. The other might be more appropriate.

Carol Busfield came in with the tea, and some digestive biscuits she'd found to go with it. 'Tell the sergeant what you told me, Miss Brinsley. What you thought.'

'Do you think I may be right, then?' Rula asked her, looking gratified. 'Oh, very well.' She focused her sharp glance on the sergeant. 'Sergeant Carmody, I told your nice policewoman here that I don't believe he was a chance burglar. I think he was looking for something. He didn't steal anything, just rooted around. Well, look at the state of this room.'

Carmody didn't say that, of course, it was the first thing that had occurred to him. The significance of the deaths of both Wishart and his mother hadn't escaped anybody. It was one of the reasons why he'd come here himself, instead of sending a DC. He surveyed the room again. The job bore all the hallmarks of a determined search. But there were still one or two pieces of old silver dotted around, and several decent pictures hanging on the walls, all of which had been there for the taking. The television and VCR were untouched.

'As far as I can tell, I don't think he took anything at all,' Rula said, 'unless he had it in his pocket.'

'Let's have a shufti, then. If he was looking for something specific, let's see what we can find that he didn't,' Carmody said.

The WPC coughed. 'He'd been rooting through the sugar and the flour in the kitchen, Sarge,' she said meaningfully, 'so he may've found it.'

'Ah.'

But what the burglar had been after was, in fact, still there. In the spare room which Rula was occupying at the moment, in a cupboard, the key of which was in the handbag Sybil kept with her in her bedroom. When opened, the cupboard revealed a pair of scales and a plastic bag of some white substance, weighing perhaps half a kilo. Plus bicarb and sugar to cut it with and make it go further, clingfilm to parcel it into wraps. Several sheets of LSD, thousands of Ecstasy tablets. Enough to transport half the population of Lavenstock into Never-Never Land. Not such an amateur as all that, after all, Timothy Wishart.

'Pretty!' Rula exclaimed, stretching out a hand to the sheets printed with a strawberry motif.

'Don't touch!' warned Carmody, pulling her back, startling her so much that she drew back as though his hand was red hot. 'In case your skin absorbs it.' Miss Brinsley thinking she could fly like a bird was a complication he needed like a turkey needs Christmas.

'So that's what Sybil was referring to,' said Rula later, recovering from the shock of the discovery with another cup of tea, 'when she said she was helping Tim out. This is the room he always used whenever he stayed here. Poor, silly Sibyl. I won't believe she was a party to what he was doing, although ... I'm sorry to have to say it, but she never did have much sense, especially where Tim was concerned.'

The news of the haul came in just before they began to interview Morgan. There was no shortage of chargeable offences to nail him with. At least three separate counts, possibly four. Abigail and Skellen had decided how to share the interviewing out between them. Morgan looked as though a little of him went a very long way.

Morgan. Long hair, waving to his shoulders. High cheekbones, good teeth, insolent smile. A handsome devil, and devil might be the least of it. Abigail took a very good look. She knew now the link between him and Wishart. The last time she'd seen that face was in a photo, as one of the crew of the *Nancy Norton*, laughing and holding up a glass of champagne.

He'd looked more at home there, on the yacht, with Wishart and Pardoe, than in the company of the motley crowd who inhabited the house at the Bagots. But living there would only be a matter of convenience; he'd only stay until he'd made enough money out of those who trusted him as one of them. Then he'd move on, leaving the destruction of wrecked lives in his wake. It was a familiar, depressing pattern.

'I suppose you know why you're here, Mr Finch,' began Abigail.

'Morgan,' said Morgan, looking pleased with himself to have so many big guns present when he was being questioned, names that had been announced to the tape. 'It's how I prefer to be known, just Morgan.'

'But not how we prefer to know you,' Abigail said, giving him a look specially designed for smart alecs. 'And your solicitor – you're going to need one, believe me – won't take kindly to representing you as Just Morgan. Sure you don't want us to get one for you?'

Morgan shrugged. He'd already twice refused. Didn't he realize what deep trouble he was in? Either the extent of it hadn't dawned on him yet, or, with nothing to lose, he didn't care.

Mayo decided not to stay. He nodded to Abigail and strode out. He'd got the measure of Morgan and could safely leave this interrogation to his more than capable detective inspector and to Skellen. Himself, he had other business more pressing than massaging some little squit's ego.

Morgan watched him go, then suddenly said, 'If I have to have a solicitor, then I'd like my father's. Name of Emma Morrison.'

In with the high flyers, was he? Emma Morrison had a reputation. She was a female crocodile who could slice a witness to ribbons with one snap of her teeth. She didn't come cheap.

'And your father's name?'

'My stepfather. Dare say he'll pay for my solicitor, on account of my mum, but don't hold your breath. Carry on, meanwhile, it's all the same to me. Don't expect him to bail me out, that's all. We're not best buddies.'

'Bail? You'll be lucky! Come on, what's his name?'

Morgan lolled back in his chair and laced his fingers through his hair and behind his head. Pulled back like that, fastened back in a pigtail maybe, you could easily have thought his hair cut short, as Amy had when she'd seen him. The photofit resemblance was now startling. 'Well, all right then,' he said carelessly, 'his name's Pardoe.'

Tony Pardoe's stepson. Marianne Pardoe's son. Abigail looked at the strong planes of the face which were too harsh in the woman but were handsome in the son; a likeness which was evident when it was pointed out. Marianne's bitterness against Wishart was explained, if she believed he'd seduced her son into the dirty world of drugs dealing. Though Morgan, with that secret, knowing, self-satisfied smile, those veiled eyes, didn't look as though he'd have needed much seducing. He looked as though he'd been born knowing the answers, she thought as she began the process of questioning him about the attack on Nick.

Timpson-Ludgate was still on holiday, and the post-mortem on Nick had been carried out by a competent woman replacement. She had been of the opinion that there had been more than one adversary, probably several. So, out of all his injuries, which was the one that killed him? And who had struck the fatal blow?

As Abigail had anticipated, Morgan professed to know nothing. There was as much likelihood of getting anything from him as prising the kernel, whole, from a brazil nut. And just as certainly, she knew he was in it up to the neck. Knowing it was one thing, proving it another.

She turned him over to Skellen and was pleased to see his cocksureness drop away as Skellen hammered away at him. He began to sweat. His cover was blown as far as the drugs scene was concerned, and he knew it. He was well aware there'd be too many people willing to identify him to save their own skins. When Wishart's name came up, after some skirmishing around, he finally admitted that the dead man had been his supplier.

'We know you went to see him on Thursday the fifteenth. You had a row with him. What was it about?'

'He was getting greedy, trying to up the ante. Every time, the price was more.'

'You're sure it wasn't because you were trying to cut him out? He brought the stuff over here when he went across the Channel with your father on the *Nancy Norton* – all right, your stepfather, then, with Pardoe. You were dealing for Wishart and thought it would be a better idea to bypass him, get in on the act yourself when you crewed for Pardoe, isn't that it?'

'Wrong. I've told you, me and Tony . . . well, I don't go sailing with him any more. We don't even meet. You ask him, I'm *persona non grata* as far as he's concerned. We had a big row when I wouldn't go into his crappy business with him and he chucked me out. No job, no nothing. That was when Wishart approached me, said he knew someone over on the other side who could get him whatever he wanted, and he offered to cut a deal with me if I could get rid of it for him. I don't touch the hard stuff personally, nothing more than the odd joint,' he admitted, suddenly willing to co-operate now that he had nothing to lose in that direction. 'I wouldn't.'

'But you knew plenty kids who would.'

The censure bounced off Morgan. He lifted the corner of his mouth. 'There'd be some other guy, if not me.'

'Oh, sure. There's always somebody else. But I think you're lying. I think you've fed us a load of rubbish. I think you got rid of Wishart because he was getting greedy, and you intended to cut him out – whether you would use your stepfather's boat to bring the drugs across or not is immaterial – '

'I had a row with him, but I didn't kill him, no way! I was nowhere near his house that day, you ask my mother! I went to see her, I was with her, all that Saturday.'

'Mothers, unfortunately, tend to be biased in favour of their sons, even when they're dirty little toerags. I thought you said you weren't welcome at Pardoe's house – why should I believe you went there?'

'She'd promised to lend me some money. He didn't see me, he was working.'

'Short of cash, were you?' asked Abigail. 'That was why you broke into Mrs Wishart's flat? Looking for the drugs her son kept there?'

Involuntarily, Morgan twitched. His hand went half-way to the long, double scratch on his face, the mark of Sybil Wishart's nails.

'We can prove you were there, Finch. And that you pulled a knife on two elderly, unprotected women.'

He almost choked. 'It was in self-defence, for God's sake! They'd have killed me between them, those two crazy old bats and the dog!'

'You admit you were there, then?'

He might have got away with it, had not Rula – and her dog – not been staying with Sybil. As it was, he knew he wasn't going to walk away from this one. The knife hadn't turned up, but the scratches on his face could be matched with skin found under Sybil Wishart's fingernails. There would be the dog's teethmarks on his ankle, and evidence, possibly, of a blow to his skull from the candlestick. There was also the matter of a positive identification from Rula Brinsley. Abigail soberly lined it all up, and then informed him that Sybil Wishart had died as a result of the stab wounds. 'So we're going to charge you with her murder, Morgan Finch. And you remain a suspect for the murder of Timothy Wishart.'

His face lost colour. His cockiness left him and he fell silent as he was formally cautioned and charged on suspicion of the murder of Sybil Wishart.

John Fairmile's wife had returned home, having been away longer than she'd intended. She'd gone to stay with her mother to help her redecorate her small sitting-room, a quick emulsion and gloss paint job which was completed in a few days. But Penny had thought the new paint made the old curtains look shabby, and her mother had to agree, and then the new curtains dictated a new carpet . . . So Penny's visit had had to be extended to help choose the carpet and run the new curtains up, and John Fairmile had had to fend for himself a few days longer.

'Was the van there again?' Penny asked after she and the children and their father had been happily reunited, and she'd had time to digest the shocking news about their neighbour that had awaited her.

'The van? I don't know – yes, it was, now you mention it. I saw it through the trees, where it was before.'

'Did you tell the police that?'

'No, why should I? It's Clare's van, after all. No reason why she shouldn't park it on her own property.'

'No reason at all, but why *there*? Not exactly a convenient spot, is it? And why would she want the van, *and* the car at home? She doesn't normally come home in it.'

'Maybe she lent one of them to Richie, and wanted the other for herself – '

'But it was there the other weekend when Richie was away for that geography field trip or whatever it was, remember?'

'Oh God, we've been over all this before.'

'I know, but this time I think we should tell the police,' said Penny forthrightly.

Although Morgan was being held on suspicion of the murder of Sybil Wishart, and on the drugs charges, they couldn't break him in the matter of Tim Wishart's death. Jimmy McKeogh was charged with possession. The rest were to be released on police bail.

Abigail was back in her office when there was a call from downstairs. Jeremy Spencer, the one they called Jem, had asked if he could be allowed to speak personally to her.

'Tell him I'll be down presently.'

She sighed. Any chance to ease off for a minute or two looked like having to wait. As in all life's crises, she needed coffee. More than usually, after the last few hours with Morgan Finch. She made do with a drink of water, splashed her face to freshen up, ran a comb through her hair, dabbed her wrists with cologne and went downstairs.

'Which one of you is Jem?'

The short, swarthy boy was the little dark waiter at the Holly Tree: it was the surveillance photos Skellen had taken which had given her the idea she'd seen him before. He stood up as she came into the room, nudged his companion to do so. Nice manners, for all his gypsy appearance, his questionable lifestyle. Well brought up. What would his mother think of him, being here? 'You wanted to see me?' she asked, motioning them to sit down.

He was nervous, and seemed to find it difficult to speak. She looked at the other one – Col, wasn't it? – who sat staring into space, as though he wasn't part of the scene. Another, stoned out of his mind? She didn't think so. Thin, gangling, his eyes behind his spectacles haunted, but intelligent and very much aware.

'You're free to go. You're being released without charges, this time,' she told them. 'On police bail. Do you understand what that means?'

Oh sure, they understood, Jem said. It had been explained to them. It wasn't that . . . He looked at his friend.

Col turned his gaze towards Abigail, and spoke.

'The thing is, we're very worried about Luce . . .'

16

'*Every* Saturday afternoon?' Farrar repeated.

He and Deeley were sitting drinking coffee and taking notes in the Fairmiles' sparkling farmhouse kitchen, which smelled of baking and floor wax, and a breath of White Linen every time Mrs Fairmile passed the table. 'The van's been parked there every Saturday?'

'For two or three weeks, anyway,' Penny Fairmile asserted firmly. 'Down there, behind that holly thicket, where it couldn't be seen from the road – or from the mill, either. Only from our bedroom window, because we're on higher ground, and I don't suppose whoever put it there would have thought of that.'

She was a forceful, pretty, plump young woman with a bright cap of straight golden hair that looked to Deeley's untutored eyes as though it had been cut round a basin. It suited her, though. 'I told John there was something odd about it being there, but we didn't feel it was any of our business, not then.'

'You're sure it was the Miller's Wife van?' Deeley asked, reducing the pile of home-made brandy snaps on the plate by two more.

Farrar cast him a pitying glance. Couldn't he see that Fairmile's wife was the last person likely to have made a mistake? She was capable and energetic, and very sure of herself. Anyone who could organize her time efficiently enough to make brandy snaps, as well as look after a couple of noisy lads, a farmer husband and a rambling farmhouse – and look so good, into the bargain – wasn't the type likely to waste anyone else's time, either. He should be so lucky, he thought, looking at the bright hair, envisaging his own once-lively, but now permanently discontented Sandra, who rarely cooked anything more ambitious than a microwave meal.

'Couldn't mistake something like that,' Penny Fairmile said decidedly, 'that white and honey colour, with the wheatsheaf logo and the name all curly in dark green and gold.'

'Oh, right.'

'I saw it as well,' Fairmile said. 'We both did. Our bedroom window overlooks the thicket, though it's a good way off, down the slope, other side of the river. We wouldn't have seen it even then, if it hadn't been for the evening sun glinting on the white paint.'

It was left to Deeley to ask the most pertinent question. Unimaginative, down-to-earth, he invariably said the most obvious thing, which everyone else declined to do, since it *was* so obvious, and thereby, very often, he hit the button. 'Why didn't you just ask Mrs Wishart?'

'We assumed Clare knew about it. I must say I thought it a bit of an odd place to leave a van, but you don't go around quizzing

177

your neighbours about their peculiar parking arrangements, do you? Not when it's on their own land.'

'It can't be coincidence, the way everything seems to lead back to Miller's Wife,' Abigail said, chewing over this new development with Mayo. 'This business of the Rimington girl going missing – she's another who worked there.' Three of them, now, though it was true that Barbie Nelson had never really been missing at all, and Roz Spalding had only gone because she'd chosen to. She was back in circulation again, perhaps wishing she wasn't. And Luce – Luce was a free spirit, an impulsive young woman, accountable to no one but herself. Perhaps there was no reason to worry about her at all.

'What does Morgan Finch know about it? Luce was his girlfriend, wasn't she?'

'Nothing, he says, but he would say that, wouldn't he? Hasn't seen her since the Saturday morning, is what he says, when he went off for a few days. He *seems* genuinely worried about her – or worried as he can be about anyone but himself.'

'Not enough to try and contact her, though.'

'They'd had some sort of argument. Then the letter from her sister came after he'd left and he was huffed she'd gone off without leaving him a message.' She flipped through the pages of her neatly written notebook. 'Seems he didn't know her mother's address or phone number, anyway. "When she goes there, she rings me," was what he actually said. "Her saintly mum doesn't approve of her friends, especially me." Sounds a sensible woman!'

Still, when Luce had heard her mother was in trouble, she'd responded like a shot, according to Jem.

'But the mother wasn't worried when Luce didn't turn up?'

'They're not on the phone at the Bagots – and Mum assumed somebody there had been getting at Luce not to go home. She was more annoyed than worried, that her daughter couldn't be bothered to help her out when she needed her. She blames the whole thing on Luce's grandfather, leaving her that house.'

'She's probably right,' Mayo said. Independence was all very well, but he knew what daughters were. His own daughter, far away on another continent, was still a source of needless worry to him. Probably would be, all her life.

He studied the report of the two detectives who'd interviewed the Fairmiles, succinctly presented by Farrar and neatly summed up. The inference about the van had seemed obvious to Farrar: the killer had been watching Wishart for some time, waiting for the right opportunity to shoot him. Not wanting to use his own car in case it was recognized, he had used the van, in the belief that if anyone had by any chance seen it parked there, they would have assumed it to be there legitimately.

'Fair enough. But who'd leave it there for any other reason than they wanted to hide it? In the middle of that scrubland?'

'It's good cover,' Abigail agreed, 'that holly thicket, although to get to the woods across the river you'd have to fight your way through the jungle first. Still, less chance of being noticed than walking up the lane to the mill house and past it, then over the bridge on to the other side.' She thought a bit. 'But of course, they wouldn't need to, they'd use the main road. Skirt round the mill altogether, there and back. I'll get Carmody to have a word with them all down at Miller's Wife. And have the security checked down there, see how easy it is for anybody other than the company personnel to get into the yard when the place is closed for the weekend.'

'Hm.' Mayo twirled his glasses, cogitating. 'You sure we're on the right tack with this? I don't want this case falling apart, going off at a tangent. You're thinking of Finch, I take it?'

'Thinking of him, yes. Hoping. But we're not going to nail him with it until we find his grubby little traces all over the van. Which we won't.'

'I want him, Abigail. Not just for the old woman's murder, and the drugs. For Spalding, *and* Wishart.'

'For anything else we can get him for, as well. There's still a chance, the company he keeps, that somebody will talk. We all know that sort'd shop their mother if there was something in it for them.'

It was still worrying. 'This Wishart business – it doesn't stack with Morgan. Why go about the job in such a roundabout way?'

'I don't know – yet.'

A break was what they'd needed, and the van had given them

that, but all it seemed to do was to rule out Morgan. As far as he was concerned, the van was probably an irrelevance. Why did he need to risk using the van – he or anyone else he might have hired to get rid of Wishart?

Abigail wasn't the possessor of an overheated imagination, though she could sometimes be impulsive, but Mayo trusted her intuitions, better than his own. He only allowed himself to have them in personal matters, nebulous and unreliable as they were, and even there he felt they often led him to wrong conclusions. She was going round to Miller's Wife, and he thought it was time he went to have a look at what was going on there himself, too.

As she'd predicted, they were open and working again. 'We've a big order we can't afford to slip up on,' Clare explained. 'A party scheduled for tonight. Mind waiting a few minutes?'

The way she was concentrating on piping mayonnaise on to that platter of salmon scaled with transparent slices of cucumber, Mayo could see how keeping up with her routine, coming in to work, could be a source of therapy to her. And perhaps the best way for the others to show sympathy was through solidarity, by carrying on as usual.

It was warm and well-lit in the kitchen, in contrast to the gloomy morning outside, and he was content, for the moment, to sip coffee and watch them working, until one or other of the women had finished what they were about. He was fascinated by the ordered bustle and harmony with which they dovetailed together, clever women's hands doing age-old tasks. Chopping, slicing, beating, kneading. Even the middle-aged woman who was fetching and carrying, stacking the cupboards with fresh supplies, had her own well-paced rhythm, not getting in any-one's way.

'There now,' Clare said, putting the finished salmon into a fridge, 'that's finished. Thanks for waiting. What can we do for you?'

She was mystified when asked about the van. 'Certainly I never left it – where did they say, behind the holly thicket? How odd. Are they sure it was our van?'

180

'Both Mr and Mrs Fairmile swore it was. Who normally drives it?'

'Barbie Nelson – or she did. But any of us do, if we have a rush order and there's no one else available.'

'Did she ever use it privately?'

'Barbie? We all use it from time to time in an emergency.'

'I used it myself last week when my car was being serviced,' Ellie Redvers offered, from the direction of the stove, where she was absorbed in stirring a savoury sauce. 'But not on Saturday.'

'Who holds keys, and to what?' asked Abigail, remembering Ellie taking the keys for Barbie's flat from the key-cupboard on the wall.

Ellie, Clare and David Neale all held keys to the main entrances. Others were kept in the locked key-cupboard, for which the same people each held a key. 'Oh, and Barbie had a set of course, but she posted them through the letter-box when she left,' Ellie said.

Abigail wasn't impressed with the arrangements. For one thing, the key-cupboard hadn't been locked on her previous visit, she recalled. Practically anyone, at any time, could have gained access to whatever keys they'd wanted.

Ellie tasted her sauce and added redcurrant jelly, a dash of mustard, then brought the saucepan and a teaspoon over to Mayo. 'Taste? An unbiased opinion?'

Sharp and piquant, the sauce stimulated his taste buds, reminding him he hadn't had lunch. 'Absolutely delicious,' he said, but nothing else was forthcoming.

'Good. Now I'll take you up to meet David.'

Neale wasn't able to enlighten them any more about the van than the rest of them, but patiently put aside his work to answer their questions.

His office was workmanlike, but there were indisputably feminine, softening touches in the subtle colours of the walls and the co-ordinated carpet and curtains. Green, thriving plants and a handsome set of bookshelves. Plus a couple of East Anglian watercolours – if original, likely to be his personal property rather than part of the office furniture.

181

Yet it was a room in which the tall, bespectacled man with the grey-blond hair and the pleasant smile didn't seem totally out of place. A good office to work in, but noisier than you'd have thought. Mayo, sitting by the window, saw that the road was very close, the traffic continuous and rather noisy. A double-decker cruised past and two big lorries in convoy rumbled down the road and turned towards the river. If they were starting on the demolition of the last of the old property, the consequent noise and mess and dust here would be unbearable for months. Shopkeepers in the area had already put in complaints, in fact, but starting meant the end was in sight, a relief to everyone.

Abigail was still questioning Neale about the van. The little runabout was at the moment parked in the yard below, drops of the moisture-laden morning dimming its white and honey-coloured paint, 'Miller's Wife' lettered in dark green above the wheaten sheaf that conveyed a subliminal message, an image of good, country wholesomeness.

The yard was surrounded by high, chain-link fencing, and a break-in was unlikely not to have been noticed. It was conceivable, of course, that keys had been obtained – by Luce, for instance, while she'd been working here.

Mayo turned his attention back to Neale, to hear Abigail saying, 'Maybe you can help us on another point. We're also inquiring into the disappearance of Lucinda Rimington, who used to work here. I believe you keep all the personnel records.'

'Lucinda – ? Oh, Luce, you mean! Disappeared, you say?' He tut-tutted but, interestingly, gave the impression that he was not altogether astonished.

'She set off to see her mother on Saturday the tenth but never arrived. She hasn't been seen since . . . You don't seem surprised, Mr Neale.'

'Well, to be honest, I'm not, really. Her sort, you know . . . here today, gone tomorrow . . .'

Abigail said sharply, 'What do you mean, "her sort"?'

Neale shrugged regretfully. 'Nice girl, basically, Luce. Respectable family, well brought up. Why *do* these pretty girls choose to dress and do their hair so outlandishly – grotesque, isn't it? And what was she doing associating with that riff-raff down at the Bagots? I tried to make her see sense . . .'

'You talked to her?'

He laughed, spreading his hands ruefully. 'She talked to *me*,' he corrected. 'She'd talk to anyone, she'd no inhibitions. Rattling away like that got in the way of her work, but that didn't matter to Luce. In fairness, however little she chose to show it, she was quick and intelligent.' Abigail could see that, despite his disparaging remarks, he'd liked the girl.

She'd worked there for several weeks in a casual capacity, he told them, as so many of them did, at Miller's Wife. Frankly, it wouldn't ever have occurred to him to employ her, not at any cost, but it was Ellie who'd set her on. 'She thought she brought a bit of sunshine to the place,' he said drily. She'd found Luce amusing, with her outrageous clothes, her chatter and her careless good nature, though not when she discovered the large amounts of food that were going missing. Everyone was entitled to their perks in a place where there was always spare food going begging, but that had been something else. Luce had been sent packing, and that was when Barbie Nelson had appeared on the scene.

'Didn't you think it strange that she'd confide in you about her private life?' Mayo asked.

'No, she was totally open about it, to everyone, but I have to say, the more she told me, the more concern I began to feel for her. Some of those she lived with were involved with hard drugs. She swore she never smoked more than cannabis herself, she didn't see any wrong in that and shut her eyes when I warned her how easy it is to get drawn into serious drugs. It's like a vicious, downward spiral. A road to nowhere.' He looked down at his well-manicured nails. 'I hated to see such degradation, especially in a woman,' he said quietly.

'Yes, I can understand that,' Abigail replied sympathetically. 'And why you're so anti-drugs. Damien Rogers, your wife . . .'

Seconds passed. 'My wife?' His facial muscles seemed to have stiffened. 'What do you know about my wife? You've actually been prying into my private affairs?'

'And into everyone else's associated with the inquiry,' Mayo said. 'Nobody can have secrets in a murder case, Mr Neale. We make it our business to know a lot more about people than they ever tell us. Don't worry, it won't get passed on.'

Not if we don't choose to pass it on, he thought. Or need to.

Something was wrong here. Mayo said thoughtfully to Abigail as he left, 'There's a lot of tension in that place.'

What he'd actually felt strongly was the sort of overheated, claustrophobic emotion generated by women in close communities, but he'd be wiser not to say that, not to Inspector Abigail Moon, or to his Alex, either. They'd accuse him of being sexist. But it was a rum set-up, was the actual phrase going through his mind.

How did David Neale, the only male, working amongst them all every day, cope with that?

When they'd gone, Neale sat immobile at his desk.

He'd tried so many times to make Luce see sense, that in the end she began to avoid him. When she'd been dismissed, he'd felt a sense of personal failure that he hadn't been able to do anything to make her see what a collision course her life was on.

And Jane, he thought. Oh, Jane!

Few people, if any, had any suspicion of what their life together had been like, when Jane was alive. Wonderful, at first. She'd been such a vibrant woman, she'd given him so much, tried to teach him that although life might be real and earnest, it could also be fun. It was a lesson he was not equipped to learn.

They had no children, a deep sadness to both of them, which they'd faced in their different ways. He had always thrown himself into his work, now he became obsessive, successful in his own right, and no longer dependent upon Jane's money. Left to her own devices, she began on the social round: bridge, golf, parties and yet more parties. It took it out of her. Always slim, she'd become thinner and thinner. He began to worry over the bouts of exhilaration alternating with periods of extreme agitation and anxiety. She found strange new friends, and began to dress carelessly. She couldn't sleep, became hyperexcitable, and still it hadn't dawned on him what was wrong. Until it was too late. Until she'd moved on from cocaine to heroin, and become careless about the evidence, uncaring. Syringes, needles left lying about for him to find.

Nothing would induce her to get treatment, and he watched helplessly until the final, inevitable, fatal overdose that killed her and left him alone, lonely, and filled with an implacable hatred against drugs and those who trafficked in them.

17

The mists had at last cleared from her brain. Her limbs felt heavy and lax, there was an overwhelming lassitude in her body, and she was so weak, but she wasn't muzzy-headed any longer; she was able to remember everything, her mind clear and lucid.

Lucid Luce. Lucinda Rimington, standing at the bus stop, waiting in the fog.

God, why doesn't the bus come? Don't think it's *going* to come. I shall miss the train, and the connection in Birmingham, and I shan't get to Guildford till Lord knows when. Why don't I get myself a car, never mind environmentally unfriendly? I can afford it, twenty cars, when I sell the house. Haven't time to walk to the station, my rucksack's too heavy, too bulky, just shoved everything in, not thinking of anything much except Mum, Jesus, I hope she's all right. Debbie said it wasn't serious, just a bang on the head when she fell against the stair, but you never know, Deb's only a kid, why didn't Mum write, herself? Where is that bloody bus?

Salvation! Who said there wasn't a God? Of all things, looming out of the fog, the twee little white van. Who's driving? Doesn't matter, I can wave and flag it down, whoever's driving will know me and give me a lift to the station. Brilliant! Cheer up, Mum, your bad little girl's on her way . . .

The Town Hall clock struck eleven p.m., loudly enough for its unmusical bong to penetrate the double glazing in Abigail's office. It didn't bother the wet and bedraggled pigeons, who were used to it, dozily huddled together for warmth on the ledges, but it caused Abigail to look up, reminding her that she had a bed to go to.

She ran a hand through her hair, then rubbed the place

between her brows where a headache had lodged. The rain had begun again, lashing the windows, bucketing down. Clean, steady rain, which might hopefully wash away the last of the dirty fog, though it was bitterly cold and if it began to freeze, there'd be trouble on the roads in the morning. If it went on like this, there might be danger of floods again.

She should have been home hours ago, but the senior staff session in Mayo's office, with the ACC present, had gone on and on. Sheering had eventually left them to it, and at last even Mayo had had enough and called a halt. He'd packed it in and gone home, expecting the rest to do likewise. Abigail had stayed on to sort the notes she'd made. She added another, this time about Barbie Nelson, then pushed the lot into their folder and stood up. She'd been through them so many times she was cross-eyed and no way were they going home with her tonight – except in her head, and that was something she couldn't escape.

She had her raincoat on, buttoned and belted, and her hand was on the light switch when the telephone rang. 'What? All right, tell him I'll be down in a few minutes.'

She passed through the deserted CID office and looked in at the incident room on her way down; it was humming quietly along this time of night, nothing going on of any significance, nothing that needed her attention. She said goodnight to the lone, yawning constable left to man the telephone and went downstairs to meet the lanky figure hovering by the front desk.

'Colin? What are you doing here? Is it Luce? Has she turned up?'

'That's what I came to ask you.'

She shook her head. 'You'd have been told. I promised, we'll let you know, just as soon as we hear anything.'

His shoulders sagged, his spectacles had misted up in the indoor warmth. His sopping hair dripped on to the shoulders of an ex-RAF greatcoat, already dark with rain, his jeans and trainers were soaked. She took pity on him and said gently, 'Come in here a minute.' The civilian inquiry officer had gone off shift, and she turned to the PC on the desk. 'I'm sure you can find us some tea, would you mind?'

'Ma'am,' said the constable, a surly individual who didn't take kindly to women who ordered him about. He didn't much like women at all. Especially policewomen, dykes or bikes, the lot of 'em.

Abigail took Col into the nearest interview room and when he'd shrugged off his wet coat and slung it over the back of his chair, she found a wad of tissues in her bag and handed them over, so that he could wipe his face and hair.

The constable's revenge came in polystyrene beakers: weak, grey and milky, scalding hot, already heavily sugared, as she found when she plucked up courage to take a sip. She pushed it aside, managing not to gag, but Col drank like a man who'd been in the Sahara without water for a week.

'I won't believe she'd go off like this! Something must have happened to her. She wouldn't have disappeared without saying anything, that's not Luce's style.'

It didn't seem to be like Luce, Abigail agreed, from what they'd learned of her, but disappeared she had. Had she hitched a lift somewhere? She seemed to be the sort of girl – sparky, independent, gregarious – who might have done so, and met the sort of trouble that might have been expected. Her physical description had been circulated. Small, slim, crop-haired, dyed blonde, stud under her lower lip. Wearing her best, least way-out clothes when last seen: trailing black skirt, heavy boots, denim jacket, Save the Whale T-shirt.

But nobody remembered her buying a ticket at the station, she hadn't been seen at either Birmingham New Street or Guildford. Since leaving the Bagots, she'd disappeared into thin air.

There'd been no reports received of any unidentified female bodies, or not yet.

Col was persisting. He was an intelligent young man, though she knew his history by now, had been warned how his moods varied, how unpredictable he could be. There was no evidence of this at the moment. He simply looked miserable and unhappy. She also knew the debt of gratitude he owed to his friends, Luce, and Jem Spencer, so that he was bound to feel like this about Luce, even in face of evidence to the contrary. When he'd first been brought in, he'd been questioned in the presence of a psychiatric social worker as a matter of course, and she'd confirmed that he could function more or less normally if he kept up his medication. There lay the problem: he hated to feel he was dependent on it and sometimes rejected the need for it. His eyes, when he took his specs off to rub them clear, were preternaturally bright; she wondered whether this meant he'd been taking his pills or not.

'Col, she'd had a row with her boyfriend, she'd be upset, maybe – '

He waved that aside. 'Only a few words, Jem says, about Ginge. Luce would've forgotten about it in a few hours, she never bears a grudge.' His mouth set in a stubborn line. 'I won't believe she's just taken off, without a word to anybody. She was due to come into big money any time. The house, for one thing ... the developers want it, you know, and she was supposed to be meeting them yesterday. She was planning what to do with the money ...'

Start a commune on a remote Scottish island? Give it to the Animal Liberation freaks?

'Well,' she repeated, 'we'll let you know ...'

Col, without seemingly noticing it, had picked up her rejected tea and gulped from it. He plonked the beaker down on the table; light and empty, it wobbled over and the dregs spread in a tiny puddle. He watched in silence as she mopped it up with more tissues. He was so tense he practically vibrated, dangerously on the brink.

'You're in charge of that murder, aren't you?' he asked suddenly. 'Tim Wishart, that bloke who was shot. Married to that woman Luce used to work for.'

She looked at him steadily. 'Yes. What do you want to know about that?'

'I'm not asking, I'm telling.'

He breathed deeply and then said, 'I'm telling you he was the one Morgan was getting his drugs from.'

'Yes, Col, we know.' There was a silence. The fact that his bombshell hadn't had the effect it should have had didn't seem to surprise him. She had the feeling he'd been aware that it was known, that announcing it was the prelude to something else. 'Are you saying it was Morgan who killed Wishart?'

'Nah, not Morgan. He's not as clever as he likes to think, but even he wouldn't kill the golden eggs, would he?' he demanded, in some confusion. 'But listen, what about that crazy, that guy Neale, works at Miller's Wife? The one who's always down at the Centre? He's round the twist, you know, about drugs. Ask any of the kids at the Centre, he's always lecturing them. He drove Luce bananas when she worked at that place, lecturing her and that. It's obvious isn't it? He knew Wishart was supplying Morgan – '

'What leads you to think that?'

'He must have known. He was watching Morgan like a hawk. I know, because *I* was watching *him*. I've time on my hands for that sort of thing,' he added morosely. 'I didn't trust him where Luce was concerned.'

'A lot of people don't approve of drugs, Col, you've told me you feel that way yourself. But that hasn't made you go around killing the suppliers.'

'You don't know him, that Neale. He's weird, really weird, sometimes.'

'Look, if there's something else you want to tell me, Col, you'd better get it off your chest.'

'I don't know anything,' he came back angrily, 'it's him you'd better ask. Ask him where Luce is. He knows. Don't ask me how I know that, I just feel it. All I'm saying is, you want to ask him. We want her back. We love her.' His eyes filled with despair and, as a slow tear trickled down his cheek, he laid his head on the table, on his folded arms.

Abigail placed her hand gently on the weeping boy's sleeve. They were going to have to confront Neale now, she thought heavily. But they'd known that, anyway.

There had only ever really been two possibles after the discovery of the van: Morgan Finch, who seemingly had no access to it – and why should he want to use it, anyway? – and David Neale, who'd had no motive to kill Wishart. At least, that was how it had appeared until they'd learned about his wife, and the part drugs had played in her death. His wife. Luce. Damien Rogers. Neale appeared to have been conducting a one-man vigilante crusade. How short a step was that to taking the role of avenger on himself?

Col believed Neale had discovered Wishart's drug-supplying through keeping a close watch on Morgan. Well, maybe knowing Luce had made Neale suspicious of Morgan, but it was unlikely he would have been able to spot the connection with Wishart, when Skellen and his team had failed to do so, while watching Morgan's every move. No, it would have been his wife's habit that had led him to Wishart, when he'd first begun to supply 'recreational' drugs to those able to afford them. Addicts in the later stages of addiction were not noted for their circumspection, and Morgan's evidence provided ample grounds to believe that Wishart had been supplying Jane Neale.

It was enough reason to kill. Any reason was strong enough, if it seemed so to the murderer. Never mind motive, Mayo was wont to say. Give me the opportunity and the means, and the possibility that the suspect was capable of performing this crime, and motive will take care of itself. Opportunity David Neale had had, and as for capability ... He showed a gentle and diffident face to the world but that, in the history of murderers, didn't amount to a ha'p'orth of beans.

There was no hard evidence that he *was* a murderer, yet. It was going to be difficult to expose him as such. But the appearance of the van had shifted the focus of the investigation inexorably in his direction.

The van's importance, so near the scene of the crime, couldn't be discounted until a satisfactory explanation for its presence was forthcoming, which hadn't so far happened. The forensic report was still awaited, but Abigail wasn't getting her hopes up about that. There wouldn't be any evidence, if whoever had used it had any sense, and Neale's intelligence wasn't in doubt. Of all those associated with the case, he was the one who had the opportunity to use it. The timing was too tight for everyone else.

He'd been seen to arrive at the Centre at twenty to four, and his car had incontrovertibly been jammed into the car-park until at least half-past five, during which time several people had seen him from time to time around the Centre – though none were prepared to swear exactly when. Plenty of opportunity for him to have slipped out of the Centre, walked across to Miller's Wife and picked the van up, made a quick four-mile dash over to Clacks Mill, then followed the reverse procedure. Not forgetting a spot of murder in between.

Moreover, Barbie Nelson might well be a possible witness. The exact time of her arrival at the hospital to see her father remained unconfirmed, the staff had been too busy to remember, but it had certainly been too soon after Wishart had died for her to be realistically considered as a suspect. But . . . Jenny Platt had been convinced at the time of the interview with her that she was holding something back. And, as Abigail now recalled, the windows of her flat overlooked the yard where the van was parked, so that she could have seen something. She'd left Lavenstock far too early last Saturday to have seen anyone taking the van away – on the day of the murder, that was. But what about the previous Saturdays?

As sure as God made little apples, she wouldn't have come forward to say so; if she'd had suspicions she was keeping them to herself. Like Marianne Pardoe, she'd be only too happy if Wishart's killer went free.

Despite Abigail's reassuring words to Col, his outburst had set up alarm bells in her mind. She was beginning to be seriously worried about Luce's fate. She couldn't see any reason for Neale wanting to harm her. On the contrary, he had seemingly been concerned for her welfare, unless – and this was a thought to make her pause – unless in some way the girl, Morgan's girlfriend, she had to remember, had also been involved in dealing drugs. Her other friends were adamant that she'd nothing to do with this, but dealers weren't known for sharing their secrets.

Whether Luce had been dealing or not, Abigail was seized with a growing conviction that they couldn't afford to make light of her disappearance.

18

The weaker she grew, the more Luce's senses were heightened. She was getting used to seeing in the dark, and her hearing had become acute. She heard the rain on the window and, she was sure, somewhere not too far distant, the lap of water, and even the distant sound of traffic. And every now and then, more of those those small, furtive scuttlings. They'd once terrified her, these noises: rats, or cockroaches, she'd imagined with horror, tensing for the clammy insect-touch on her skin, the red eyes in the dark. But as time went on, she identified the sounds as coming from behind, not inside, the walls of her prison. They were comforting, in a way, now, sounds of life.

The end for her must be very near. You couldn't survive without water and she had none left, and no hope either, that he would ever return. He was going to leave her here until she died. It was hard to believe this of him, but then, the whole story of her imprisonment was bizarre.

When she'd flagged him down at the bus stop, David Neale hadn't looked very happy, but you never expected that from him, he was a glumchops at any time, and anyway, he'd agreed after a moment to take her to the station. It wasn't much out of his way after all, and she might just, if he got a move on, get that train. She'd bundled in and thrown her rucksack down anyhow on to the floor beside her. He was in a funny mood, very quiet, and she didn't push her luck by trying to make conversation, which would only turn into one of his boring lectures. It was when they'd reached the railway station and she was getting ready to jump out as soon as he stopped that she realised her bag was somehow stuck and gave it a jerk. One of the straps had caught around something pushed under the seat and as the rucksack was freed, what was under the seat came with it. Of all things, the barrel of a shotgun!

At first, she thought his reaction was because he knew that killing animals was something she thought obscene – she'd once told him about taking part in anti-foxhunting demos – but it wasn't that. His face had gone a queer clay colour, and then, before she had the chance to get out of the van, he'd swung it round with a screech and driven off like a bat out of hell, throwing her sideways. She'd had thoughts about opening the door and jumping because, Jesus, he frightened her. She'd never seen David Neale in a fury before, and it was something she'd rather not see again. But she'd been too awkwardly placed by then to make a jump for it, wedged inextricably into her seat as she was by her lumpy rucksack, hampered by her long skirt. And besides, she didn't fancy the idea of being spread out on the road in front of whatever might be coming up behind.

He drove into the yard at the back of Miller's Wife. And that was the last thing she remembered until she'd wakened up here.

'Bring him straight into my office,' Mayo instructed the two detectives sent to bring Neale in next morning. They returned without him. He was, they reported, neither at home nor at Miller's Wife, where they'd also called.

'Keep trying.'

They had scarcely departed before Abigail received a call from the civilian SOCO man. Ex-Police Sergeant Dexter had news. Several short peroxided hairs had been found on the back of the van's passenger seat.

Abigail's heart lurched. 'The missing girl's a dyed blonde, Dave.' The quick stab of excitement faded. 'Thanks, anyway, for letting me know. But they're no use without *her* – unless . . .'

'Right, so get me a sample,' Dexter said tersely, 'from her clothes at home.'

A few minutes later, Deeley and Scott radioed back that they still hadn't been able to obtain an answer at Neale's house, everything appeared to be locked up. But Deeley gave it as his opinion that their quarry could be in the house. 'There was a bottle of milk on the step when we came earlier, and it's gone now. We've had a look around and there's a light on in a room at the side, and the computer's going.'

'Tell them not to do anything until I get there,' Abigail said crisply. She picked up the telephone and spoke to Mayo.

'I'm coming with you,' he said. They picked up Sergeant Carmody and Farrar and, within minutes, were on their way.

None of the houses on this side of the river were small, and that included Neale's. Stockbroker Tudor, surrounded by a spacious, well-kept garden, it had rosy bricks and sweeping roofs and diamond latticed windows that must have been a window-cleaner's nightmare. A battering ram would have been needed on the studded door. They didn't waste time on it. After knocking and receiving no reply, Deeley was sent round the back to break the glass on the door of the modern utility room extension to let them in.

In a wood-panelled hall as big as the average-sized sitting-room, an arrangement of flowers that looked almost real, in a Chinese jar half the size of a man, stood in an ingle-nooked fireplace. A settle and chintz-covered chairs were arranged around it. Thick rugs were spread on polished boards, and as they moved from room to room, only the occasional whirr of the freezer motor broke the silence, and presently, the noise of men's footsteps and voices as they began to swarm around the house.

Not a thing was out of place, every item of furniture shouting its value, shining with care and attention. The house was cold, and smelled of pot-pourri and furniture polish, of unused rooms, like a National Trust house; only the guide, sitting on a chair by the door of each room, was missing.

'Where's the room with the light on?' Abigail asked, emerging from a dining-room with a refectory table long enough to seat twenty, if ever it had, in this house.

'Over here.'

Mayo's voice came from a doorway further down the hall, opening on to a small room, evidently a study, comfortable and informal, unlike the rest of the house. Lamps cast a warm overall glow, the electric fire was full on, a half-empty cup of coffee, cold as Abigail found when she touched the side, stood on the desk next to a word processor where the cursor flickered on an otherwise empty screen, and the desk chair held the imprint of the occupant's rear on the cushion.

'Just like the *Marie Celeste*,' said Mayo, even as footsteps descended the stairs and Farrar came in to report that there was no one upstairs, either. But somewhere in this waiting house was Neale. The air held his presence. However, he mattered less than Lucinda Rimington. The bottom line was her safety.

'Sir,' Deeley said, emerging from the kitchen, 'there's a light coming from under what seems to be the cellar door.'

'Well, don't waste time telling me. Get down there.'

'The door's locked or bolted from the other side. We've shouted but nobody's answering.'

'Then what are you waiting for?'

An audience gathered to watch Deeley as he applied his shoulder and, despite the tension, there were a few muffled laughs as the door flew open and steps leading directly downward caused the big lad to stagger back in an effort not to tumble straight to the bottom. Whoosh! You could almost hear the air expelled as he hit the pneumatic Scotty.

Mayo waved them back and went in first.

It was, in fact, only a short flight of wooden steps, leading into what was more of a basement than a cellar, a big space that had been converted into something approaching a small gymnasium, with exercise machines all over the place and, at one end, a target practice area.

On a wooden chair facing the steps sat David Neale. A shotgun was balanced across the chair arms and his finger was on the trigger. He had removed his spectacles and without them his gaze was unfocused, his eyes rolling in a way that said he was out of control. But the gun was pointing unerringly at the doorway.

There was a moment when everything halted. Without turning round, Mayo told the men behind him to get back. Those who could see past him saw the man with the gun. No one wanted to leave Mayo there but no one wanted to stay, either.

He said, quietly, 'Give me the gun, Neale.'

There was no response. He looked into the mad eyes he had once thought gentle and compassionate and saw the mistake he'd made. This man had destroyed life at least once before, without a qualm, and would never be sorry. He repeated his request quietly, moved his hand slowly forward and the world exploded in a deafening roar.

The sound ricocheted from wall to wall and in the enclosed space it was as if the end of the world had come.

For a split second afterwards there was silence, another roar, and then pandemonium.

Mayo, his face spattered with blood, lay still at the bottom of the steps. Neale, or what was left of him after he had spun the gun round and aimed it, full into his own face, was still sitting in the chair.

Abigail bent over her boss, her ears ringing, her heart still. His eyes opened. 'For God's sake somebody get me something to clean up with,' he said, scrambling to his feet in an undignified manner.

*

'Yes, yes, of course I'm all right,' he said testily. It had only been a combination of self-preservation and shock which had thrown him to the floor.

This wasn't the way he liked a murder investigation to end. Neale shooting himself was tantamount to a confession in his eyes, but the law wouldn't recognize him as a murderer with that as the only evidence. There was nothing that would stand up in court. However much Mayo might be convinced about what had happened, there would be no case to answer.

He felt cheated. He'd have given a lot of what he possessed to have interrogated Neale. To have got out of him how he had killed Wishart, just what it was that had made him do it – apart from the consciousness of his own righteousness. He had set himself up as judge and jury. But that first killing had set in train other murders.

'He's got away with it, the bastard.'

'And what about Luce?' asked Abigail, pale with the after-effects of shock. If Neale had had any hand in her disappearance, where was she now? There was a silence. Was she still alive, or was she, too, dead? How were they even going to begin looking for her?

Mayo was more shaken by the whole thing than he would have admitted. He wanted a shower, a change of clothing and a stiff drink. He'd been inches away from his own death and what had made Neale turn the gun on himself instead, nobody would ever know.

He was on his way out of the house when Farrar appeared at the doorway of the study.

'There's a lot of stuff on his computer, sir ... He'd been putting it all on disc, for months.'

'Been putting what on disc?' The DC was obsessed by bloody computers.

'Mostly a record of his investments. He liked to play the stock market and he'd made a packet. He was very systematic, and all the information he'd been gathering is here ...' Mayo's eyes had begun to glaze over. '... I can print it out for you, sir.'

'Do that,' Mayo said, ignoring the implication that scrolling through a screen was beyond him ... though that might well be a justifiable doubt, given his avoidance of computers. He'd nothing against them, they smoothed the path of superintendents of police considerably, but the operating thereof he left strictly to others. No use having a dog and barking yourself was not a maxim he always followed, except in this case. 'Send it up to me as soon as you've finished.'

The sounds started again. The thumps and bangs overhead that had penetrated the shallow sleep in which Luce now passed the whole of her time.

She fancied she'd heard the sounds some time ago, but they'd gone away quite soon and she knew she'd been hallucinating again. This time the noises went on, and she heard shouts and voices. There was a deafening crash as something fell to the ground just outside the window, another which made the floor above her vibrate.

This was what it had sounded like at the Bagots, in that wild storm when tiles and coping stones and a chimney pot had blown off the roof of number six. For a moment, time stood still. Was she – could she possibly be – in the cellar of her own house? Except for one shuddering foray half-way down the steps when she'd first seen the house, she'd never been into the cellar, preferring not to know what it was like. Only Jem ever went down there, under some compulsion to keep a check on the damp. Had they started already on the demolition work? Fear crawled over her skin like worms.

She imagined one of those huge balls swinging against the walls, causing them to cave in. Tons of bricks, concrete and rubble, the world smashing down on top of her. Exposed ceiling beams at crazy angles and plaster, the smell of old concrete. Choking grey dust, making her cough, blocking her throat and her sinuses. God, how thirsty she was!

She tried a shout which came out as a hoarse croak, a scream that sounded like the mewling of a seagull. But nobody heard her.

The indefatigable Farrar had two print-outs on Mayo's desk with a speed that had Mayo commenting, 'He'll meet himself coming back, one of these days, that lad will.'

He handed one to Abigail, glancing at it without much interest until he saw what it was, what Farrar had meant by 'gathering information'.

He wished the reports of investigations his DCs sent in were as precise and ordered as Neale's record of how he had taken justice into his own hands against the man he blamed for his wife's death. He skimmed through it but not as quickly as Abigail.

'Luce!' she said. 'It's all here, where she is.'

David Neale had been appalled when he saw the girl Luce at the bus stop and realized she'd seen him and was flagging a lift. Fractionally, he'd hesitated, but then decided he'd be better off complying than refusing to stop for her and thereby fixing the incident in her memory. It was quite feasible, after all, that he should have the use of the van, and if she became too nosy he could always concoct an excuse. She told him she had this train to catch, but not why. She was in fact unusually quiet, for her. He thought she might be afraid he was going to preach at her again. But he was more wary nowadays than he had been. She never had listened to reason, she'd been so pert when he'd tried to convince her of the error of her ways. And scornful when he'd tried to warn her of the dangers of drugs. She didn't do hard drugs, she said, she only smoked the occasional spliff, by which she meant cannabis, and that didn't do anyone any harm, it was practically legal anyway, these days. He had been so angry with her naïvety, her refusal to listen.

He knew he'd reacted badly when she saw the shotgun – he should have passed it off with some casual remark about potting rabbits or something. She'd have been disgusted, he knew she was vegetarian and disapproved of killing and eating animals, but at least she'd never have suspected that he'd been using the gun for any other purpose. But it had been a gut reaction to swing round and drive out of the station forecourt and into the yard of Miller's Wife.

She screamed at him all the way, even tried to grab the wheel at one point, and immediately they stopped in the yard, she'd tried to leap out of the van, but the rucksack was in the way and trying to clamber over it, she'd fallen. By the time she'd picked herself up he was round the other side, grasping her shoulders and shaking her. Then, horrified at the violence she'd unleashed in him, he had abruptly let her go and she'd fallen again and hit her head on the ground, losing consciousness.

He'd felt the blood drain from his heart, he was sure he'd killed her, but when he knelt beside her he could feel her slow pulse. She wasn't dead, and that meant that she would probably come round sooner or later. And would certainly tell what had happened.

For the second time, he panicked. He couldn't let that happen! On the other hand, he didn't want her to die. Only people who were evil deserved to die like that, and Luce wasn't that, only incredibly silly – and unlucky, coming across the gun like that. He felt her pulse and his panic subsided.

His mind began to work quickly, seeking possibilities, and presently it came to him what he could do. In his mind's eye, he saw the view across the river from his house: the old houses at the Bagots, the defunct warehouses and factories not yet demolished to make room for the flats and houses that would take their place. In particular, the building which had once been a sweet factory: humbugs, mint imperials and liquorice all-sorts a speciality.

He'd always taken a lively interest in every company he had shares in. Artemis Developments was one of them, and since the properties they intended to demolish were practically on his doorstep and he had a natural curiosity, he'd taken the opportunity to poke around. It was a good, solid building, pity it had to come down. Some of the machines were still there ... the boiled-sweet drums like cement mixers, where mint imperials were rolled until they were rounded and smooth, the toffee pullers, the sugar-boiling vats. Sometimes, he fancied he could still smell the peppermint and liquorice of the old sweet factory. Perhaps he could. He'd learned that if your imagination is strong enough, anything can happen.

His interest in the old building had been casual at first, but the basement floor and the small room whose function at one time, he guessed, had been to serve as some sort of counting house, for some reason fascinated him and remained lodged in his memory.

The room had a heavy lock with its rusty iron key still *in situ*, and offered the perfect place in which to leave Luce for a while now. She was already coming round when he left her, and each time he visited her with food and drink she tried to talk to him, but he never replied. From what she said he knew that she'd no idea who he was, and that she'd no memory of how she'd got there. This suited him very well.

He hadn't intended it to be for long – it wasn't part of his plan that any permanent harm should come to her. He was still angry with her but this captivity would make her come to her senses, he was sure. When he told her the truth, she'd forgive him and be grateful to him for making her see the error of her ways, and she'd understand why he'd had to get rid of Wishart, the source of so much human misery.

He hadn't reckoned on her losing her memory for so long, but gradually, insidiously, he began to enjoy the thought of her being there, not knowing who her captor was. The knowledge of his secret stimulated him, keeping him in a permanent state of excitation. This was another country, something other than the dull monotony of his normal daily life. It was almost as good as planning to kill Wishart.

As the days went by, however, these pleasurable feelings began to be clouded by doubts. He wondered if she really *would* keep quiet about Wishart when her memory returned. Luce was incapable of keeping her mouth shut – and she could take up a strangely moral stance about some things. No, he couldn't ever let her go now, she knew too much.

She would never escape from that prison, and the thought that she was going to die wasn't pleasant to him. He wrestled with his conscience for some time, he searched through the Bible, as his father had done before him, for some text which would give him guidance. He found many that he could have twisted to suit his purpose, but he had become accustomed to lying to himself and in the end, he found it easier to tell himself that her death would be painless and gentle. She would gradually sink into a coma until the end came. And then he could go and remove her before demolition work started on the warehouses and the possibility of her body being found occurred.

It was then, from his bathroom window, that he saw they were beginning work on the factory.

*

The contingent of three police cars and an ambulance drew frantically to a halt and officers piled out beside the three-storey building that Deeley, locally born and bred, had immediately and familiarly, if inaccurately, recognized from Neale's description. 'That's Toffee Taskey's! Down by the river.'

The almost indistinguishable sign actually read: 'G.W.Taskey & Sons Ltd. Purveyors of Fine Confectionery.' Instead of the busy confusion of big cranes and steel balls swinging on chains, the piles of old bricks and stinking bonfires they'd expected to be met with, they saw two high-sided lorries standing empty. There was also a mini-crane, lifting gear and cutting equipment, with half a dozen burly demolition workers wearing hard hats and a leisurely air, standing outside a temporary hut from whence the smell of bacon wafted.

Mayo asked one of them for the foreman.

'Jack!'

Jack appeared from the hut, the last quarter of a bacon sandwich in one fist, a pint mug of thick mahogany-coloured tea in the other.

'Knocking it down? Not yet, we aren't, squire. First we have to gut it. Stuff in there worth a bob or two, so they tell me.' He stuffed the sandwich into his mouth and spoke through it. 'Nobody chucks nothing away, these days. Old machines, old fittings, somebody'll want it, somewhere.' He washed the sandwich down with a swallow of tea. 'Architectural salvage, industrial archaeology, summat of that sort, that's what the boss calls it. You'll have to ask him, be here in an hour.' He threw a wary glance at the posse of police. 'It's all accounted for, though, matey, nothing funny going on here.'

'Not that kind of funny, anyway,' Mayo said, and told him why they were here and what they wanted to do. Jack looked disbelieving, but professed himself willing to allow them to search.

'Is it safe, inside?'

'Solid as the Rock of Gibraltar. Start at the bottom, I should if I was you, we're working down from the top and haven't found nothing up there.'

There was no light in the boarded-up building; the cavernous spaces echoed to the sound of feet and monolithic shadows from the heavy machinery danced in the torchlight as they progressed steadily from one section to another. The ground floor revealed nothing, except steps in one corner, leading upwards, and in another, a heavy door that was locked or bolted.

'Are there cellars, a basement?'

Jack nodded. 'I reckon that's where most of the offices were, where they used to put the clerks to work, poor buggers. No unions in them days.'

'Do you have keys?'

'No, but there's no need. There's steps outside.'

The basement was below the level of the river. The land sloped upwards on its far side. On the other it had gratings above a sunken areaway created to give some light and air to the basement. The windows here were, like those in the rest of the building, boarded up, and the flight of stone steps leading down to the door was half covered in a heavy overgrowth of elder, buddleia and bramble, which perhaps explained why there were no signs of anywhere having been occupied by dossers or junkies, anybody sleeping rough.

They began their search through the numerous chambers which had once comprised offices and storerooms. The mechanism for a hoist still partly existed, from the time when, long ago, supplies had arrived by water and been lifted into the factory.

It was Deeley who found her. She was obviously in the last stages of starvation and dehydration. She could barely speak. He picked her up bodily and carried her out.

19

Abigail said goodnight and left the rest of the team getting pie-eyed at the bar of the Black Bull where they'd repaired to celebrate the wrapping up of the case.

It was a cold, starry night. She stepped outside and took a deep breath of the clear air, pulled the collar of her jacket up and walked on towards the river. She was going to Ben's flat, to wait for his return, but there was no hurry. She was in the mood for a solitary walk, through a town she was beginning to see through

Mayo's eyes. He'd come here as a stranger, but by now knew it better than she did, had walked every inch, in daylight and in the dark, too, when it was more likely to give up its secrets. It was her town, she'd grown up here, been educated at the High School, haunted its coffee bars and discos as a teenager, but never really seen it, never breathed in its atmosphere as he did, until she joined the police and began to know its darker side.

Ben was another of the same ilk as Mayo. For the duration of his time here, he'd made Lavenstock his town. He was coming home, later this evening, having fixed himself up with a Middle East assignment, then as soon as he could wind up his job here, he'd be off.

'We're none of us very good judges of men, are we?' Ellie had said last night when she'd heard this – none of us meaning herself, and Clare and Abigail, and perhaps even Barbie Nelson and Roz Spalding – but Abigail didn't want to be included in the list. As far as Ben was concerned, she'd no reason to feel her judgement was at fault. She'd decided to be positive about the situation. There might even be advantages. Might. Well, no relinquishment of her independence, for instance. The joys of a sweet homecoming after a separation . . .

But she knew what Ellie meant about wrong choices. Tim Wishart had been bad news for anybody, particularly the women who associated with him. The shot that killed him had injured them all. Clare especially. It was easy to conclude she was better off without him, but living with that knowledge wouldn't be comfortable . . .

'He offered me cocaine, you know,' Ellie had told Abigail, 'a few nights before he was killed. Wanted me to try a snort. Or something else, he said. There's plenty more where that came from. Go on, give yourself a treat. I realized what he was up to, later, when he asked me for a loan to pay back what he owed Tony Pardoe. He said it was only short term, he'd be solvent again within a week or two. I guessed Tony had staked him in for his latest lot of drugs, but I don't know where he thought I could lay my hands on anything like such a sum. I hope', she finished grimly, 'you get Pardoe.'

It gave Abigail a sense of the greatest satisfaction to inform Ellie that Pardoe was probably at this moment shaking in his handmade shoes. He must know that this time, despite the first-class lawyers he no doubt had ready to defend him, he was unlikely to slide past the law.

She cut through Cat Lane, and as she emerged, the houses at the Bagots were a dark huddle against the sky. The doomed Toffee Taskey's stood further along, reminding her of a girl's life which had almost ebbed away.

Some people talked and got things out of their system, some couldn't. Luce was a talker, and was prepared to talk about everything, except Morgan. He'd abused her trust and maybe her love. How much he meant to her, Abigail didn't know, and Luce wasn't saying. But Abigail sensed a lot of sadness in her.

Luce, however, was a survivor, one who lived in the present. She was gutsy, and she'd already put her ordeal behind her, after plugging whatever gaps she could for them. Gaunt and hollow-eyed as she was, in her hospital bed, it didn't stop her from telling everything. 'I want to. Then I can forget it. Though I still see it in my head, when I go to sleep,' she admitted, filling her eyes with the sight of the sky as she looked out of the window, as if she could never get enough of it. Yet those same eyes had, amazingly, brimmed with tears when she'd learned about Neale's death. 'He was a good man, basically, you know.'

'A good man,' Mayo had repeated caustically. 'He killed Wishart in cold blood. He left that girl to starve to death, and she still says he was a good man.'

'I think she means his motives . . .'

Mayo rolled his eyes to heaven. The situation was black and white to him, he saw no grey in it. 'His motive was revenge. And not wanting to be found out. He was deluding himself if he thought he ever meant to free Luce. When he saw they were starting on the demolition of Taskey's, he knew there was a chance she'd be found still alive, and didn't give a damn about her. The possibility of shooting himself must always have been there – otherwise why that smug little record left on his computer, letting us know how clever he'd been?'

A man in check trousers and white apron came out from behind the Nag's Head with a bucket, tipped it into one of the bins, leaned against the wall. A match rasped, flared, and a cigarette tip glowed in the dark. Some people came out of the Holly Tree and went to inspect the river level before walking away. It had gone down, the long-term weather forecast gave promise of a sustained spell of dry weather.

She heard footsteps behind her. She turned round and there he was, Ben, coming towards her and smiling.